Time for Raine

by

C. Barry Denham

Time for Raine

Cover Art by *Kristian Norris*

The Wild Rose Press, Inc.
PO Box 708
Adams Basin, NY 14410-0708
Visit us at www.thewildrosepress.com

Publishing History
First Sweetheart Rose Edition, 2017
Print ISBN 978-1-5092-1426-6
Digital ISBN 978-1-5092-1427-3

Published in the United States of America

Noelle had never seen a more beautiful man.
He stood across the room like a deer in headlights, gorgeous. He wore a navy sport coat, khaki slacks, bright white shirt, and peach tie. Each piece of clothing seemed designed and tailored perfectly for those broad shoulders and slim hips. Time stood still as she walked slowly toward him. His eyes fixed on her advance. The closer she got, the more her heart hammered. She stopped a few feet from him and smiled.

"You look…stunning," he said.

"I was about to say the same about you."

He moved ever so slowly toward her, stalking her, drinking her in with his eyes. She willed her legs to take her closer. She thought she might keel over, yet strangely, she had no fear. If she did faint, she hoped she would fall into his arms. He licked his lips and leaned closer still.

If he doesn't kiss me right now, right here on this spot, I will die.

"Daddy?"

The sleepy sound came from behind them.

The spell was broken. A different Sean Sampson appeared before her eyes. The passion in his eyes faded. Noelle found humor in the moment and laughed. From the look on his face, he did not.

Praise for *TIME FOR RAINE*

"The story unfolds at a pace that kept me enthralled, and dialogue and characterizations were crisp and completely relatable."

~The Romance Reviews (5 Stars)

Dedication

For all the little girls from China,
especially those lost or left behind

Chapter One

Ono Island, Alabama—the first day of fall

Raine was too young to have memories of her mother. Sean Sampson remembered everything. The scent of her lotion and subtle taste of mint from her good night kiss. The way her long, thick, chestnut hair refused to stay put over delicate ears, no matter how many times she pushed it away from her face. The salty tears she tried to hide from the intense pain she suffered, knowing there wasn't one thing he or anyone else could do to will a different fate for her.

The days before, during, and after the long trip to China to get their daughter marched through Sean's mind like so many bands in a parade. Some of the memories were melodic and beautiful. Others were loud, ugly, and etched deeply into his heart. The pain of her absence refused to loosen its grip. A small tear leaked from the corner of his eye.

"Are you okay, Daddy?" Little fingers held tight to his index finger. One of his steps meant two for her along the desolate sandy beach.

The warm air promised to extend the long summer. The light salty breeze off the Gulf of Mexico played at the senses and eased the soul. The sun raced across the western sky, burning its way to the end of day. It took aim at a cluster of sea oaks perched on one of the many high dunes that stretched inland.

"I'm fine, sweetie. Daddy has something in his eye." It was only a little white lie.

Having her next to him made it a little easier to keep the memories distant.

"Daddy, why do they call today the September eck…eck…qwi…not?"

He stopped, knelt, and frowned at the barefoot child. The breeze threw a bracket of raven hair over her face. She pushed it away. Eyes as black as midnight searched his. What she said wasn't what one might expect from a child barely two and a half years old.

"September equinox?" he whispered.

Raine lowered her chin toward the soft sand that bubbled and sizzled around her toes. A docile wave receded. She nodded and looked again at him. "Did I say it wrong, Daddy?"

He gently took her shoulders. "Oh, no, sweetheart, you said it fine. I was just surprised you know what today is."

Until then the significance of the date hadn't registered. He smiled, squinted, and tilted his head. "How *did* you know today was the first day of fall, little one? Have we been watching too much TV?"

He goosed her. She giggled and tried in vain to escape. He lifted her into his arms and gave her neck a smooch, before setting her gently back onto the sand. They resumed the walk as the last of the sun faded to a blazing sliver on the horizon. A sea gull swooped in and landed squarely on top of the remaining orange yoke.

He waited for an answer. His mind raced through his memory for any books on seasons he might have read to her or TV shows on the subject. Was it from the Animal Planet shows they watched together? The Learning Channel? He could think of nothing that could have prompted such a question.

"I don't know. I guess I saw it somewhere."

At the end of the day, she would sit on the carpet next to his chair and rustle through the pages of the daily newspaper. Or, from a lower shelf in the den, she would haul down one of the ancient, heavy *World Book Encyclopedia* volumes he had for some time meant to put in storage. It became part of the routine before he read to her at bedtime. Until that moment he assumed she was playing, looking at the pictures, pretending to read like Daddy. "So you saw a picture?"

"I read about it." As if any fool should know it was the only way for a thirty-month-old child to top off her evenings before bed.

"In the books or in the newspaper?"

"Yeah."

He stopped and knelt once again. His mind regressed to times she had reacted to words and sentences in books he read to her, even before he read them aloud. *The Swiper's trick on Dora…The Cat in the Hat's antics…*He had thought about her doing this at times, but assumed she had memorized portions of her favorite books.

"So you look at the words in the encyclopedias and in the newspaper?"

"Duh." She grinned and planted her hands on her hips, the way he did, and then said, "That's how you read, isn't it?"

He smiled and popped his forehead with the heel of his hand. "Of course it is. Silly Daddy, huh?"

She giggled and gave him a look that melted his heart.

His weak laugh sounded more like a whimper. His mind churned. He wanted to grab her up, gallop back to the car, take her home to the novel he was reading, and find out if what she said was true. Instead, he took a deep breath and continued walking toward the last light of day.

Why did he suspect his daughter's gift meant trouble?

He might need some help to figure out the answer to that one.

Chapter Two

Raine's pediatrician had been right concerning Dr. Victor. The doc warned Sean might need to get on a list and could have a long wait to get in to see the popular child psychologist. Indeed, she was booked solid through the fall and beyond the holidays. He opted to be put on a list for cancellations. Fortunately, the week before Thanksgiving, the office called.

The next Tuesday, he and Raine arrived to a packed waiting room. Sean looked around the room as they stood before a young, pretty receptionist with flaming red hair. A woman in the corner stared at him.

"Excuse me, aren't you Sean Sampson, the writer?"

Raine turned toward the woman. "Yes, ma'am, and he's my daddy. But he hasn't written in a long time."

Leave it to Raine to hit the nail on the head. He *hadn't* written since Patty died. The inspiration seemed to die along with her. Try as he might, he couldn't convince himself to hit the power switch on the old desktop he had once frequented. He couldn't hold on to ideas long enough to get them down on paper. The words were prone to evaporate, along with the balance in his bank accounts. Royalties dwindled, and he was well into rainy day money, just to make ends meet.

The woman looked as though she wanted to say something but instead turned her attention to the magazine she was reading. Another woman from across the room spoke up. "Well, I for one love your books."

"See, Daddy?"

Fortunately, the receptionist ushered them into the doctor's office and introduced them. She looked up, walked around her desk, and gave Raine a surveying smile. Sean felt strange as the doctor stood looking at her, then him, over narrow reading glasses. As a man of words, he was suddenly without them. He hoped he wouldn't have to speak. Light-blue eyes set in a pretty face seemed to look into his soul. The way her lush lips curled slightly had him searching for air. He hadn't expected the doctor to be so young and attractive.

She offered her hand. It was small, warm, and soft, but the handshake firm. He wasn't prepared for how natural her hand felt in his. She wore business attire, but it failed to hide her tall, shapely, slender body and long, sleek legs. Her dark and flowing hair shone in the office lights. Dr. Victor appeared to be in her late twenties or early thirties. She asked them to sit, and he took a chair. Raine climbed onto his lap.

"My mommy's name is Patricia, too," Raine said.

The doctor leaned toward her. Raine's greeting confused Sean, but if it had caught the doctor off guard, she didn't show it. She threw a perfunctory glance in his direction. Sean cleared his throat and shifted nervously in his chair.

"And I bet everyone calls her Patty?" She walked behind the desk and sat. "When I was younger, I wanted everyone to call me Patty, which you might think would work since it *is* my first name. But my parents insisted on calling me by my middle name, Noelle. And over the years, it stuck."

Raine's expression changed, and she fiddled with a button on her light jacket. For a moment, it appeared she might burst into tears. The doctor gave him a questioning look. He opened his mouth to explain, but then thought of Raine's revelation. "Honey, how did you know Dr. Victor's name is Patricia Noelle?"

"Duh, Daddy." The doctor stood and put her hands on her hips. "From the name on the door?" She turned to Raine. "Right, sweetie?"

"Right." Raine laughed and flipped her hair from her face. She turned and gave him a loving look before turning back to the doctor. "My daddy and I say 'Duh' a lot, too."

The ice was broken. The doctor was in charge. But as pleasant as she seemed, Sean remained cautious.

The conversation continued for better than a half hour. Most of the time, Sean just listened. He couldn't seem to get a word in edgewise, although he hadn't a clue what he would have said anyway. The easy exchange between the doctor and Raine continued through cookies and milk and a sugar-free sucker. The doctor seemed not only impressed with the conversation but delighted as well. Sean was impressed by some of Raine's responses.

"And what is your favorite color?"

Raine gave the doctor that look, as she propped her little hands on her hips. Sean braced for a "Duh."

"Red, of course. I *am* from China, you know."

"Of course." The doctor took it all in stride and didn't miss a beat. She glanced at her notepad. "And what's your most favorite thing you and your daddy do together?"

Raine hesitated and then giggled. "Playing poker

on Sunday afternoons."

Sean wasn't prepared for the answer. Reading to her, maybe. Fishing, working on the boat? She could have named a number of things. But poker? In spite of his attempt to brush her answer off, he blushed and smiled nervously. The doctor chuckled and looked at him, which gave him a funny feeling in the pit of his stomach.

"Interesting." She turned to Raine. "And who usually wins?"

"Me mostly. Although sometimes I let Daddy win."

The doctor made notes, but the smile never faded. She knew what questions to ask and how to ask them to get the clearest response from Raine. She seemed genuinely interested in Raine's favorite toy, stuffed animal, and even her favorite food. Sean thought the exchange might never end.

"Well, I think that does it for now." The doctor pressed a button on her phone. She informed the receptionist the appointment would be running over a few more minutes and to please handle the next patient for her. "I hope you don't mind?" She glanced to Sean. It was one of the few times she acknowledged his presence in any way.

"No, no," he said, unsure of what to do with his hands, yet strangely happy to have her attention. "Of course not, please continue. I have a few questions, but I assume there will be time for them?"

"Of course." She smiled. "Just a few more minutes, and you and I will take some time to chat."

Ten minutes later, the doctor summoned the receptionist into the room.

"Connie, would you please show this delightful young lady to our recreation room for a few moments while I talk to Dad?"

Sean was reduced to "Dad." Not Mr. Sampson. Not the man who was paying for all this. Not the signer of the checkbook. Just "Dad." In spite of efforts to deflect his feelings, he remained cautious and wondered how much more this extra time would cost.

"Is that all right with you, sweetie?" the doctor asked.

Raine took Connie's outstretched hand.

Alone with the doctor and a hint of an unknown, yet intoxicating perfume, Sean's pulse quickened, and the uneasiness returned full force. What was going on with all the conflicting emotions? Why was he feeling this way, knowing he might be staring into the eyes of the enemy?

What the hell do you think you're doing? Of all the women in the world, why be attracted to this one?

He was sure he might be a shade crazy. This lady could well be a threat to the quiet life he had worked so hard to create with Raine. All his instincts told him to keep things in perspective and heed the many warning signs.

Yet he continued to ignore them all.

"Mr. Sampson, I would like to…" She paused and looked into his eyes. "Mr. Sampson, have we met?"

He blinked and shifted nervously in his seat. "No, I don't think so. I'm sorry, forgive me. I was thinking, well, I was just, ah, thinking."

Noelle raised her eyebrows.

"Never mind. Sorry, it wasn't important."

"Of course." She leaned forward and touched his

arm. "Mr. Sampson, based on my initial interview with your daughter, I'd like to administer some standard aptitude tests. Raine is extraordinarily intuitive and bright. The tests will give us an idea of how bright she is. You and/or your wife could, of course, be present during the tests or watch from the observation room we have at this facility."

Sean let the wife comment go. Other questions remained. Besides the costs, his main concern was how Raine would react to taking any kind of tests, and what issues might surface if she didn't do so well on them or even if she *did*. He wanted nothing to do with anything that might upset the continuity of their relationship.

"Doctor, I must be honest." He made a conscious effort to avoid those eyes. "I'm concerned about testing her. Although you might not believe it because of the way she's opened up to you, she can be very shy and most times doesn't relate well to people. I'm afraid if she doesn't do so well, what it might do to her."

"Mr. Sampson—"

"Please, call me Sean." He frowned. "The mister part makes me feel old."

The doctor smiled.

God, what a nice smile she had!

"Of course, Mr…Sean." She moved a strand of hair behind an ear. Her gaze locked on his for a moment, and she swallowed. "I-uh-I'm sorry, where were we?"

"I was relating my concern that these tests might frustrate or confuse Raine."

"Yes, of course. Sean, you can halt the proceedings at any time during any of the sessions. You can—"

"Sessions?" What was going on here? On the one

hand, he had convinced himself he was doing the best thing for his daughter by being here. On the other he wanted to stop all the proceedings, load up, and go back to the sanctity of their home on Ono Island.

"I'm sorry," she replied. "These tests are designed to be given during three sessions. That way Raine doesn't get so tired. And it also allows for the possibility she might have a bad day, if you will. The tests are pricey, but I believe strongly they're essential in our evaluation of her and will provide us with great information to determine the best plan for her education and development."

Doctor Victor continued for a few minutes, relating the details of the tests. Her soft, feminine voice and demeanor were mesmerizing. Her subtle and unassuming nature made her so very…interesting. There was no other way to put it. And that perfume. But as much as he enjoyed being in her presence, Sean couldn't shake an underlying uneasiness. Was the room getting warm?

"Sean, you don't have to make a decision today regarding the direction I'm suggesting for Raine." She stood and produced a manila envelope from the corner of her desk. "Here are a few brochures and collaterals concerning the tests, along with the costs involved. Most health insurance providers will cover at least a portion of the costs. There are also references, if you and Mom care to check them out. So, if it's okay with you, I'll ask Connie to set up a follow-up appointment we can use as the first testing session, or if you want, to set another plan of action in evaluating your lovely daughter. And she is very lovely. And it's plain to see she adores her father."

"Thank you."

What? That was the sum total of his response after all his concerns? His face felt hot, but if the good doctor noticed, she didn't bring attention to it. Did she notice how he was perspiring?

"Now let's see how Raine is doing, shall we?"

He stood and followed her toward the door, like a little lost puppy.

****

The last patient was gone, and the front door to the office suite was locked. It had been a long day.

Noelle couldn't stop thinking about him. *What a nice dad this man is, and not to mention a hunk. The strong silent type. His wife is very lucky.*

"Well, I must say…" Connie dropped a few files on Noelle's desk. Noelle flinched, caught thinking about things she shouldn't be thinking about. "Things are looking up, wouldn't you say?"

"What do you mean?" Noelle straightened the files on her desk and hoped Connie wasn't somehow tapping into her thought.

"Uh-huh. Noelle, my dear, you don't fool me. You know exactly what I'm saying. I mean, if you didn't notice Mr. Major-Hunk-What's-His-Name-Sampson-Man, well then honey, you better check your pulse."

She agreed, but wasn't going to let Connie know how she felt. Sean Sampson was a good-looking man—the entire package—at least from what she had witnessed. But that meant nothing to her, did it? For heaven's sakes if there were any man who was off limits and out of her league, it was this one, right? Not to mention the fact he was married!

"Did you see those biceps? And that six-pack?

12

Why, you could see those flat tummy ripples straight through the fabric of that thin shirt."

Connie was milking it for all it was worth. Noelle didn't know if she was trying to get a rise out of her, or if Connie was expressing interest in him.

"And the dark hair and those piercing brown eyes?" Connie was relentless, like a dog on a bone.

"Okay, Connie." Noelle flipped hair from her face. "I get it. And yes, he is quite an attractive man." *It's getting hot in here, right?*

Connie laughed. "Honey, the UPS man is attractive. This Sampson man is drop-dead hot!"

Noelle couldn't hold back a laugh. It *had* been a long day, and she was giddy. If Connie only knew how much she had thought about him since the moment he and Raine walked into her office. And if she were honest with herself, thinking about him made her very uneasy. It was far too soon to be thinking about any man, especially one like Sean Sampson. It would take more than a few months before she could trust anyone of the opposite sex. She wanted to kick Connie for suggesting she might be attracted to someone married. No way. Not when she had generally cursed all men since the day she caught Scott cheating.

"You know, honey," Connie said, "all men aren't pigs. There are still some good ones out there. And there's a good one out there for you, too."

"Well." Noelle shuffled the files on her desk. Had Connie jumped inside her mind? Her friend had an uncanny ability to read her. "I have to tell you, I'm not interested in finding that man right now."

"Too bad, lady. I think this could be one of those rare ones." Connie's expression turned solemn. "Umm,

umm. Well then, if you're not interested, would you mind if I took a shot at him?"

"You can't be serious." Noelle was shocked. *Wait a minute! Jealousy?* Who was she kidding? She couldn't be jealous, not of a married man. Could she? She shook her head, as if trying to rid herself of the thought.

Connie broke into a smile. "I'm just messing with you, honey. I've got my hands full right now with the UPS man."

Noelle frowned.

"No, really." Connie lost her smile. "He asked me out this weekend." Connie studied Noelle closely. "Wait a minute! You were jealous, weren't you? When I said I might be interested in this Sampson guy, you were jealous. I can see it all over your face."

"I was not," she said, louder than she had planned. "I told you. I'm *really* not interested."

"Not interested, or not ready?"

Noelle sighed. "Well, maybe you're right. Maybe I'm not ready. But really, I think it would be better if I concentrated on my work. After all, Sean's little girl is a very interesting and unusual case."

"*Sean's* little girl?" Her friend's eyebrows lifted. "It's *Sean*, now. Y'all are on a first name basis, I take it?"

"I'll have you know he insisted I call him Sean."

"And did you tell him he could call you Noelle? No, wait. Let me guess. You also told him he could call you for a date, right?"

"Very funny. That'll never happen. His little girl let me know right off the bat her daddy was taken. She told me her mother's name is also Patricia. Let's not kid ourselves. Neither one of us goes for married men."

"Married? Uh-uh." Connie shook a finger at Noelle. "Not this time, honey. I checked his file. There is no Patricia Sampson listed in the 'name of spouse' section of the forms. Under mother's name, it had an N slash A, not applicable."

"I don't understand." Noelle mentally replayed the conversations she had with both Sean and his daughter.

Connie looked confused. "I'm sorry, maybe it's me who doesn't understand. I thought you knew he wasn't married. Didn't you notice he wasn't wearing a ring?"

"Lots of men don't wear their wedding bands."

"So you noticed?"

"Yes. I mean, no, I didn't." Maybe Connie was right. Maybe all men *weren't* pigs. Sean Sampson seemed to have it all—good looks, kindness, gentleness, admiration for his child, courtesy. She looked up, but her friend was no longer there. Maybe she should leave well enough alone. It *had* been a long day.

A long, but very interesting—and confusing—day. The appointments with Raine were strung out over the next weeks, and she couldn't help but wonder if time around him would bring clarity…or more confusion.

Chapter Three

All though dinner and bath time, a myriad of questions buzzed around in Sean's head. Through the constant banter of his sweet daughter, he replayed the conversation with Raine on the beach and the visit to the doctor over and over in his mind. The test results would surely yield some answers, but he couldn't wait. They settled into his favorite chair for bedtime stories, and he took matters into his own hands.

She snuggled against his chest, and he breathed in the clean, sweet smell of her bubble-gum shampoo. She was a little doll, clad in her red and blue *Dora the Explorer* pajamas. Although she asked for one of her favorites, he pulled out a new, more advanced book and convinced her he should read to her from that one. He read slowly and was on the second page when she giggled and made a comment concerning a line he had not yet read aloud. He paused and searched the page for any illustration that might have clued her to the humor but found none. He cleared his throat.

"Now, my little sweet-smelling picadee, how did you know the pig was going to say something funny?" He wrinkled his forehead and raised an eyebrow.

She wrinkled the corner of her mouth. "Uh, Daddy, I read it."

"You can read this book?"

"Uh, yeah."

"Okay, Miss Smarty Dora Pajama Pants, read it to me."

And she did. At a pace he could barely follow.

As proud and as surprised as he was, his heart pounded. This might not necessarily be a good thing. He pushed the envelope and suggested she read to him from an old physics textbook. Surprisingly, she nimbly navigated her way through several chapters of the book. In the process, she asked questions regarding the concepts and theories of the subject that were astounding.

"Daddy? Why are you looking at me like that?"

Sean stammered for an answer and smiled. "Well, I was...Daddy was thinking of how proud I am at how well you can read."

Clearly, he had to take this issue further. Remembering the promises he made to Patty, he was torn between wanting what was best for Raine and taking the best course of action to protect her. Would Patty approve of the doctor's plan to test their little girl? The first two years without Patty were difficult, but he had always been up to the task. However, nothing like this situation had arisen. He had to hold it together, and not fold with the first adversity that happened along. He would do whatever he needed to do to ensure that did not happen.

Later, in bed, he was unable to turn off his mind. How had he missed the clues to her ability to read so well? How long *had* she been reading like that? For most of the night he continued to struggle with the right course of action—stick to the testing appointments, or find a reason to cancel. Before falling asleep he knew there was but one thing he needed to do.

He needed to get a second opinion. Not from another doctor, but from a source close to the subject.

****

When he woke, the sun shone through his blinds, confirming ideal conditions for step one of the day's plan. He had slept later than usual, courtesy of the absence of his normally early-rising daughter. He slipped shorts on and made his way to her room. She was awake, lying in her bed, deep in a conversation with Belle, her stuffed nighttime sleeping partner.

"Hey, sweetie," he whispered.

She looked up at him with the smile that always made his day. "Hey, Daddy." She sat up and tucked Belle back under the covers.

"What say we take a trip to the beach today?"

"Yippee!" Sean moved closer, and she jumped into his arms.

Step two was complete.

Soon they finished breakfast, dressed for the beach, and were out the door. On to the final step of the plan.

As a widowed dad, Sean often found it challenging to wedge himself into a group of mothers at the beach or at a playground, at least not without an open romance novel in his lap or flipping through *People* magazine or *Southern Homes and Gardens*. He'd learned to improvise, however, and managed to find ways to get within hearing distance. Through strategic positioning, he could inconspicuously cash in on tidbits from their conversations. Such an informal gaggle of ladies was often a wealth of information concerning any number of pediatric subjects. The plan today was to find out if any of the ladies had taken a child to a psychologist. If he got lucky, he might even garner some opinions of Dr. Victor and her battery of tests.

He strategically claimed a spot a safe distance away yet near a cluster of moms, and watched his sweet child mold wet sand into an unknown object, one he suspected only she could identify. He didn't have a clue what to do next, but resolved to find some way to eavesdrop on some answers.

"You know, you are welcome to join us if you like."

The statement came as a shock, and he hoped it didn't show as he looked up, shielding his eyes from the sun. A half dozen ladies, positioned a few feet behind him on the sugar-white sands, giggled in unison. A tall, slender woman had materialized next to his folding chair.

"We won't bite, you know. Especially big handsome dads like you."

She offered her hand, to the *oohs* and *aahs* of her friends. Sean's face flushed. He took her hand and stood. She removed her shades and gave him the once-over. Clad only in his swimsuit and baseball cap, he felt naked.

"What are you, anyway, six-one, six-two, and let's see—one-eighty-five, one-ninety?" She glanced to her friends for validation. "We'd all like to know the secret behind those arms, legs, and abs, and that hint of cologne I'm getting. It's very subtle but quite delicious. Oh, really, there's no need to blush. Although I'm told my bite is much worse than my bark."

This brought laughter from the group. It was quite the icebreaker, and in spite of his discomfort, Sean smiled. Despite the publicity his book signings and personal appearances had given him, he was never quite comfortable in the limelight.

This voluptuous, bikinied beauty led him to a spot next to her chair and in the middle of the coconut-scented covey. The circle of bikinis, blankets, and lounge chairs was a kaleidoscope of color. From the edge of her sandcastle a few feet away, Raine giggled. He turned to find his daughter watching the entire scene. After a few moments of silent appraisal from the group, he removed his favorite, albeit sweaty, cap and took the initiative.

"Good morning, ladies, my name is—"

"Oh, we all know who you are, Sean Sampson," interrupted one of the women. She lowered the book she had been reading and looked around the circle of ladies. "I think all of us have read at least one of your books. Just because we read *romance* doesn't mean we don't enjoy a good action-adventure story once in a while."

"Action adventure?" argued a woman who looked no older than eighteen. Her bright yellow two-piece left little to the imagination. "I think, Mr. Sampson, we all agree there are enough hot love scenes in your books to seriously consider a new genre for your stories."

"Like the scene with Matt and Ginger in the cockpit of the boat in *Down Island*?" added a blonde woman in a pale green cover-up.

"Or that sizzling love scene under those Maui waterfalls in *Above Suspicion*?" purred another dark-complexioned and dark-eyed beauty.

"I think our author friend is blushing again," said the ringleader. She extended her hand once more. "I'm Elaine. The only unattached one in the group, incidentally. Well, currently, at any rate, and if you don't count past divorces."

She faced the circle, holding firmly to Sean's hand. "This is Brenda, Alice, Rene, Tammy, and Susan."

Sean nodded. Consistent with his newly acquired writer's block, words were elusive.

"Well, it's nice to see you again, Sean," said Rene, her book still in hand. "Although I am disappointed you don't remember me."

He searched his memory. After a few moments, he folded his arms and rubbed his chin. "I'm sorry. We've met?"

"Well, yes. But that's okay." She poked her lip out. "I guess I'll forgive you, considering there were a lot of other ladies lurking around when I met you."

"I don't understand."

"At the signing for your first book *South Winds* a few years back?"

"Ahh," he acknowledged, although he didn't remember. He ventured a guess. "At the Barnes and Noble in Mobile?"

"Close enough."

"So, Sean," asked baby blue bikini. "When can we expect another one of your stories? I haven't seen a new release in quite a while."

He wasn't prepared for the question. Not from a stranger. He had gotten the question quite often from Derek—his best friend and agent—and from his publisher. And he had asked himself that question.

One of the ladies seemed to sense his frustration and broke the silence. "Well, you can believe that when the next one comes out, Sean, we'll all be there in line for a copy. And as for myself, I want a steamy, very personalized autograph."

Sean smiled, happy she had bailed him out. "It would be my pleasure."

This brought more *oohs* and *aahs* and seemed to render her silent. After an awkward moment, he glanced around to check on Raine.

"She is so adorable," Elaine said, recovering from her sudden shyness. "You and your wife must be so proud of her."

Sean looked at the expectant expressions around the group and became aware he must have kept his personal life more private than he realized. Never had he spoken of his daughter or her mother at events, nor written of them on the flaps and inside covers of his books. If he had his way, there would be no bio or photo of him. Building strong characters in his stories for his readers was one thing, but keeping his private life from the public was another. He had never quite understood why some found it so difficult to separate the author from his creations.

"My wife passed away, soon after she and I got home from China with Raine."

After a long silence, Elaine replied, "I'm sorry." She seemed near tears.

The uneasiness hung in the air like a fog, and it was his turn to break the silence. He turned toward Raine, who was intently examining a cache of multi-colored shells. A few other children had joined her.

"Don't let her size fool you." He laughed. "That little girl is an eating machine. She can surely pack away the groceries."

Several ladies laughed.

"Such a beautiful name. How old is she?" a woman asked.

"Thirty-two months."

"No!" another argued. "I would have guessed she is closer to four years old, even considering her petite size."

"Four?" Sean asked.

"I would agree," said the woman at the end of the line of chaises. "From hearing her talk to my son, I thought she was at least that age. She seems so mature and—"

"Smart," Elaine interrupted. "There's no other word for it. Sean, your daughter's vocabulary and reasoning are very advanced for being—did you say thirty-two months?"

"Are you sure?" asked one of the ladies. "I've read there may be some confusion in determining the age of adopted Chinese children." She covered her mouth. "I'm sorry, I didn't mean to—"

"It's okay," Sean added quickly. He smiled and lowered his voice. "I've read the same reports. But we adopted her when she was seven months old. If there is an error in her birth date, it can't be more than a few weeks."

"Well, at any rate," another woman said and looked at Raine, "you should have her tested. There's a doctor—a Dr. Victor, Nancy…no, Nell, Noelle! Yes, Dr. Noelle Victor has a practice in downtown Pensacola, on Palafox Street, I believe. She specializes in gifted children. I hear she's very good and worth the money and the drive. I don't think I'm stepping on any toes by saying that developmentally, that little girl of yours is head and shoulders above our guys and other children in her age group as well."

The group of ladies echoed agreement.

Sean looked at Raine and then back to the ladies. "Well, it looks like my little one is emerging from her shyness. Looks like she's made a few friends today. Really glad to see that."

"Like daughter, like father," one of the ladies said.

Sean smiled and tipped his cap. "Touché."

He wanted answers. He had certainly gotten them. Dr. Victor was the consensus choice.

But were they the answers he wanted to hear?

****

Sean hosed down a squealing little girl on the back patio, wrapped her in a towel, and shuffled her inside. His land line rang as he scooted her off to her bedroom to get dressed. He reached inside the refrigerator for a bottle of water before picking up the phone. The digital display indicated the call was from Derek.

"Hey, buddy, how goes it?" He took a long pull on the water.

"If I were any better, I couldn't stand myself."

He smiled. Derek was never one for any lack of self-confidence. "You really need to work on that self-deprecating monologue, my friend. You're going to give me a complex."

"Never claimed to be anybody other than the great person I am. How goes it with you? Haven't heard from you in a while."

"You mean still no work out of me, right?"

"Hey, you know that's not me. I love you, man. I figure you'll hit it again when the time's right. Someday you're gonna get tired of carrying that cloud around, and you'll ditch it and let the sun back in. Hey, that wasn't bad. I give you full permission to use that line in your next book. And I'm confident you've got quite a few more bestsellers in you, buddy. You'll cough 'em up when you're ready. As for your publisher, you let me worry about them for now."

"Yeah, the writing's easier said than done, pal. Hey, nobody wants another bestseller more than me. But the thing is, it's hard to write with the inspiration gone."

And most of the money. But that was another issue. He couldn't believe how fast the money was dwindling.

"Life goes on, as they say," Derek said. "It *has* been two years, my man."

"And every day still hurts like the day I lost her."

"I understand, I really do. But you have to be feeling the pinch in the ol' pocketbook by now, man."

"I'm fine." He wished he could convince himself and his agent otherwise.

Raine skipped into the room with red shorts and an orange tee that was on inside-out. She circled him, hopping and skipping. He jammed the receiver against his shoulder, caught her, peeled the T-shirt off, and put it on correctly, but ignored the clashing colors.

She cast her eyes downward, in that familiar resignation, and became very quiet. "Did I pick the wrong clothes, Daddy?"

Sometimes Sean forgot how sensitive she was. "No, no, sweetheart, you did just fine. I love what you picked out. You're getting so big to pick out your own clothes. I'm proud of you. Hey, wanna talk to Uncle Derek?"

"Yeah!" Her eyes lit up as she held the receiver to her ear. It dwarfed her small hand. "Hey, Uncle Derek."

He could hear Derek's muffled response, but couldn't decipher his words.

"We went to the beach today…yeah…yeah…Oh, and Daddy talked to a bunch of ladies."

Another few seconds of muffled comments from Derek.

"I gotta go pee." She had an urgent look on her face and handed the phone back to him. Derek let out an audible laugh.

"Okay, sweetie." He put her down. "Off you go. And don't forget to wipe!"

He raised the receiver back to his ear.

"You see, big man? You should be more like that little daughter of yours. Tell it like it is, I always say."

"Yeah, well. You have no idea. You should have heard what she said to a lady at the grocery store yesterday."

"Yeah?"

"Took one look at the unsuspecting woman's backside and was nice enough to tell her the margarine she was looking at had four more grams of fat per serving than another brand."

"Jeez," his friend said and laughed. "Where'd she get that? More importantly, what'd you do?"

"I just smiled, grabbed Raine, and got the hell out of there. It looked like the woman was thinking about throwing something."

"I can imagine. So what was the deal with the ladies on the beach?"

Sean briefly described his new acquaintances, but his friend zeroed in. He decided he would wait before telling him about the doctor, and his purpose for going to the beach.

"Of all the luck. So, break it to me gently, were there any in the group that *weren't* hot? Sounds like you had the pick of the litter. The sole man in a flock of bikinis? Where the hell are these babes when I'm at the beach?"

"Hiding?"

"Very funny, jerk wad. So did you see anything you liked?"

"It wasn't an auction, buddy." He wanted to say he *had* seen someone he liked, but she wasn't at the beach. He turned serious. "No, I'm not—I don't—"

"You're not what, man? You're not 'ready'? You don't 'deserve' it? Which one is it?"

The same old conversation was evolving, and Sean didn't want to feed it.

"Look, I understand," Derek said, lowering his voice. "I really do."

"No, you don't." Sean glanced around to make sure he was alone. Raine was in her room singing. "You don't have any idea how I feel."

"Maybe not, man. And I do know you're hurting still, but I know for some reason you think you're to blame for Patty's death. Buddy, you know I love you, but jeez, you spend your days like a monk, scared out of your mind something's going to hurt that little girl of yours, and you're afraid there won't be anything you can do to prevent it. I really don't understand that because I also know you're a smart man, Sean. There are simply life events you cannot change or stop from happening. Things happen to people, things you can't always explain or shield them from. It wasn't your fault Patty got cancer. Surely you can see there was nothing you or anyone else could have done?"

"There's where you're wrong. There was *everything* I could have done." Sean lost the fight to

27

keep his voice under control. "I could've insisted Patty get immediate treatment. Hell, we could have put off the trip for a few weeks while the treatment took effect. I could have told the Chinese authorities that Patty had a family emergency and could have gone alone to get Raine. I could've grown bigger balls and insisted on any of those options. Do you realize that from the time she was diagnosed until she received her first treatment was seven weeks? And do you know how fast that cancer progressed? If I had only talked her into putting the trip off for a month, things might have been different."

"Oh sure, man, and Patty would have smiled and said yes, dear. Let's forget about getting Raine, another child will come along. After all, somebody else would love to have her.'" Derek stopped abruptly. "Buddy, I'm sorry. I don't know where that came from."

"Forget it. Water under the bridge."

A few long moments lapsed before Derek continued. "Look, there's something I want to say to you."

"If it's about the missed deadline, I told you. I'll give the advance back. I lost interest in that story long ago. The words just aren't there. I can't think about writing right now."

"It has nothing to do with writing, man. Look, I trust you on that. Someday that will come back. You're my friend first, *then* my client." Derek's tone became serious. "It's something Patty said to me before…well, you remember the time toward the end when I came over and practically forced you out of the house for a while? Raine was asleep, and Patty was in and out from pain medicine?"

"Yeah, I remember. There's not much I don't remember about those days."

"Well, Patty woke up, saw me sitting there, and tried to speak. Her voice was very weak, so she asked me to come closer. I told her I would get you, but she said no, she wanted to talk to me."

"She wanted to talk to *you*?" Sean's throat constricted. "What did she say?"

Derek sighed. "She told me you might be this way, you know, holding on to her for so long." He paused.

"Go on."

"Then she made me promise I would try to help you to move on with your life. I'll be honest, it seemed like the hardest thing for her to say, but she told me she wanted you to find someone else. She wanted you to love again, man."

This was vintage Patty, to solicit help in getting him to move on.

"And it's funny," Derek continued. "Right afterwards, as if she'd thought about what she had said, she sounded as if she was having second thoughts, like she was jealous of you and someone else. Then she smiled and told me it was all right to wait a couple of years before I told you. So, here I am, buddy. I don't have to remind you—it's been two years now."

Sean smiled as a tear traversed his cheek.

"She said it seemed all right if you pined over her for a while before moving on, and then she started laughing."

"That sounds like the Patty I know and love, all right." After a moment, he took a shaky breath. "Thanks, buddy. I know that was hard for you. Are there any other words of wisdom you want to drop my way? If not, I need to hang up."

"One of the blondes from the beach is due there any minute for a little afternoon delight during Raine's nap?"

"Right."

"Later, big guy." Derek's voice was gruff and he cleared his throat.

"Hey, one more thing before we hang up. You think you can let me talk for a second or two?"

"You officially have the floor."

"I took Raine to a child psychologist."

Derek was quiet. Sean could almost hear the wheels turning in his friend's head.

"Do you think Raine needs to see a psychologist? Are you having problems with her?"

"No, nothing like that." He told Derek about the episodes with Raine, starting with their walk on the beach. "So now that I know she's special, I want to make sure I get her in the right setting, when it's time to get her into a school. And I figure in order to do that I need to know how special she is. I was able to get in to see the doctor Raine's pediatrician put me on to, who specializes in gifted kids. The ladies on the beach confirmed she was the best choice."

"She?"

"Yes, Dr. Noelle Victor, in Pensacola."

"So, was this doc another of the wanton babes you seem to be a magnet for?"

"No. I mean, maybe. I don't know."

"Whoa, buddy. What is it? Is she hot or what?"

"I guess she's attractive. But this is about Raine, buddy."

"Wow, guess I hit a nerve. Anyway, I knew you

had a smart cookie, there. But I had no idea…at any rate, sounds like a plan. Let me know if you need anything from me. A character reference, maybe? If the good doctor's worth her salt, it might be difficult for her to believe you're smart enough to be her father. And from the sound of her, wouldn't hurt me to get face to face with her."

"Very funny. Now tell me what you really think. Do you think I need to go dabbling with my little one's head? I really don't have a warm and fuzzy feeling about all this. What if there's more to this than meets the eye?"

"How do you mean?"

"I don't know, really." The uneasiness returned. "Just wonder if it's the best thing to do."

After a short silence, Derek spoke. "Do you want my honest opinion, or do you want fluff?"

"I think you know me better than that. Let me have it straight."

"Okay, here goes. I think you're making more of this than you need to. Look, you're in control here. Let the hot doctor look inside Raine's head. If you don't like what she finds or suggests, walk away. Take what you need from all of this, get Raine in the right educational setting, and throw the rest out."

Sean thought about this for a moment. Derek was right. He *was* in control, and he could temper whatever he learned from the tests the doctor had scheduled. "As hard as it is to believe, what you say, oh wise one, makes sense."

"Promise me, if you blow the doc off, you'll get her personal number for me. Seriously, I do think it sounds like the right thing to do. Now, can I talk?"

"As if I could stop you?"

"Look, why don't you and Raine come over next weekend? I could throw some dogs and steaks on the grill, and we could suck down a few brews. What do you say? Maybe you could call up a few of your beach bunnies and invite them along. Hell, invite 'em all. Tell them you've got this good-looking, hunky, divorced, brilliant literary-agent guy friend who happens to need to get laid. Or if you can bring one of 'em for me and one for you, a hot and horny redhead would be my first pick, in case I have a choice."

"Big boobs, right?"

"Exactly. You know me well, my friend."

"You got it," he agreed, but knew the party would never happen. "Make sure you call the grocery store ahead of time, so they can stock enough meat to fill my kid up. Oh, and get plenty of booze. That redhead will need it when she gets a load of you in shorts."

"I don't do shorts, man. You know that. But I *could* wear a Speedo, I guess."

"Yeah, that would work," Sean replied with as much sarcasm as he could muster.

"Just remembered, I don't have a Speedo. Maybe I could borrow one of yours? No, no, that won't work either—too tight in the crotch."

He laughed. "Just get the food."

"Way ahead of you, man," Derek said, laughing. "Way ahead of you."

Chapter Four

Two months later

Sean fidgeted in his chair, alone in the observation room. Behind the glass, Raine sat in a small chair across a low table from the testing technician. She seemed alert and offered quick and succinct answers to the questions. Sean was amazed at the depth of her knowledge concerning a variety of subjects, restoring his faith in the *Daily News*, as well as the archaic encyclopedias, which were her primary sources of information.

He glanced at his watch. She was an hour and a half into the tests, and seemed as fresh as a flower, while dear ol' Dad continued to sweat bullets. A side door to the observation room opened.

"How are you doing, Dad?" The doctor smiled and leaned inside the room.

"Not as well as Raine, I suspect."

She smiled that smile Sean had grown fond of over the last several weeks. He had learned to relax during the last two sessions—and become a little less wary of making eye contact. The jury was still out on how those piecing blue eyes were truly affecting him. Her smile was infectious and time spent with the doctor was becoming less stressful. Acceptance of the doctor's role had come much easier for Raine—she had continued to

33

build on the relationship sown during the initial appointment. The two ladies had quickly become two peas in a pod. It was difficult to keep up with their banter. At times they seemed in their own little world, oblivious to such outside factors as the dad.

"She's doing so well." She sat in the chair next to him. "She's such a bright, delightful child." She touched his arm lightly, and Sean wanted to cover her delicate hand with his. After a moment, she withdrew and stood. "Let me know if we can do anything to make this more comfortable for you. We're almost done. Because we haven't had to use the extra time slot for testing, this should be the last appointment for a while. From here, we wait for the results and then reconvene for the next step."

"The next step?"

"Yes, the hard part's over—we then have to determine the best choices for her education and development based on what we'll have learned of her intellect, weighing of course the social impacts."

"I assume you mean to make sure she is emotionally and socially equipped to thrive in whatever environment we decide for her?"

"Exactly," she said and gave him another one of those smiles. "I see you've been paying attention."

"I try."

"I'll check back in a little while, when this last round of advanced testing is over."

She moved toward the door, but Sean wanted her to stay, if for nothing more than to look into her eyes and listen to her voice. He searched for words to stall her exit but could think of none. He continued to examine the intense feeling he had known her for much longer than the several weeks since their first meeting. He watched her walk toward the door. His initial skepticism had made an about-face.

That, in itself, was of great concern. The conversation from the testing room registered once again with Sean, and he noticed the doctor had stopped mid-track at the door and turned toward the glass. She slowly made her way back to the chairs and sat next to him, listening intently. She turned toward him.

He met her eyes momentarily and then focused on the exchange between Raine and the technician. Another look at the doctor's face told him she too was astounded. Raine's answers had reached a new plateau. At a break in the conversation, she muttered, "My colleagues aren't going to believe this one. Her depth of knowledge. That perception. My God, she seems to know the next question before it's asked."

Sean shot the doctor a worried glance that seemed to go unnoticed. He continued to look at the doctor, as though he was seeing her for the first time. Tiny bells of alarm sounded in his brain.

This type of comment was not something he wanted to hear from someone entrusted with his child's well-being.

****

Raine glanced into the mirror and waited for the next question. Daddy or Miss Noelle or maybe some other people were on the other side of it, though Daddy had never mentioned watching her after the other testing sessions. She found it funny that the grown-ups didn't know she was aware she was being watched. Not only had she read about it in the books at home, she had seen a one-way glass once on Daddy's television.

Sometimes he left the TV on in his room during the night. She guessed it helped him get to sleep. One time she came to his room in the middle of the night and was distracted by a program where a bad guy was being questioned about something bad the police thought he did. She watched the people watch the bad guy through the one-way glass and thought it funny when the man in the room who was questioning the bad guy walked up and fixed his hair in the mirror while everyone in the other room watched him. She never quite understood why they didn't laugh like she did that night sitting on the carpet in Daddy's room.

"Miss Raine, I wonder if you could tell me who makes the laws in our country?"

The question brought her back, and she turned toward the technician. "You mean our Congress?"

"Yes, can you tell me how that happens?"

"Do you mean what the Congress is supposed to do, or what they really do?"

This seemed to confuse the technician. She flipped some paper, took her pen, and wrote something in a notebook. "Let's stick to what the Congress is supposed to do."

Raine explained how the House of Representatives voted on bills and passed them on to the Senate, how the House controlled the funding of laws, and how the representation was determined by districts, based on the population, and how the Senate was composed of two senators per state. She went on to name the various sub-committees that existed and what a few of them were working on. She had found a website once on Daddy's laptop that went into great detail concerning each congress person's staff and what the function of each person was but figured the technician might not be interested in that—or have enough time to listen. There was much more she wanted to say concerning what the Congress did that they weren't supposed to do, and how other branches of government seemed to take liberties outside their authorities, but the technician interrupted her.

"That's—that's fine, Miss Raine," she said. Her hands shook as she looked through her notes. "Let's move on to the executive branch of the government. Can you tell me who the President is?"

The technician looked sick as she recited both the names of the President and each member of the Cabinet. She went on to the vice president after that but was stopped before she had finished with the names and staff positions of the First Lady.

"That's very good." The technician poured water from a pitcher into a glass. "Would you like some water?"

Raine shook her head. "Don't you want me to finish? Don't you want to know the names of all the members of congress and what state they represent? I also know the names of most of the state congress members, too, if you want."

The technician's face was very pale and she couldn't seem to find words. Instead, she glanced nervously toward the mirror. She turned to Raine with a funny look on her face and stood.

"Miss Raine, would you excuse me for a moment?" Her arms shook as she leaned across the table toward Raine. "Let's take a short break. I-I'll be right back."

Guess she wasn't interested in hearing about the White House staff.

****

Noelle sat in her office and reviewed the events of the day. The session with Raine Sampson had been surreal. Never in her entire career had she witnessed such perception and intelligence from a child, especially considering she was not yet three years of age. When she thought of her reaction to Raine's answers posed by the technician, she put her hands over her face and shook her head.

"Everything all right?"

She flinched and looked at Connie, who stood in her office doorway.

"I'm sorry—I didn't mean to startle you. I was just closing everything down and getting ready to leave."

"No, that's fine." Noelle took a deep breath. "It's been one of those days."

"You're talking about the Sampson child, aren't you?" Connie moved closer and leaned against the desk. "I read your notes before I filed her chart."

"Yes, extraordinary."

"To say the least. Something else bothering you?"

Noelle frowned and looked at her friend. "I'm afraid I might have stepped over the line with her father."

"How do you mean?"

"I guess I let the excitement of the moment overrule my professionalism."

"I'm not following you." Connie sat in a chair across from her desk.

Noelle guided a strand of hair behind her ear. "As you might imagine, as a single parent, Sean is very protective of his child. I don't know where Raine's mother is, but it seems he's on his own in raising her, and dealing with all the ups and downs that come with it. And then I go and make a stupid comment."

Connie inquisitive expression was not unexpected.

"My first thought was that I couldn't wait to discuss this case with some of my colleagues." She shook her head and examined a cuticle on her right hand. "I'm afraid Sean might have misinterpreted my priorities. Believe me, this little girl is so precious, and although at times she is on the top of her game, at other times I have observed her shutting down at the least bit of cross-examination. And Sean, in a way, is so much like her. He seems so vulnerable when Raine might be threatened.

"Connie, there is no way I would ever do anything to hurt him or Raine."

"Whoa, doc." Connie frowned. "Where is this coming from?"

"What do you mean?"

"Well, I've never heard you so concerned about a patient's or parent's feelings."

"I'm concerned about *all* my patients. *And* their families."

"Down, lady," Connie said. She held out her hands in defense. "I didn't mean to strike a nerve. You seem, well, overly involved with this one."

"Connie, she's a special little girl."

"And he's a special daddy, too?"

"Well, yes."

"Uh-huh."

"What's that supposed to mean?"

"You and I go back a long way," Connie said. "I think you know me well enough to know I call it like I see it, right?"

"Of course."

"I think this little girl and her father are more special to you than you are willing to admit." Connie stood. She didn't wait for a response and moved toward the door.

Noelle sat quietly and thought about Connie's comments. In a moment, Connie called out from the reception area and bid her good night.

"Good night," she whispered, but Connie was gone.

Her friend was way off base, wasn't she? She couldn't possibly be getting personally involved with Raine and Sean. This was something that could not happen.

Could it?

Chapter Five

There is an adage that claims the two greatest days of a boater's life are the day he buys his boat and the day he sells it. Sean carried Raine aboard *Time for Raine,* his vintage forty-five-foot Morgan split-cabin sailboat. To him a different saying seemed more appropriate—"A boat is a hole in the water into which you constantly pour time and money." *Time for Raine* required a lot of both, contradicting a third adage that suggested, "Sailing is free."

"Daddy, when did we get our boat?"

"Oh, honey." He paused from the arduous task of polishing the teak. "We've had this boat for a long time. Even before you came along."

"Did you have it before you met Mommy?"

He was surprised by her curiosity. He adjusted his sunglasses. "No, Mommy and I got it a year or so before we went to China to get you. She gave the boat to me for my birthday."

"For your birthday? Wow."

"Yes, it was the best present I've ever gotten. Your mommy knew how much I love sailing."

"How old were you when she got it for you?"

"Thirty years old." The words sounded ugly, as if he had spit something bitter from his mouth.

"Then, you're thirty...thirty-three years old now?"

"That's right, sweetie." Lately, he felt every one of

41

those years and a few more.

"And you named the boat after me?"

"Well, yes and no. We named the boat before we named you. And then we changed the boat's name because of you."

"Huh?"

Sean couldn't leave it at that, given the boat was named a few days before the trip to China. The boat and their daughter-to-be had been nameless for a year before the idea was hatched for either. They kicked around prospective names for both but couldn't decide. It wasn't a time he wanted to dwell on. On the day he and Patty learned of her cancer, they spent the night on the boat, trying to drown the news in drink and optimism that too soon turned to tears. Heavy rains poured down that night, a product of a weak tropical storm. They made love in the cockpit of the boat, lashed by the hard-driving warm rain, and resolved to christen the boat *Time for Rain*.

He looked at his sweet daughter, whose face begged to hear more.

"We named the boat on a night it was raining and decided Raine—with an 'e' on the end, of course—was also the name we wanted to give to you."

Raine gave him a wrinkled expression. "So did you name me Raine because of the rain or because of the boat?"

He laughed. "Neither. We liked the name. The boat was renamed after we decided on that name for you. Since it rained that night, it all seemed to fit."

She grew quiet and returned to scrubbing. He resumed his attack on some mildew on the starboard teak rail.

"Daddy, am I doing this okay?" Raine looked up through the straps of her life jacket. She had a small bucket of water with mild soap and was cleaning the Plexiglas pane of the bow porthole to the forward cabin. She frowned. "Daddy, it looks like your back is burning."

It was early March on Ono Island, but the sun was hot enough to cook winter skin. Sean glanced at his shoulder.

"Yes, dear." He smiled and stood. He stepped into the cockpit, applied sunscreen, and shaded his eyes.

"You're doing a great job, little one. If I didn't know better, I'd say you took the Plexiglas out to trick me. It's so clean, I can't tell it's there."

She laughed and took a deep breath.

The back porch ringer from the house phone broke the silence.

"My little missy, what say we take a break and get something to drink?"

"Daddy, do you think that's Miss Noelle calling? Maybe she has the tests back? It's been a long time since I answered all those questions at her office."

"Maybe." He pulled on his shirt, knelt and faced her. "Sweetie, you don't have to worry about the tests. It's only to see which school Daddy needs to take you to when you're a little older." He smiled and gathered her into a tight hug. "Daddy's going to love you the same, no matter how those old scores come out, okay?"

She studied his face, and a smile crept onto her face. "I just kinda wish we could see Miss Noelle soon. I miss her. She's really nice."

He wasn't sure he was ready for her comment, but it all made sense. She was more interested in seeing the doctor than in how she did on the tests. He stood, grabbed her hand, and contemplated how to respond. He opted for silence.

They walked the finger pier toward the house, and the outside bell for the telephone again shattered the silence. Sean flinched, and Raine giggled. "I guess somebody else is anxious to hear from Miss Noelle, too, huh, Daddy?"

The doctor had said it would take two to three weeks to get the results. With them overdue, he had imagined all sorts of reasons why they were so late. Were the results bad? Had the nature of Raine's answers indicated other issues with her? What if she did exceptionally well? What would that mean? All the questions were getting to him. Perhaps his daughter sensed this, in spite of his efforts to downplay the results. He found consolation by assuring himself that no matter what the test results revealed, life would go on as usual. More than once, he had reminded his daughter of the doctor's assurance there was no pass and no fail. According to her, the tests were quite difficult, designed to push the limits of a child's knowledge.

"Daddy, what happens if I did really well on the tests? Will I have to go somewhere far away to school?"

Sean paused again and knelt. Since that day last fall, the way he communicated, the way he related to his daughter had changed dramatically. He was forced to stop treating her like a toddler and start treating her as an older and more mature child. And yet she was still only three years old. In terms of his relationship with her, it was as if years had passed in a matter of a few months. He wasn't quite sure how he felt about this. In some ways they had been robbed of those precious years of her growing up. He would watch her closely and do what he could to protect her from her own speedy maturation process.

"Of course not, little one," Sean said. "Daddy wouldn't send you off somewhere to school." He looked into her eyes. "You know Daddy couldn't spend even one day without seeing you. And even if that were so, you know Daddy would go with you and be with you the whole time, don't you?"

She giggled and threw her arms around his neck. "I love you, Daddy."

Inside the kitchen door, he picked up the phone on the fifth ring, beating the answering machine. Dr. Victor responded, and he put on his casual face. His hands shook slightly, and he wondered if it was for the anticipated test scores or from getting a chance to speak with the doctor again.

"Hi, doc, can you hold on a minute?"

"Sure." There was excitement in her voice. "Oh, and don't you think it's time you called me Noelle?"

Sean turned to Raine. "Honey, why don't you get a juice box from the fridge and if you can reach it, would you get Daddy a bottled water?"

Raine nodded.

"Sorry, doc—I mean Noelle, we were out on the boat."

"Hmmm, that sounds great. I'm envious. Well, we got the test results in late yesterday. I wanted to call you then, but I know you're busy that time of the day getting dinner and settling Raine in for bed."

"No problem. You can call me any time, day or

night." He took the bottled water from little outstretched hands. He covered the phone for a moment, and whispered a thank you to his daughter, who stood looking at him expectantly. "So what's the story?"

After an audible deep breath, she spoke slowly. "I don't know any other way to say this but to say it straight out."

There was enough pause to give Sean worry. Little dark eyes watched him closely.

"So, is my daughter a genius, or what?"

"I've never seen anything like this…ever. Neither have any of my colleagues."

"Go on," Sean pleaded as calmly as he could muster. He gave his daughter a thumbs-up. His heart continued to race. The phone went silent. "Noelle?"

"Sorry. I was reviewing the charts and summaries again." She took a deep breath. "On the cognitive tests, she made the highest rating."

"You mean higher than the other tests?"

"No, Sean," she said as if he had asked an absurd question. "The institution's highest rating ever recorded for that phase of the testing. For any child. Anywhere. Anytime. I thought it was a mistake, so I called to confirm. They verified to me no other child had ever come close to that level of score."

"Wait a minute. Did I hear you correctly?"

"Yes, I'm talking the highest score ever registered by the testing engine. And this institution tests over ten thousand children a year, from all over the world."

His legs were weak, and he made his way to the chair.

"What is it, Daddy?" Raine hopped onto his lap.

He covered the receiver.

"Sweetie, you did really well on the tests. I am *so* proud of you."

"Sean?" Noelle asked.

He had taken his ear from the phone, totally forgetting about the receiver. He held it to his ear.

"Are you there?"

"Yes, I'm here."

"That's not all. On all the other tests, the quantitative ones, she made near hundred percent. Ninety-nine-plus percent average, in fact. No child has ever done that before in even *one* of these tests, let alone all of them. Few adults could do any better than eighty percent. She got an average ninety-nine point four percentile. That's on all of them. Essentially, what that means—"

There was a shuffling noise, and the doctor counted in a whisper. "Of the three hundred fifty-three questions on the tests, she missed two answers. And as I recall, her answers could be argued."

At this point, Noelle's voice had become loud enough for Raine to notice.

"I see," he said, as he moved the receiver away from Raine. "So…"

"When these scores make the rounds at the testing institute—and I'm not sure that hasn't happened already—people will be contacting us, wanting to talk with you and Raine. In fact, it might be difficult to convince some people the scores are legit. Fortunately, these tests are so closely held, the people who matter know they are legit. Since there is an annual award given for the highest score—and she will definitely blow the competition away—this will eventually get out to others in the scientific and academic community. I don't think anyone can stop that, HIPAA privacy laws or not. And then it will be a matter of time before the media and a whole lot of other people get thrown into the mix. I know this is probably as overwhelming to you and will be to Raine as it is to me, but Sean, your daughter is absolutely—"

"Wait. Wait. Hold on a minute. Can we just slow this down?" Although Raine was not facing him, she was very still, and he sensed she wasn't missing a beat from his reaction to the phone call. His heart hammered, and he fought a wave of panic. To make matters worse, he had to keep his cool with Raine. "Give me time to let this sink in and talk it over with Raine, and then we'll call you back. Can you fax or email the test summaries to me?"

"Of course."

He recited his email address, and after a long hesitation she said, "So." Her voice sounded much calmer. "I'm sorry, please forgive me. It's...well, it's just I've never run across a child like Raine before, and it's all exciting. Take all the time you need to review the information. Can I call you tomorrow? Wait, no. Check that. Oh, I'm sorry. You call me when you are ready to talk about the next step."

"Next step?"

"Sorry, shouldn't have gone there. You're right, let's slow down and digest what we have so far. There will be plenty of time to regroup."

"Thanks," he said, somewhat relieved the conversation might soon be over. "I'm sure you'll be hearing from us in a few days. At any rate, it probably won't be tomorrow. Tomorrow morning is Raine's birthday party."

Raine tugged at him and whispered loudly in his ear. "Can Miss Noelle come to my party?"

He was caught off guard. "Honey, I'm sure Miss Noelle has other things she has to do tomorrow—"

"Forgive me, Sean. I overheard. Actually, I don't have any plans. I mean, if you'd prefer I not be there, I would certainly understand."

From the first planning of the party, he had known Raine would want to invite her. He was surprised she hadn't asked earlier.

"No, please. Forgive me for not inviting you. Besides, I'm not sure how many mothers are coming. My agent and best friend Derek usually helps me with things like this, but he's on a book tour with one of his other clients. If you're up to it, I could use some help with the party."

"Really, I would completely understand if—"

"Raine would really like for you to come."

The moment of silence seemed much longer. "I would be happy to come. And help. Thank you for inviting me."

"Sure, I'll add your name to the list of guests at the bridge guard shack. Tell the guard you're coming to our house. Number eleven, Ono Way. Party starts around ten. Can you come early to help set up?"

"Of course," she replied. "I'll see you nineish?"

"Perfect."

He ended the call and tried to process all that he had heard. Raine laid her hands on his cheeks and turned his head toward her. For a long while she stared at him, her face inches from his nose. He stared back and tried to hide his apprehension. Soon, a smile crept onto her face. She shrugged and held out her little palms.

"The questions were easy."

Sean made wild eyes and showed his teeth. He messed up her hair and ran his hands over her head. "So easy for you? Hmmm, I see. Ve must remove dis brain and see vhat is causing dis smartness. I must call my assistant. Igor! Igor!"

She giggled and tried to escape his grasp. He held onto her tightly and cackled. "Your brain is mine, all mine!"

She laughed as hard as he remembered her laughing in a long time. Making a joke was what the doctor ordered. At least for his daughter.

As for him, all he wanted to do was make it all go away and will their lives to magically go back to normal. He had the feeling things would never be the same.

When things settled, after a few moments she smiled again. "I'm glad Miss Noelle is coming to my party."

"Me, too." For some insane reason, he really meant it.

****

Sean woke face to face with dark eyes staring at him. Those eyes were attached to a little body that sat directly on his chest. He'd had trouble getting to sleep and struggled to open his eyes. He glanced at the clock. It was barely six, four hours until the party.

"Are you awake yet, Daddy?"

"Aaghh, let me sleep, please?"

Raine had a different agenda and bounced on him, forcing the air from his tired lungs.

"Get up, Daddy," she pleaded. "Today's my party. We have to get ready."

"We're ready. Five more minutes?"

"Okay." She was still and quiet for perhaps five seconds before jumping again. "Time's up."

He gave up on the losing battle, sat up quickly, flipped her playfully, and caught her before she vaulted from the bed. He tossed the covers and swung his legs over the side of the bed. Light was beginning to show through the curtains.

"Okay, okay," he growled, hugging his bright-eyed daughter. "And how long have we been up?"

"You've been up a few seconds. I don't know how long I've been up."

He suspected she had been up since long before first light.

"I'm hungry," she said and took a deep breath.

"How would you like some birthday pancakes?"

"Yippee!" She was off to the kitchen. "I'll get the eggs!"

"Wait till I get there, young lady!" He rose from the bed slowly. Several joints popped and creaked in rebellion. He made his way to the kitchen, purposefully avoided looking back at his bed.

Three pancakes and a messy kitchen later, Raine leaned back in her chair and belched loudly. Sean looked at her and raised an eyebrow.

She giggled. "What, Daddy?"

"I'm waiting." He folded his arms.

She belched again, louder this time. "Is that better?" She broke into a belly laugh.

He laughed, too, in spite of efforts to the contrary. Discipline would have to take a back seat to birthday excitement. In an effort to save face, he wiped the smile from his lips with his hand. "What do you say, young lady?"

"Excuse me." She tried to mock him by repeating his action. It didn't work. The smile was still plastered to her face. Her expression turned solemn for a moment.

"You know, Daddy, if we were in China, those beeps would be a compliment."

Beep was the designated word for the expulsion of bodily gas—from either end. Because of her age, he had never considered teaching her the proper words for those bodily functions. He never imagined she would be able to pronounce belch or flatulence, let alone be able to understand the meaning of the words. And teaching her to say burp and fart seemed out of the question. As the magnitude of her statement caught up with him, he did a double take.

"Wait a minute, you excessive pancake eater." He followed her as she took her plate to the sink. "How did you know about the customs of your native country? Was that in the encyclopedias also?"

"Nuh-uh." She put the syrup back in the lower shelf in the refrigerator. "You're going to tell me about that custom."

"Oh." He rinsed the plates. "I see. So I was going to say 'Raine, in China it is considered a compliment to belch'?"

"See?" Her eyes lit up. "You just told me. I knew you were going to say that."

A weakness settled into his knees, and he stopped in his tracks. "What?" he cried, a bit too urgently. "Wait a minute, how did you know I was going to tell you that? You were guessing, right?"

Her demeanor changed, and she lowered her chin. "No...I mean I don't know," she whispered.

His mind raced, and he had the strong urge to shake himself awake. More than anything he wanted to press his daughter for an explanation, but he was treading on thin ice. Because of her sensitive nature, the wrong comment or tone could shut her down on the subject. She peered at him cautiously as if she thought she had said something wrong. Did she even understand how she had known what he would say? He made a conscious decision to table the matter. There would be a better time to broach the subject she had raised with her strange epiphany. In a couple of hours, Noelle would arrive. Maybe she would be able to shed some light on the subject. After all, he didn't want to upset Raine, especially on her birthday.

"Okay, birthday girl," he barked, forcing a smile. "Off to your bathroom to brush your teeth and then on with your party duds. I expect you to fall in at oh-eight-hundred hours for full inspection."

"Yes, sir, cap'n," she bellowed, saluted, and then marched from the kitchen.

The blood drained from his head. What had just happened? What else would surface concerning his daughter's intellectual gifts? Was he reading too much into her perception? His mind raced with the latest twist to her situation. This could not help in his quest to ensure that his little girl have a safe and normal life that all three-year-olds deserved. The whole situation was spiraling out of control, and there seemed to be little he could do to stop it.

****

Sean's chance to talk with Noelle came later during the party. All the mothers and kids were enthralled in a pin-the-tail-on-the-donkey effort outside on the back patio. He and Noelle were in the process of cleaning up from the cake fest. Noelle broke the silence.

"The cake was beautiful," she said. "You did a good job with the *Toy Story* theme."

"Thanks."

"Wow. Raine got a lot of nice gifts, too. Especially from Derek. I would say he made up for not being here with the motorized car. I think she likes that gift best of all."

"Yeah."

"Are you all right?" she asked. "You know, if there's anything you ever want to talk about, I'd be happy to listen. After all, I hate to waste all that training and studying."

He smiled.

"It's not often I offer a freebie." She stopped. "I mean—"

"It's okay, I know what you meant."

He put the dishrag down, took a deep breath, looked at her, and shook his head.

"What's wrong?" She backed away, a concerned look on her face.

"It's probably nothing."

"What?"

"Well, this morning after breakfast, Raine said something that's been bothering me all day." He proceeded to tell her, word for word, what Raine had said. Noelle was quiet for a long moment, stopped what she was doing, and looked at him with a frown.

"And she said you *were going to* tell her that?" she

asked. "That's exactly what she said?"

"Yes. And when I pressed her, she shushed up and became very uneasy."

"Can I ask you a question?"

"Of course."

"Did you and Raine go over the test results?"

"Yes, we looked at them for quite a while."

"Did you go over the questions and answers in detail?"

"Yes, she wanted to. Why do you ask?"

Noelle became quiet, walked to the kitchen table, and sat down slowly. "Well, I guess that fills in a few blanks for me."

Sean moved to a chair across from her. "Okay, let's hear it."

A scream came from outside. Sean was out the back door before the sound stopped echoing in his ears. Raine was on the concrete patio with blood on her face. Although it was a small amount of blood, Sean saw it as much more. He lifted her into his arms and frantically examined her face. Before he could turn to ask, Noelle held out a wet paper towel. Raine reached out for Noelle.

"I am so sorry," said one of the mothers. "We were playing a game, and she slipped and fell."

"It's okay." Sean took a deep breath. He reluctantly gave Raine to Noelle and wiped blood from his daughter's lip. Noelle held fast to Raine as if she were her own daughter, although she had told him she had no children. Raine had never expressed interest in being held by anyone other than him. She was not one to have social interaction with anyone, especially during stress or trauma. She had only recently become comfortable interacting with kids on the beach and at the playground. Never had she so willingly gone to another adult, not even Derek. To add to his bewilderment there were tears in Noelle's eyes. She held Raine's head against her breasts and rocked her slowly. Luckily, it was only a small cut on her lip. Her teeth and gums were unharmed. When he was sure the bleeding had stopped, he tossed the paper towels in a waste can. He returned and reached for her. Raine put her head on Noelle's shoulders and sniffled. He dropped his arms awkwardly.

Sean felt threatened. Yet he was blown away at how natural Raine and Noelle looked together, there in the morning sun on the edge of the patio. Noelle glanced at him and gave him a slight shrug of her shoulders, as if to ask, "Do you want her back?" He shook his head ever so slightly and followed them into the house. He only hoped his daughter wouldn't get too attached.

The three of them sat quietly at the kitchen table. Raine remained in Noelle's lap, with her head against her shoulder.

"Does your lip hurt?" Noelle continued to lightly rub Raine's hair from her face. Raine shook her head and sighed.

Noelle looked at Sean, and for a moment he was unable to glance away from her eyes. She seemed to be equally confused at how Raine had taken to her. The little girl lifted her head and leaned toward Sean. She reached out for him. Noelle handed her to him. Their hands touched as he took Raine. Strange, conflicting emotions caused Sean more confusion, as he took his child into his arms. Noelle's face continued to show concern. Sean turned his attention to Raine.

"Are you all right, now, sweetie?"

She nodded. "Can I go back outside?"

Sean lowered her to the floor, and she made her way out the door.

Through the excitement, he had forgotten about the conversation he and Noelle were having. He looked across the table to Noelle, who continued to look at him. She soon looked away and stood. He followed her back to the sink. He felt he was standing by a totally different person, one softer and more feminine. Shoulder to shoulder by the sink, he continued the task of rinsing silverware and plates for the dishwasher, as she wiped cake from them. As she handed him the last dish, her hand brushed against his. He gently placed the dish in the sink and turned toward her.

"Thanks for—" His eyes froze on her glimmering blue eyes, which seemed to search into his soul. Her supple lips parted seductively. He wiped his hands for a moment and then cupped her face in his hands. She met his advance with urgency by throwing her arms around his waist. He kissed her. To his surprise and pleasure, she relaxed in his arms and kissed him with equal urgency.

The back door opened, startling him. They separated and returned to the dishes seconds before the mother of one of the children walked into the kitchen. They turned and looked at the other woman, who looked uncomfortable.

"You two seem awfully busy in here," she said. "Do you need any help?"

They answered in unison, stumbling over each other's words. "No, thank you."

"Everything is under control." He waved her away.

The mother backed away and couldn't get out of the kitchen fast enough.

He had not been truthful with his response. Everything seemed anything but under control.

Where did the kiss come from, and what the hell was he thinking?

Chapter Six

"Do we have to move, Daddy?"

Sean sat with Raine in his Lazy-Boy chair, the place where he had soothed her through many sniffles, rocked away fevers, and shooed away bad dreams. This question was not one he expected to hear. He placed the test results on the table next to the chair.

"Of course not, sweetie. Why would you think we have to move?"

"I don't know."

"I like it here in our house. Don't you?"

"Yeah, I guess so."

"You guess so?" Sean wondered where this discussion was going and what was behind her concern. Nothing he had said about the test results should have prompted that, had it?

"Daddy, someday can we live on the beach?"

"The beach?"

"Yeah, I dreamed last night I woke up and heard the ocean."

Sean drew her close and kissed her cheek. "You know what, little one?"

"What, Daddy?"

"If you listen real closely, you can hear the waves from the beach right here in our house. Especially if it's not too hot or cold, and we leave our windows open."

Raine smiled and shrugged. After a few moments,

she crawled down from his lap.

"So you're okay now with the test results? Anything else you want to ask Daddy?"

She shook her head and bounded off to her room. For the most part, she took it all in stride, as if their several-day, thorough examination of it was old news. It was a different story for Sean. He continued to have long and hard thoughts about the tests and couldn't quite shake his concern over what the results *did* mean. The discussions with Noelle during the party kept resurfacing in his mind. They had never gotten a chance to resume the conversation concerning Raine's newly discovered gift. Instead, they agreed to table the discussions for a future meeting.

And of course there was the kiss. They had spoken a few times since then, but neither had mentioned it. He refused to dwell on it, and yet the guilt and confusion surrounding that kiss hung out there like a giant albatross.

He shook it all away. It was the end of the week, and following dinner and a bath, Fridays were spent with Orville Redenbacher and the movie of the week. This week's entertainment included popcorn and *Dr. Doolittle*. It was ironic that the movie he had chosen featured someone with an extraordinary gift, in this case the ability to talk with animals. Raine's was a much different gift, one that was as yet not fully understood or quantified, yet the world kept spinning as it did before. She was still a daddy's girl, and he was the daddy. If anything she seemed to need him more, not less. There was an air of excitement in the house but also a twinge of uncertainty hanging over them, which hovered just out of reach throughout movie night.

The test results and the discovery of Raine's extraordinary perception hung in the air like a thick fog. So many things could spin off out of control from here. Would there truly be a school nearby that could provide her with the environment she needed for learning? Would there be emotional issues for her from that intelligence? It was a lot for a little girl to deal with, not to mention what he as her father would face. How would he temper and protect her from all the inevitable recognition her intelligence would bring? There was too much new information, and not enough time to process it. Yet Raine seemed happy dumbing down with the old man, popcorn, and the flat screen.

He couldn't stop admiring the special little girl who snuggled next to him on the couch. Eddie Murphy's antics brought giggles and laughs, but the distraction of the movie also bought him some serious thinking time to digest what the events of the last few days had brought to them.

He fought to stay focused on the mindless movie for most of the early evening. Raine was exhausted. As the night and movie pressed on, her eyelids drooped. She nodded and was soon asleep, as cute as a bug in her long pink princess gown. He carried her into her bathroom, sat her on the toilet, and prepared her toothbrush. She flushed, stood, and staggered, while he brushed and flossed laboriously. She let out a big sigh and a "Daddy, I love you," and was asleep before Sean laid her between Ariel and Belle. He kissed her rosy cheek and watched her for a moment before turning out the light.

As always, standing for a moment next to her bed, he thought of her mother. Patty was always there in spirit, sharing every part of his day, every thought in his head. He thought of her countless times during the day, and often found himself thinking, *What do you think about that, Patty?* or *Can you believe our daughter, sweetheart?* Raine grew and changed every day, and he had to remind himself that most of the memories Raine had of her mother were the ones he had shared with her. Raine remembered nuances from looks Patty gave her, and time spent during midnight feedings. Yet with the recent parade of events, all the memories seemed more elusive of detail. Sadly, it was becoming harder and harder for him to picture Patty. Her image had blurred, especially in the past few weeks.

He always tried to keep the memories alive, yet in perspective. Strangely, his daughter aided in that process. Although he continued to answer the many questions concerning her mom, Raine asked them with less frequency now. As much as Sean missed Patty, it was better not to dwell so much on the past. Except for a small, framed photo of her mother, which sat on the bedside table in Raine's room, there was little indication of her in the house. He felt guilty. Had he removed most of the mementos because they made him miss her more? Maybe, or was it because they reminded him how lonely he was?

There were times when he dwelled on his need for a woman. But never so much as he needed one at that very moment, alone with his thoughts and the darkness of Raine's room. This thought, in itself, represented a big change for his life, one he hadn't felt during the last two years. But he didn't need just any woman. She would have to be a very special one to fill the void left by Patty.

In spite of his efforts to divert them, his thoughts drifted immediately to Noelle Victor. Of all the beautiful and successful women in the world, why was he dwelling on the very one who could damage his relationship with Raine the most? Her excitement and reaction to Raine's answers that last day of testing made him question what she hoped to learn or gain from his daughter's gifts. Although his initial doubts concerning Noelle had faded, he still wasn't sure what her motives were. And why were some of the things Derek related, concerning Patty's desire for him to love again, surfacing in his thoughts?

Never mind what anyone said. It wasn't time to move on. It was too soon to think about loving someone again. Raine was still the only person who mattered. He would continue to remind himself of this each time he looked into the doctor's hypnotic blue eyes.

****

There was no use lying in bed any longer; the battle for sleep was lost. Might as well get up and get going. The unseasonably cool, late April morning dictated indoor work. Sean resolved to bury himself below deck in the Morgan and attack jobs put off far too long. Most of the chores entailed work on the Yanmar inboard engine. Raine brought a few books to pass the time. She expressed a desire to help but, when faced with the prospect of icky grease on her hands, chose to read instead. She yawned and settled in below deck with Sean and Mark Twain, as cute as a doll in her jeans and sweater, red socks, and boat shoes.

Sean was astounded by her insatiable thirst for reading but remained vigilant in filtering what she read. He begrudgingly relented to her requests to read about a variety of topics, including high school math and science books as well as an occasional medical journal. She also loved the classics—at least the ones Sean allowed her to read. Trips to the outlet mall in the nearby town of Foley were more frequent now, simply because she had read her way through every allowable book in the house. To save money, he took her to the library. The increasing frequency of the trips and size of the stacks of books she blazed through soon required a different tack. After some thought, and despite the strain on the budget, he bought her a laptop and Kindle, albeit after paying extra to have the proper restrictions installed. It was worth it for the peace of mind alone. The last thing he wanted for her was to get the wrong education from the vastness of cyberspace.

All throughout changing the oil in the Yanmar, the house phone continued to ring. The thin hull of the boat did little to drown out the shrill of the outside bell. The caller or callers were persistent and weren't giving up easily.

"Let's take a break, sweetie." He stepped from the engine room into the main cabin, where Raine lounged on a settee. She closed the book she was reading.

"Daddy, it's sad what Mr. Twain said about the people in India," she said and sat up. "Do the people in China have the same kind of problems they have?"

"Ah, from *Following the Equator*. How do you mean, sweetheart?"

"Well, it seems there's nobody to take care of them," she said. "A lot of people don't have enough food and stuff."

"Unfortunately, sweetie…" He caught his breath and sat next to her. "A lot of countries, including China and India, don't value life like we do here in America, and don't have a lot of the things we take for granted here."

"We're very lucky, aren't we, Daddy?" she asked, nodding. "And I can't wait to help them all."

"Help who, my little one?"

"All the people of the world."

Sean thought for a minute and resolved that her pledge was generic, somewhat like a child wanting to be a fireman. Still, his curiosity was piqued.

"How do you mean, my little fix-the-world girlie?"

"I don't know."

"Well, I think that is a very nice wish you have." He smiled. "But before we go off saving the world, how does a snack sound? Somebody keeps calling the house phone, and I think we should maybe check out who's calling."

"Yeah, I heard all the ringing." She hopped up and took Sean's hand. "Wonder who it is?"

"Let's go see."

The phone rang again, as they reached the kitchen door. Sean grabbed a juice and water as he picked it up. He handed the juice to Raine.

"Sean," Noelle sounded frantic. "I've been trying to get you all morning. I tried your cell phone, too."

"Sorry, we were out on the boat," he said. "My cell phone is charging in my bedroom."

"Are you sitting down?" There was an excitement in her voice that made him smile, in spite of his apprehension.

"Should I be?"

"Guess who called the office this morning?"

"I give up, who called?"

"*World Cable News*," she said. He could have sworn she giggled.

"Serves you right," he said and winked at Raine. "You should've paid your bill."

"Very funny," she said.

"So, I have two questions," he said. "First, did they call concerning my brilliant and lovely daughter? And second, how did they know about my brilliant and lovely daughter?"

"Sean, the test results have been out over a month now. Not specifics, just generalities," she replied. "It was bound to leak out to the media sooner or later. I don't know, maybe some friend of a friend of an employee of the testing agency has a friend who has a friend who works at a network. You have to understand, this kind of news can't be contained for very long. Word had to leak out eventually."

"So, what happens now?" he asked. He ignored the signal that another call was waiting. He looked at the display but didn't recognize the area code or number.

"Nothing."

"Nothing?"

"I can't and won't divulge anything concerning Raine, although Connie said most of the callers knew a lot about her and you."

"Callers, as in more than one? Who called besides *World Cable News*?"

"I think an easier question to answer would be who *hasn't* called. After all, the test scores are quite a story. You should prepare yourself to be bombarded by the media. It won't take very long for all these callers to find your numbers."

"Cell phone too? Even though all my numbers are

unlisted?"

"Of course. They'll find a way. I want you to know I'm doing what I can to deflect them. Besides, you know I wouldn't or couldn't give out any information anyway, not without your permission."

"Are you asking for my permission?"

A short silence followed.

"Quite honestly, I don't know," she admitted. "I'm not sure *I* know exactly how to handle all this newfound notoriety. So I can imagine how you're feeling. I'm not sure what happens next."

"Thank you for that."

"For what?"

"Never mind," he said, relieved she was trying to temper the newfound fame. "Look, I know it's Saturday and you're off the clock, but I was wondering if you might be free for dinner tonight? Maybe we could talk more?"

Another short silence.

"Noelle?"

"I'm sorry," she said. There was an immediate change of tone in her voice. "I...can't. I have other plans. Maybe some other time?"

"Okay, sure," he replied. "I understand."

He didn't understand. What had happened? Why had her tone changed? It was as if someone had walked into the room, surprising her. As if she was trying to cut the conversation short.

After he hung up, he thought about the conversation for a long while. He felt terrible. Had he said something wrong? The suspicions again surfaced. What were her motives in evaluating Raine? What did she hope to gain from all this? Would she put her own aspirations above the interests of her patient? That's what Raine was to her, wasn't it, just a patient? No more, right?

There was so much he didn't know about Noelle Victor. And the more he thought about it, the more he wondered if the kiss had been just another strategic move to her. Was it a ploy to reel in his trust? No doubt, Raine could be a feather in her professional hat. The doctor could stand to profit greatly from the notoriety, not to mention draining him dry with her fees.

He had never felt so vulnerable. Why was he so drawn to her, given all his suspicions? With that one kiss, he had allowed his heart to venture out onto his sleeve. Now it was being slapped around by someone he hardly knew. All the bells of alarm were sounding loud and clear. And yet one fact came into crystal clear view.

He was falling hard for her.

****

Noelle hung up the phone and cried. She had willed the tears away during the conversation with him, but after hanging up they flowed.

How could he be so insensitive as to ask her to dinner after prefacing it with *I know it's Saturday, and you're off the clock*? Just like a man. How impersonal. What must he think of her? Was she also off the clock at Raine's party when she kissed him? And why had he not said anything about that since? Did the kiss mean that little to him? Apparently, at least not as much as it had meant to her. Yes, it was true; she was embarrassed. At first she considered what happened to be highly unprofessional. She certainly had no intention of becoming attracted to Sean, especially since his daughter was her patient. That didn't make her a bad person, did it? She thought not but still had a measure of doubt. Was her attraction to him having an effect on her professional judgment? How quickly she had grown attached to Raine! So many questions swirled around in her head about them both. She couldn't seem to make sense of any of it.

And if this notoriety of Raine's played out as she suspected, it could monopolize more of her time than she could afford, given her goal of growing her practice. Yet she was drawn to Raine and Sean like a fly to honey. Why was she allowing herself to get so involved?

That kiss. Understand it or not, it had happened. One thing was for certain—it wasn't a casual kiss, at least not to her. It had meant so much more. It seemed so right. She hadn't seen it coming, yet when it happened, she had absolutely no control over stopping it. At first, she thought it was something that was going to happen and then be done with. A kind of celebratory kiss of relief that Raine's fall had resulted in only minor injuries. Frankly, she wasn't expecting much from the kiss, given that Sean didn't seem to show much interest in her. What harm could it do? And then when his lips crushed her mouth, she was lost. Lost in another world she had been unaware of. The kiss had possessed her and made her so willing to be dominated. Her arms grew weak around his muscular chest, and for a moment she had felt faint.

Had a kiss ever done that to her before? She would be fooling herself if she thought so. Scott certainly never made her feel that way. Sure, Sean was bigger and stronger, but it was more than that. There was gentleness in his hands as he took her face and drew her to his lips. It was an urgent yet gentle need she had never felt from, or for, any man before. And then he had pressed her against his body. She was on fire as she felt his body react. What would have happened if they had been alone? She had fantasized about that. It was like a scene from a movie. Would she have been able to temper her passion? Would he? Did he harbor the same passion?

Other plans. Why had she told him that? Why hadn't she told him right then and there how she felt? With that thought, she admitted she wasn't quite sure how she felt.

And what do you know about him, Noelle?

Plenty, yet nothing. Just that he was a loving father who adored his daughter. But with adoration came his exclusivity. He was solely intent on protecting his daughter and had little interest in anything or anyone else.

God, he was gorgeous. Was that the only thing behind her desire for him? She refused to believe she might be that shallow. What she felt had to be deeper than that. He seemed to be so much more than a pretty face and body. He was successful and intelligent. He was the strong, silent type, and one of his best attributes was humility, something she hadn't seen in many single men. Instead, most eligible men were more concerned about the level of testosterone they could display than anything else.

Could she trust him?

She hadn't a clue. Something had to give. Her nerves and well-being depended on resolution concerning this matter of Sean Sampson and demanded it fast. Her desire to help Raine had to trump everything. And that meant having to keep her romantic interest in Sean at bay. She had known Raine a matter of weeks, and she was so attached to her, more than to any other patient she had treated. The little girl displayed a great many of the positive attributes her father possessed. She was very well adjusted, considering being separated from her mother and being raised by a single parent. Sean had truly worked miracles.

She thought long and hard about his wife. Or ex-wife. Or whatever she was to him. Had he ever actually been married? Did she live close by? Why did Raine live with Sean and not her mother? Did she ever talk to her mother, or visit with her? Noelle found herself wondering what she looked like. She would bet she was a beautiful woman, although he didn't seem to be the superficial type. Then again, he was extremely attractive and might demand that in a woman. Noelle was sure they made a beautiful couple.

How could she compete with that? She couldn't get her head around it all. She was having severe feelings of inadequacy and was not at all prepared to deal with them. Not with all that remained to be accomplished with Raine.

Chapter Seven

Three major cable networks, seven universities, including two Ivy League schools, and several corporations and foundations left messages on Sean's land line voicemail. Messages and texts piled up on his cell from various magazines, research institutions, and one think-tank, scattered among those from friends.

He had no clue what to do next. If he had his way, he would do nothing at all, but that didn't seem like a viable option. He doubted any of the callers would simply give up.

He tried to shield Raine from most of it. He returned the calls from friends and acquaintances, including Elaine and others from the beach bunch. Most seemed genuinely interested in Raine, with the possible exception of Elaine. Sean was sure she had ulterior motives for her calls, but she held no interest for him. He politely and diplomatically fended off her invitations and innuendoes.

Parks, the guard at the bridge gate to Ono Island, handled the local traffic. Sean called him immediately with a warning, after hanging up with Noelle. Sean hated to think what the situation would be without the security provided by Ono. He couldn't imagine what a nightmare he would be facing otherwise, from news vans, reporters, and TV stations, all parked outside his home. Thank goodness none of them would make it that close! Living in a gated, island community did have its benefits.

Nothing, however, could compare with an incident that occurred at the Sampson household. It stirred a hornet's nest of speculation on how smart Raine was. A couple of weeks after the news leak, when Sean was helping his daughter develop the motor skills necessary for faster Internet surfing on her new computer, he left her to practice, while he took a quick shower, confident the restrictions built into the device would render the situation safe for the few minutes needed for his shower.

He hadn't thought about restricting the house phone.

After his shower, he returned to the den and found Raine talking away with someone, her little face plastered to the receiver. At first, he refused to panic and was confident the call was from someone she knew, maybe Derek or Noelle, both of whom routinely called. It soon became apparent, as he finished towel-drying his hair, that the call was from persons unknown. Before Sean could ask, Raine noticed him and told the caller she was sorry, she had to go. She abruptly hung up the phone.

"Who was that, sweetheart?"

"I don't know." She twirled a strand of her hair. "Some professor. I forgot his name, but he was from some school in Massachusetts."

"A school in Massachusetts?"

"MIT or something like that," she replied.

Aware of his daughter's sensitivity level, Sean feigned disinterest. "Oh, really?" he asked. He grabbed a book and sat across from where she sat with her

73

laptop. "And what did *he* want?"

"He first asked for you, but I told him you were in the shower. Then he asked if he could talk to me for a minute."

"And you said—"

"I said sure."

"Of course," he said. "And what did the two of you talk about?"

"Cosmological Pendulum and other stuff like that," she said so matter-of-factly it shocked Sean.

"Which is?"

"Oh, it has to do with the theories of the origin of the universe. Stuff like that."

"I see," he said, but in reality was aware of how little he did know about the subject. "And what was the outcome of this conversation?"

"I think he understands now." She continued searching for characters. She typed slowly but deliberately on the keyboard. He found it strange that as smart as she was, she still had age-appropriate dexterity, and struggled to find letters, numbers, and other characters on the keyboard.

"Understands it now, does he?"

"Yeah. I think he understands where he was getting confused about that kind of stuff."

He stood, put the book on the table. and knelt by his daughter. "Well, I'm glad you enjoyed your little chat with the professor from MIT. I am so proud of you, my little angel. Daddy loves you very much."

She smiled and hugged him. "I love you, too."

"Okay, well, if there isn't any other professor, scientist, theologian, or world leader you need to chat with tonight, what say we head for bed? I'm sure we can find an astrophysics textbook to read before you go to sleep if you want?"

"You're teasing me, aren't you, Daddy?" She giggled. He lifted her from the chair and spun her high in the air on the way to her bedroom.

Her giggle turned into a guffaw.

In no time, she was asleep. Dealing with such high level scientific and philosophical subjects had worn her out.

It certainly had for Sean.

Sean lay in the bed, the television volume low. On the screen was a suit jabbering on concerning the stock market, a newly discovered disease that hit a cruise ship, the fluctuating price of oil, and tension in the Middle East.

His mind drifted to the conversation he had with Raine before bed, and her pontification of science and technology. He tried not to overthink it. Her range of knowledge on many subjects and the intuition she displayed was simply beyond his comprehension. As he allowed the events of the day to soak in and he became drowsy, his daughter's picture flashed on the screen before him. He turned up the volume.

"Get this, Sheila," the suit said, and looked at the co-anchor. A chart flashed up on the screen. "This graphic was released today by the American Foundation—a renowned think-tank. Dr. Robert Seldwin, director for the institution, explains the graphic you are looking at on your screen."

A gray-bearded man appeared on the screen. The doctor's name flashed across the bottom of the screen.

"The American Foundation was able to secure the tests taken recently by the adopted Chinese three-year-old girl from south Alabama. From our intelligence models and based on research by several learned colleagues, we were able to postulate and compare the estimate of the three-year-old child's intelligence quotient with many scientists and scholars, both living and deceased."

A narrated short film of various scientists and suits followed, ending with the same graphic. Raine's estimated IQ was at the top of a list of several names, some of which were familiar to Sean. Notably, Einstein and Socrates were somewhere mid-list of the dozen or so names. A numerical IQ was listed to the right of each name. The numbers ranged from 140 up, bottom to top, with Raine at the top. But instead of a numeric value to the right of her name, the chart displayed a range of 185 to 200+.

Sean swallowed hard and shook his head as the camera panned back to the anchors.

"How would you like to figure out what grade this one should be in when she starts school, Bob?" Sheila chuckled as the background music faded in, and she straightened a stack of papers.

"Not me, Sheila," Bob said, checking the knot of his tie and feigning discomfort. "I have enough problems helping my ten-year-old with geometry homework. How could you possibly keep this child from becoming bored?"

The credits rolled up the screen, and the music cued louder as the anchors chatted silently back and forth.

"You have no idea," Sean said to the television screen. "Not one clue."

****

The calls began early the next morning.

"Thank you for your interest...Yes, I have your number and will consider your request." This was the fourth call in the last ten minutes. If there was anything positive about all the offers, it was that some were offering quite sizable fees for an appearance by Raine. Sean continued to prepare breakfast as Raine sat at the kitchen table with a coloring book. Before he could make any progress on the food, the phone rang again.

"Hello?" Sean's patience thinned. Worse, this was the third time someone from this particular tabloid had called. "Look, I told your other colleagues I'm not interested. Please don't call again." He hung up harder than he intended. Raine's eyes grew big as she looked up from the table.

"Daddy, why are so many people calling?"

"Well, sweetie, it looks like a lot of people found out how well you did on the tests, and they're curious." He glanced at her. She simply shrugged and continued coloring.

Earlier he had invited Noelle over for an informal cookout. It would be the first time she had returned to Ono since the party. They had spoken a few times, but the conversations continued to be icy. Her comments and answers were short and to the point, as if she couldn't wait to end the call. He hadn't pushed to find out the reason for her aloofness, figuring when she was ready, if ever, to talk, he would be more than willing to listen. He feared her change of heart might have something to do with a man or something else going on in her personal life. Try as he may he couldn't stop thinking about her. First chance he got, he was determined to find out what was going on. It had taken a while to admit it, but he was attracted to her and he wasn't giving up easily on pursuing the chemistry between them.

****

"Noelle," he pleaded, stepping in front of the door after putting Raine to bed. She was so close to making her escape. "Can you give me five minutes? It's concerning a conversation I had with Raine last night."

She nodded. The question sounded more like a command.

"Please sit down." He indicated a chair in the living room. As she made her way to the chair he took a deep breath.

"Have I said or done something to upset you?"

Like kiss me, while I was off the clock? "What do you mean?" She shifted in the chair and avoided those dark beautiful eyes.

"It seems you're very uncomfortable around me lately."

You have no idea. "No, I'm fine." She had to look away. "What is it you wanted to say?"

"Raine had an interesting conversation with a professor at MIT yesterday." He related the details. She sat quietly through it all. "Not to mention the countless offers for Raine to attend any number of functions and interviews virtually all over the country. I'm not sure where to go from here."

It was apparent he needed more than five minutes of her time. "Sean, I'm not at all surprised. Her scores aren't something that happens every day. In fact, we might never witness this kind of achievement ever again. Or at least not for a long time."

"So where does that leave us?"

What she was thinking was important, so she wanted to say it right. She had thought of little else since she had first reviewed those test results.

"There are really two courses of actions we can take. We sit this out until the news blows over, which in all honesty could take a while. Or we give Raine her 'fifteen minutes of fame,' if you will, and then get on with determining what the best plan of action for her should be."

He stared at the floor during her spiel. He sat very still with his hands folded.

"Sean, I understand how you must feel. This is all, well, very scary. I've been dwelling on this for a while now, and I really think the latter option might be the way to go. Set her up for a few selected appearances, and then let it all blow over. Oh, and I know this is getting expensive, but most of the national venues who have called will offer a fee for her appearance—some could be substantial. I don't know what your financial position is, and I certainly don't mean to pry, but that money could ease the pain of the costs of her evaluation, with enough left over to set aside for the future."

Sean looked up at her during the last part of her statement, but it was hard to read his thoughts. He sighed and rubbed his eyes with the heels of his hand.

"I'm not sure what's best for her," he said. "She's never been comfortable in a lot of limelight."

Like father, like daughter. "Have you talked to her about it?"

He smiled, and Noelle had to look away. A sexier smile she had never seen.

"It's funny." He gave her one of those twinkling

glances. "She seems fine with all the notoriety. She seems to be enjoying it. Can you believe it? My shy, sweet little girl?"

"Would you like for me to talk to her?"

His expression seemed guarded for a quick moment, then he nodded. "I think that's a good idea. And I'm sure she would love it."

She could guess it was a leap of faith and love for him to be considering any options that would put his daughter in any situation where he might perceive he would lose control of her surroundings.

"Daddy, I think I would like to do something to help people."

Sean flinched. Noelle turned to see Raine standing at the opening of the hallway to her bedroom.

"Maybe going on TV or talking to people might help," she murmured timidly.

Sean looked at Noelle and then to Raine. "Honey, if that's what you want, then I would be very proud of you. And I'm sure Miss Noelle would be, too."

"Absolutely," Noelle agreed and smiled.

Sean stood and guided his daughter back to her bedroom. Noelle's heart raced. At that moment, she knew she had vastly underrated the wisdom of this child.

Do I have what it takes to help this little girl?

In the few minutes it took Sean to return, she managed to regroup. To show any weakness now would be fatal in her quest to effectively evaluate Raine. She regained control and began charting a course of action, mentally reviewing the offers that had been extended.

When Sean returned, he looked perplexed.

"Is everything all right?"

"Yeah, fine." He sat across from her. "I was thinking back to that day on the boat."

"How do you mean?"

"I was taking a break from working on the engine. She was reading *Following the Equator* and was concerned about the people in Asia. And then, out of the blue she said she couldn't wait to help those people."

"Maybe this is what she meant," she said.

He didn't respond and seemed deep in thought and very uncomfortable. He continued to look at her, a deer in headlights.

During the next hour, Noelle and Sean planned a three-event trek for Raine, which included appearances and interviews in New York, Washington, DC and Atlanta. Noelle thought it best if Raine first accepted the offer from *Global This Morning*, mainly because that cable morning show had consistently gotten high ratings and was offering a hefty fee. From New York, they would go to Washington to accept a special invitation from an Alabama representative to observe a House session. Finally, they would go to Atlanta for a taped interview with *World Cable News*, which would be aired later that month in a special gifted-children documentary. To somewhat prepare them for the major networks and events, Noelle suggested a brief appearance at a local TV news show.

"Thanks for planning all this." His look melted her heart. "This kind of stuff isn't my strong suit. I really appreciate you laying it all out. Makes things so much simpler."

"I would be happy to have someone at my office make all the arrangements if that's okay with you."

Noelle couldn't remember why she was so unhappy with him. Tonight, he was absolutely adorable. The memory of the kiss kept running through her mind.

"That would be great," he said and gave her one of those sexy smiles. "You don't know what a load off my mind this is."

In spite of her efforts to the contrary, she found she couldn't stay mad at him. He was just too damned gorgeous. Even his groveling was sexy, and he was so sweet and personable to her during the time they spent planning.

But at no time did he say a word about the kiss.

Even worse, he never tried to kiss her again.

Chapter Eight

"Can Miss Noelle go with us?"

Raine's question came out of the blue. Sean wasn't expecting it, although Noelle had been on his mind all day.

"You know, Daddy," she said and tugged on his sleeve. "On our trip next week?"

He nearly flipped a burger off the grill.

"Are you going to drop my hamburger, Daddy?" Her gaze followed the rolling hunk of meat as he caught it with the spatula before it fell onto the patio.

"Well, sweetie," he said and cleared his throat. "I'm not sure that's a good idea."

"Why, Daddy? Didn't you tell me we would have connected rooms at the hotels where we are going?"

"Well, yes," Sean said tentatively. Before he could offer another objection, her face drooped and she climbed back onto her patio chair. He suspected this wasn't the end of the conversation. He had never known her to give up so easily. As he paused for a moment to drink some ice water, she confirmed he was right.

"Hey, Daddy? Didn't you say each room had two beds?"

"Well, yes, that's right," he said. "But I'm not sure—"

"Noelle could sleep in one, and you could sleep in

the other."

Sean almost choked on his water. "No." The word was louder than he intended. But nothing was going to deter his daughter's persistence.

"Hey, wait." She rocked in her chair. "Miss Noelle could stay in the room with *me*. That would be neat! Girls in one room and you in the other."

He stood in front of the grill. His face felt hotter than the coals. He glanced at his daughter and suspected he had been set up. As innocently as her conversation had meandered around to the two ladies staying in the same room, he wondered if she had planned it this way from the start. Propose the preposterous, and then offer a solution that seemed doable.

He looked at his daughter. *Why, the little sneak. She set me up.*

Her smile widened, as if she knew she had been caught. "Can we ask her, Daddy?" She flashed that pitiful look she was becoming so skilled at. "Please?"

There was no denying her.

"She's due here in a few minutes. We can ask her later, maybe after we eat, so we don't spring it on her when she first walks in. And don't be disappointed if she says no. She is very busy and a very good doctor. She has a lot of patients."

"Oh, thank you, Daddy." She sprang from the chair, hugged his leg, and skipped toward the kitchen door. "I'll go watch for her."

As Sean finished the grilling, Raine walked outside, hand in hand with Noelle. He did a double take. She looked even better than the last time he had seen her. In fact, she seemed to look better every time he saw her. Had she done something special with her hair? Was her makeup different? Did she even wear makeup?

During the pleasant conversation before and during dinner, he couldn't seem to take his eyes from her.

"So which princess is your favorite?" Noelle asked, taking a break from the food.

"I like Belle the best."

"Why is that?"

"Because she isn't afraid of the beast," she said, her mouth still full of food.

"So you like her because she is brave and isn't intimidated by big ugly beasts?" Noelle glanced toward Sean, and Raine giggled.

"You mean like my daddy?" Her giggle turned to a belly laugh, and in spite of the implication, he was more concerned she might choke.

"Oh, no, sweetie, I didn't mean your daddy was big and ugly." Noelle's face turned red, and she dropped her fork on her plate. She glanced back and forth between them and, after noticing the smile on his face, joined in the laughter. Raine regained her composure and the conversation continued between them.

Sean sat back in the cushioned chair and enjoyed the banter. The sun made its late-day escape, but the warm temperatures were holding. The spring rains had been light, and tourist season was beginning to kick into gear. It was beach time in coastal Alabama, but given recent events, he wondered if they would ever again be able to go to the beach and enjoy a simple uninterrupted session of sandcastle building and boogie-boarding.

He finished his food and continued to watch the ladies' feeding frenzy. When it came to eating, they were two peas in a pod. He couldn't figure it. Raine ate like a horse and never seemed to gain an ounce. Noelle's appetite seemed as ferocious, yet she was quite slender. Where were they putting it?

"Daddy, why are you staring at us?" Raine paused from the mêlée and glanced at him with a concerned look on her darkly tanned face. She was so beautiful in her pale yellow sundress. It seemed a perfect complement to Noelle's floral spaghetti-strap dress.

"Your daddy is wondering where you put all that food you're eating," Noelle offered with a smile.

"Me? All the food *I'm* eating?" Raine shot back playfully and glared at Noelle's plate. "How about *you?*"

This seemed to catch Noelle by surprise, and she gave Sean a quick look. He gave her a palms-up gesture and an inquisitive smile. Noelle countered with a frown. She then looked back and forth between them. Sean tried valiantly to suppress a laugh.

"Oh, I get it." She dropped the last bite of burger onto her plate. "You two think I eat a lot, huh?"

He shrugged. He wasn't going there. Raine was another story. She was fearless.

"Weeell?" she said and laughed. Noelle started for her, but the little girl anticipated the move and escaped. Noelle chased her around the patio. Raine allowed herself to be caught and let out a belly laugh as Noelle tickled her. Sean sat in his chair, watching it all with a silly grin on his face. The two ladies settled back into their chairs.

After a few more bites, Raine looked at Noelle. "You can finish your hamburger, Miss Noelle," she said without a smile. "I promise Daddy won't say anything else."

Sean raised his eyebrows and shot Raine a piercing look. "*Daddy* won't say anything else? Daddy never said anything to start with, little Miss-Behavin'. You keep this up, and you are gonna get Daddy in a lot of trouble."

A few moments of silence passed, and Noelle eyed the unfinished burger. "Well, if you insist." She picked it up again. "I'd hate for your daddy's good cooking to go to waste."

After dinner, during a game of Scrabble, Raine yawned. Destroying her competition was quite tiring for her. Although both adults had challenged some of Raine's words, Mr. Webster confirmed without fail the authenticity of Raine's array of offerings.

"I can't believe that's a word," Noelle pointed to one of Raine's seven-letter creations that ran to a triple word square. "And how does one get eighty-five points for one word?"

"And how, young lady," Sean added, pointing to another quadrant of the board, "can you tie a long word like that into three other words?"

"I don't know, matey," Raine growled pirate-like, through another yawn. "The words just pop into me head."

"Arr, missy," Sean barked, standing and twisting an imaginary mustache. "Maybe ye can think over it during bath time, and then tell us yer secret. Or it'll be walkin' the plank for ye!"

"Can the lassie give me bath, Cap'n?"

Sean glanced to Noelle, who didn't seem to want to wade into the pirate talk. She simply smiled and nodded.

"Sure, sweetie," he said. "If she…the lassie doesn't

mind."

"Of course, sweetie," Noelle replied.

"I'll put the game up while you get your bath and get ready for bed." He poured the letters from the board into the box and began turning them face down.

As the ladies left the patio, Raine stopped and turned to Sean. "Daddy, aren't you going to ask Miss Noelle?" She had quickly dropped the pirate script. It was all business now.

The smile slipped from Noelle's face, replaced by an inquisitive look. "Ask me what?"

Sean's mouth went dry and his pulse raced. He wasn't sure why he was so nervous. Other than the fact she would probably say no quicker than he could get the question out. And if she passed would it be because someone special to her might object to her going on a trip with another man? Or would it be due to the restraints of her practice? Surely she wouldn't be able to arrange the time off, not with such short notice. Whatever the reason for the anticipated rejection, he wasn't going to let it keep him from asking.

He took a deep breath and bit the bullet. "Noelle, Raine and I were wondering if maybe you would like to accompany us on the trip," he said. He geared up for a rejection.

"I'd love to."

"I know you have patients and a schedule—" He did a double take. "What did you say?"

"I said I'd love to go with you on the trip. I assume you mean New York, DC, and Atlanta, and not just to the warm-up local appearance?"

Sean was shocked. Raine squealed and nodded. She looked back and forth between the adults.

"I thought you would never ask," she replied to Raine and took her hand. "You and Daddy might need me there with you, you know."

The two ladies walked into the kitchen, leaving Sean alone in awe. She had wanted to go all along. Was it because she had known all along they needed her? Could he let himself believe she might want to go with them for other reasons? He resolved that it really didn't matter what her motives were, he and Raine *did* need her.

At the moment, he couldn't quite decide which one of them needed her more.

****

Noelle's heart rate slowed while she was bathing Raine, who all the while rattled away about how much fun they were going to have in New York. She tried very hard to temper her own excitement. It would be a working trip for her, and she had to keep that fact ever present in her mind. However, she couldn't deny how attached she had become to Raine, and how attracted she was to Sean.

She had hoped she would be invited on the trip. She had gone so far as to have Connie arrange a light week, with a back-up plan of taking a few well-earned days off if she wasn't invited.

And now she was going. She wanted to jump up and down and squeal with joy like a teenager. "What about other parts of the trip? You haven't said much concerning Washington and Atlanta. How do you feel about the interview with *World Cable News*?"

"I don't know." Raine shrugged. Her eyes lit up. "But I can't wait to go to Six Flags Over Georgia after the TV thing."

"I thought you and your daddy might need a break after the interviews and tours." Noelle wasn't going to push conversation about the interview. There would be plenty of time to prepare for that.

"Miss Noelle?"

"Yes, honey?"

"Do you like baseball?"

"Baseball?"

"Yeah." Raine was so cute, smiling through a beard of suds. "Daddy likes the Atlanta Braves team. Sometimes after I go to bed, he watches baseball games on TV. He doesn't know it, but sometimes I wake up and see him watching the games. Do you think we could take him to a game after Six Flags?"

"That would be nice, sweetie." Noelle tried to picture Sean watching a game. Her mind could even make that scene sexy.

"Sometimes baseball makes my daddy cry."

"Cry?" The comment confused Noelle. She thought about saying something to Raine to get her to expand on her comment but remained silent. She should not let her curiosity concerning Sean's personal life distort her relationship or purpose with Raine. She wondered if the comment had anything to do with his relationship with Patty. In the course of evaluating Raine, whenever she tried to broach the subject of Raine's mother, Sean always seemed to change the subject.

"I think Daddy cries because Momma went to live with God."

The stab in Noelle's heart caused a weakness in her arms, and she nearly fell into the tub with Raine. Try as she might, she couldn't stop the tears. She was filled with sadness and shock. It had never occurred to her that Sean's wife had died.

"Honey…I'm sorry, I—" Noelle couldn't finish her sentence. Instead, her lip quivered, and the tears dripped into the tub behind Raine, as she washed the little girl's back. She was thankful Raine wasn't facing her. She wiped the tears away, and with all of her inner strength and will power, she managed to regain control. "That's so sad."

"I miss her, too."

"I know you do, sweetie." She willed more tears away. Her thoughts shifted to Sean. It was now clear why he avoided talking about his wife. She felt like a fool for her attempts to find out about her. Why hadn't she done the research and found out on her own? She was surprised Connie hadn't made the discovery.

"My daddy doesn't sleep very much." Raine's comment brought her back. It occurred to Noelle that the child might not remember her mother as her father did. Her pain wouldn't, couldn't be as deep as her father's. It was no wonder he didn't sleep, dealing with his grief alone.

"I'm sorry your daddy is so sad," she whispered. Her mind raced, still trying to process the news.

"It's okay." Raine's eyes lit up. "He doesn't seem so sad anymore. I think my daddy likes you, Miss Noelle."

Noelle blushed. The bathroom seemed suddenly warm.

"I think it's time for you to hop out of the tub, little one. It is way, way past your bedtime."

The prospect of facing Sean again took on an entirely different light.

****

Sean tucked Raine into bed and hurried back to Noelle, although she didn't seem overly anxious to leave. When he suggested they talk for a few minutes about the plans for the upcoming trip, she readily agreed. He offered to make drinks and was surprised to find she liked beer. He opened two bottles and handed one to her as they moved outside to the patio. The last of the day's light held onto the western horizon. A million stars twinkled above a cool breeze that promised to keep the mosquitoes at bay. They sat for a few minutes, quietly sipping beer. The silence seemed comfortable. The door to the kitchen opened. Raine stood in the doorway.

"Daddy, can we take Miss Noelle to the beach tomorrow?"

He looked at Noelle, but it was hard to read her expression. When she hesitated, Sean took the initiative.

"Honey, I would love for us all to go to the beach," he said. "But I don't think that would be much fun. You know you've become a celebrity of sorts lately, and I doubt if people would leave us alone long enough for us to enjoy the visit."

"I have an idea," Noelle offered. "Why don't you and Daddy come out to my beach house tomorrow?"

"You have a beach house?"

"Well, yes, I do, in Gulf Shores. My house is one of the last houses on Dolphin Way before it bends around to the north, away from the beach. Tourist traffic doesn't get out that way. Besides, it's also a gated community."

"Yippee!" Raine jumped up and down at the back door. "Let's go early, Daddy."

"Okay, okay." Sean stood. "But unless you go to bed and stay there, little lady, we aren't going anywhere."

He walked her back to her room and tucked her in again. She instantly squeezed her eyes shut and pretended to be asleep. It was nice, he thought, to see her excited and acting her age.

Outside again, alone with Noelle and fresh beers, they talked about the details of the trip. Soon the final preparations were made and a detailed agenda settled for the trip. He walked Noelle through the house to the front door. She surprised him by turning and giving him a quick kiss on his cheek. For a moment, she seemed to want more, before his surprise and uncertainty killed the moment. He rebounded, held the door for her, and told her good night. He watched her walk to her car and whispered loudly. "Are you sure you're all right to drive?"

"Of course," she whispered back. "It usually takes more than two beers to ground me. Especially when I'm only driving a few miles. I'll see you guys tomorrow morning. Don't bring a thing, just yourselves. I'll fix some snacks and lunch for the beach. Oh, you might want to bring sunscreen. I don't have much of a selection."

"You got it."

She walked away, and he remembered what had been tugging at his mind all evening. "Hey, Noelle?"

"Yes?"

"It occurred to me we never discussed how we should handle Raine's...special gifts when we get to New York."

She shut the car door and returned to him. "I've

been thinking about that, too." She seemed more somber and sober than she should have been. She seemed to want to speak, then shook her head. "We can talk tomorrow."

"Okay," he answered. "Good night. Drive safe."

She kissed her forefinger and placed it on his lips. "Good night to you. See you tomorrow."

He wanted to kiss her again but instead stood as if he were paralyzed. He managed to smile as she backed her car out onto the road and drove away.

Strangely, he missed her already. Tomorrow couldn't come fast enough.

****

Noelle stared at the laptop screen. Sean and Raine weren't due for a couple of hours. Why had she not thought about Googling her? There before her was a photo of Patricia Anne Sampson, adjacent to the article reporting her demise. Although cause of death was not reported, it stated she passed after a short illness, soon after returning from China with Raine.

She cried inconsolably, like she had never cried before. Why did this have such an effect on her? She had been working with Sean and Raine for a very short time, and she had never known or even met Patty. Was it because the relationship represented something she had always dreamed about for herself? Given she had loved only two men, she wasn't being fair to herself. Both relationships had failed. She had simply made the wrong choice in each case, hadn't she?

Dr. Victor, a master of analysis, was perplexed. On the screen in front of her was the perfect love story, tragically ended. She could see what made relationships work; her own parents were a case study in a successful courtship, engagement, and enduring marriage. Many couples in this country and across the world managed to find each other, sometimes in easy fashion. There were literally thousands of boy- and girl-next-door stories out there. Why was this type of fairy-tale love so elusive for her? She was pushing thirty fast and had not experienced true love, had never been *in* love, and never had someone be in love with her.

She studied the article once again, paying close attention to Patty's picture. The pretty chestnut-haired woman looked the pinnacle of happiness, glowing with the assurance she had found her true love. The photo must have been taken long before her death and gave no hint as to how she had died. A short illness could be any number of things. It did, however suggest a heart-wrenching end to her life and relationship with Sean. They simply wouldn't have had time to prepare. Two young people with a new baby, preparing for a long life of happiness together wiped out with the sudden realization that something horrible was going to end it all. This must have been excruciatingly painful for Sean. Raine was too young to remember her mother, but Sean would have been cursed with all the memories, good and bad.

Her first inclination was to take Sean in her arms and never let him go.

Her next thought was to run from him as fast as her legs would carry her.

As the hour drew near for their arrival, she stood at her bathroom sink, repairing the damage to her face left by her outflow of emotions. She flinched as the doorbell rang.

****

Noelle answered the door, wearing sandals and a white cover-up, looking better than the law should allow. Modest sunglasses sat atop pony-tailed hair. She smelled wonderful, courtesy of some sort of tropical-scented lotion, which gave her delicate arms a shine. Even though Sean was outfitted for the beach in his swim trunks, baseball cap, sandals, T-shirt, and shades, he felt underdressed and doubted seriously if he smelled near as nice. He stood dumbfounded, wondering if he could keep from staring at her all day.

He had surveyed the exterior of her beach house as they drove up. It was a modest structure, well maintained. White storm shutters adorned the big-paned windows and were propped open, inviting the sun in. They were a perfect accent to the pastel blue exterior. The frame structure sat securely on sturdy concrete stilts.

The interior entryway of her house was as beautiful as the exterior, painted a pale yellow. No expense had been spared in decorating. Yet the room was not pretentious and in fact was subtle and tastefully inviting.

"Come on in," Noelle said, but Raine had already made her way toward the back of the first level of the home, following the sunlight. She returned and looked up at Sean.

"Now that's what I'm talking about." The little girl smiled and in a flash was gone again. She accented her compliments with *ooos*, *ahhs*, and *wows*, heard as she moved through the house.

Sean thought of Raine's dream about living on the beach, and for a moment, he felt uncomfortable. He would not share this tidbit with Noelle.

"Sweetie," he called out and made his way toward her voice.

"It's okay." Noelle brushed his arm. "She's fine. Let her explore."

"Beautiful," he said. He never took his eyes from Noelle.

"Thank you. It's taken a lot of hard work, but I think I finally have it like I want it. A pity though, since I have so little time to spend here."

"You're not going to tell me you don't live here year round?"

"Yes, I'm afraid I am. Wish I did, though. As you might imagine, my office hours prevent me from spending a lot of time here. I do try to stay here a couple of weeks each year if my caseload allows. But even then I like to spend what free time I have traveling, so it doesn't leave much time for the beach."

"I guess this would be a haul to Pensacola each day. What, over an hour's drive?"

"Something like that, more during the tourist season. So, I spend what little downtime I have in my apartment in Pensacola, even though if you were to see it, you might think it an extension of my office. It's a small one-bedroom, but for the time I spend there, it suits me enough. Most days I pretty much grab a bite and sleep there, and that's about it."

"Daddy, come look," Raine shouted from out back.

He and Noelle walked through the kitchen out onto a beautiful wooden deck. Raine stood looking at the beach. An endless sparkle of docile waves stretched to the horizon. The sun danced on the turquoise waters of the Gulf of Mexico. A patio below was partially shaded by the upper deck but extended outward twenty feet or so into the sunlight, affording ample space for a small pool and for soaking up the rays. A path led to a private beach. Not a single person could be seen in the distance in either direction. The sugar-white sand hardly looked walked on and resembled freshly fallen snow.

He stood mesmerized as a peace settled in. What was it about the beach that seemed to mend matters previously thought to be unfixable? He found Raine's desire to live in a place such as this one prophetic.

The deck held a scattering of lounge chairs and small tables. A large rectangular canvas bag and folded beach chairs sat in the corner of the deck. As he noticed these, Noelle motioned toward the bag.

"That's your job, Mr. Sampson. That's a tent-type tarp that should provide us with some much-needed shade today. 'Some assembly required' has never been my strong suit. Why don't you and Raine head out to the beach and set it up? Instructions are on the bag. Oh, and take a couple of those beach chairs, if you can carry them. I'll bring some towels and a few drinks and snacks out in a few minutes."

"You got it." Sean turned toward his daughter. "Sweetie, let's check out the beach."

Raine was off, shedding her cover-up and sandals on the way, and was to the surf before Sean reached the bottom of the steps.

After he set the bag and chairs down, he quickly shed his shirt and sandals. In a few minutes, he had read the instructions and was ready to get to work. Ten minutes later, the rectangular tarp was up. He positioned it over a patch of sand that looked ideal for sandcastles, only a few yards from the surf. He rechecked the last of the four post anchors and tightened the lines. He looked toward the house to see Noelle appear on the deck. She made her way toward the beach. She was overloaded with the cooler and food, so he hurried up to help. Sweat trickled down his spine. He wondered if it was from his efforts concerning the tarp or from seeing her walking gracefully across the sand. He met her and took some of her burden, and they walked together to the tarp. Raine had wasted no time and was sculpting a sandcastle.

Noelle spread two towels over the sand, in the sun next to the tarp, and positioned a small pillow on one of the towels. He offered her something to drink and retrieved two small water bottles from the cooler. He watched her remove and fold her cover-up and lay it with her sandals, at the head of her towel. He was thankful for the shades he wore, which hopefully masked his expression. She wore a tastefully skimpy white bikini. He struggled to swallow a mouthful of water.

****

She packed a small cooler with drinks and snacks and watched Sean assemble the tarp. She found herself making small, quiet, almost obscene noises when he peeled away his T-shirt and attacked the job. His broad shoulders glistened in the sun and the ripples of his abs created rows of narrow shadows across his stomach. Spellbound, she watched as his arm and shoulder muscles moved in perfect harmony while completing the task at hand. The dark hair on his chest was visible, even from a distance, as were his calf muscles when he bent down to jam the anchors into the sand.

Oh my God!

Connie was right about those abs. The dark hair, as

it protruded from the baseball cap, made his image the perfect poster photo for any billboard ad that wanted to accent sexy. Anywhere. Selling anything!

She took a deep breath, checked the contents of the cooler, grabbed the towels, and walked out onto the deck, forgetting for a moment to close the door behind her. She was totally flustered. She wasn't at all sure she could walk. Her heart beat wildly. He looked up and trotted toward the deck. For a moment, she took him in through her sunglasses, and his god-like movements seemed to be animated and in slow motion, his firm muscles and abs glistening as they moved in perfect harmony with his tall frame. When he reached her and took the cooler from her, she almost dropped everything else. A trickle of perspiration formed on the small of her back. Her body responded to his being so close. Even though he was sweating, he smelled very nice, primal and definitely all man. She resolved to get in the water quickly, just to cool off.

Where was all this coming from? She had never experienced this kind of problem before, had never been so out of control, so excited from the sight of a man. Did he notice? Did he have a clue what he did to her?

At the beach, there would be no way she could keep the cover-up on the entire day, so she reluctantly took it off. He offered a drink, and she folded the garment and laid it neatly on her sandals at the head of her towel.

He turned toward her with his drink, and she lay down on the towel.

He hardly seemed to notice her bikini at all.

Maybe some conversation would get his attention.

"The tarp looks good. I can't believe how fast you got it set up."

"Piece of cake," he said, but seemed hesitant to make eye contact. Had she gone too far with the bikini? She tried hard to stay fit and slender. Had her efforts not been good enough? He busied himself with adjusting and stabilizing the anchors.

"You must spend a lot of time outside," she said, trying to extend the conversation. "You've got a good start on a tan. Such a nice skin tone—I'm envious. It seems all I can do is burn."

"Yeah, well, thanks," he said but only glanced at her for a moment before diverting his attention away. "That little girl likes to spend a lot of time outdoors. Between the patio, the pier fishing, and working on the boat, we do seem to be out a lot. Makes it tough for her, though—her skin's similar to yours."

With that comment, his glance meandered from her shoulders to her legs. He quickly looked away and cleared his throat.

"She…ahh, it's hard to—anyway, if I don't keep her slathered down with sunscreen, she gets burned."

Noelle took sunscreen from her bag. *Me, too. Please offer to put some of this on me!*

Sean seemed more interested in the sandcastle Raine was sculpting.

Okay, I get it! You're a great dad, watching your child. But what about me?

She lay back, frustrated. Obviously, he wasn't going to be distracted.

No matter what tactics she applied.

****

Noelle seemed happy soaking up the sun. Sean

joined Raine in the construction of a sandcastle. He doubted if he could carry on a conversation with Noelle without drooling on himself and gawking at her anyway.

Give me a minute to get used to that drop-dead body, please.

To say she wore the bikini well was an absurd understatement. He had suspected she looked good but never dreamed she was put together so well. She didn't seem to be aware that it made her all the more attractive. She was so unassuming, unlike a lot of women he had seen on the beach who continually flaunted it. If anyone deserved to flaunt it, it was her. It seemed that type of self-centered behavior wasn't in her make-up.

Oh, great! Something else hard not to like about her.

"Last one in the water is a rotten egg!" Raine shouted from behind a mound of sand.

Before he could react, Raine made a beeline for the surf. He quickly shed his shades and cap and ran after her. Before he could reach her, Noelle sprinted by him. He was definitely about to become the rotten egg. He kicked the waves and dove past his daughter, who had stopped in the very shallow waves. Noelle surged past him, out to deeper water. She laughed. The salt water played on her shoulders, and she wiped wet strands of hair from her face. Her smile was as beautiful in the sun as it had been that night in the moonlight on his patio.

"Okay, Miss Noelle, how did you get from there to here so fast?" He deliberately spoke loud enough for his daughter to hear. "And how did you get up from that towel and past me before I could get halfway to the water? I thought I was pretty fast, but you blew me away. Are you some kind of closet sprinter?"

"As a matter of fact, I am. Or at least I used to be. If you're ever near Pensacola High, you should take a look at the trophy case. You might see a few shiny objects with my name on them. Some track, but mostly for swimming. You might have to dust them off—it was a few years ago—but I think they might still be there."

"You're kidding me. What else should I know about you?" *I would really like to know!*

"Sorry, buddy." She swam closer to him. "That's it. I'm afraid what you see is what you get."

He checked on Raine who was back on the beach, playing at the edge of the water. He looked back to Noelle. It would be hard not to like what he saw.

"I'm impressed!" He struggled to tread water. Noelle moved effortless, barely making a ripple. "And I don't buy that 'what you see' stuff. I think there's a lot more to you than you let on. But be aware—I've read up on you. Your résumé is quite impressive and extensive. I think if you laid out your honors and awards, you might cover up a great deal of the track you used to run. Psychologist of the Year two years ago? Featured in *Psychology Today*, *Newsweek,* and *USA Today*?"

"Everyone gets featured in *Psychology Today*."

Sean scoffed.

"And if we're talking awards, you've got a few in your pocket also." Her smile lit up the day. She treaded water in a semi-circle around him. He moved around in pace to face her. "*New York Times* best-sellers list three books in a row. All kinds of literary awards."

Although he tried to hide it, his expression must have said all. Her narrative faded as he looked away.

"I'm sorry, did I say—"

"No, not at all." He looked toward Raine, who sat at the edge of the waves digging into the sand. "What say we see what that little girl is up to?"

To her credit, she never lost the smile. "Is that a challenge for another race?"

He held up one hand, shook his head and smiled. "Concede!"

"You're no fun," she said and frowned.

You have no idea, lady.

Together, they swam toward the shore.

Chapter Nine

In his book *The Winds of Time,* Sean created a scene set in Puerto Rico, where his protagonist was drugged during a crowded Cinco de Mayo celebration on a street in Old San Juan. When his hero woke, he was bound and gagged in ankle-deep water in a small, dark, and dank cistern. Snakes swam in circles around him. The water rose quickly from a sudden torrential cloud-burst.

On this fifth of May, as the plane descended toward Kennedy, a similar storm shook and rattled the wings and fuselage of a very old and worn 757. Sean sat with hands folded and looked out the window. He was doing his best not to look terrified. The plane tossed around in nasty turbulence, and it occurred to him that being drugged and surrounded by snakes might not be a bad alternative right then. At least, in his book he could write his way out of danger. His daughter was busy working a crossword, oblivious to the frightening situation. On Raine's other side, Noelle sat white-knuckled and smiling, trying very hard not to look scared out of her wits as well. The plane took a sudden dip in altitude, and several passengers screamed as if on a roller coaster.

Raine kept right on filling in words.

Earlier, a flight attendant serving juice and sodas smiled and patted Raine's head. "Aw, pretending to do the crossword, like Mommy and Daddy." Sean had looked at Noelle to catch her reaction, who did her best to keep from laughing. Raine gave the attendant a funny look, as if to say *I'm not pretending. You want to try and see if you can do better?* Instead, to Sean's relief, his little girl smiled at the attendant and filled in a nine-letter word for "wanting to succeed." Sean had seen the clue earlier while looking over her shoulders, and had come up empty. Raine said the clue, and it took her all of five seconds to pencil in a-m-b-i-t-i-o-u-s. As she wrote the word in, Sean frowned and glanced at Noelle. She again appeared to be stifling a laugh.

Another jarring bump turned Noelle's knuckles whiter, and Sean squirmed in his seat. Raine looked at him, then Noelle.

"Don't worry," she said and patted Noelle's hand. "This plane is built to withstand a lot more structural stress than the bad air we're getting right now."

In spite of his own uneasiness, Sean resolved this was sufficient reassurance they were in no immediate danger of crashing and dying.

An older gentleman seated across the aisle heard this wisdom from Raine. He gave Noelle a puzzled look. "What did she say?"

Sean couldn't hear Noelle's response, but the man smiled uneasily and nodded. A few seconds later, his puzzled look was back.

"Are you sure *Global This Morning* is okay with plugging the adoption process?" Sean pulled out all the stops in an effort to distract from his apprehension. The plane continued to bounce around. Noelle seemed relieved to have the subject changed.

"Yes, they were fine with it. It might have to be

quick, given we are scheduled for only a three-minute segment. And I let them know you don't want to talk about your books. At first they questioned this, but I think they finally understood we want to keep this about Raine."

"Thanks." He scoffed. "As you might imagine, Derek wasn't too happy about that. Oddly, he said sales of a few of my books have spiked since this whole matter leaked. What time did you say we go on?"

"After a break around eight a.m. I couldn't get a script of what questions they were going to ask. According to the producer, they keep it informal—a getting-to-know-and-introducing-Raine session."

The little professor was right; the plane was quite structurally sound and touched down in one piece, a few minutes behind schedule. A large, dark-skinned man wearing a chauffeur's hat and uniform stood at the exit to the ramp. He held a sign that read *Sampson*. They made their way through the hordes of people toward him. He smiled when he saw Raine. From behind his back, he produced a large stuffed lion with a mouthful of tickets. Raine's eyes opened wide, and her mouth flew open. She took the lion and gave the driver a hug, which turned the man's face a maroon red. He seemed instantly enamored with her and spread his arms. She jumped into them, and he held her all the way to baggage claim. He summoned help with the luggage and then carried her to the limo.

The driver knew the city quite well and tried to point out landmarks on the way to mid-town. Raine yawned, too tired to notice. By the time they reached the hotel, the droopy-eyed child offered little resistance to a pre-planned nap. Tomorrow was going to be a long day, and with the excitement of the city, Sean doubted she would sleep well that night.

Raine was soon snoring in her adjoining bedroom. Sean joined Noelle in the sitting area of the large suite. She stood in front of a bar, preparing to make drinks. She took two glasses down from a shelf. "You look like a Scotch man."

"Lots of ice in a tall glass, half-water, please." In a matter of seconds, she handed him the drink, and he fell into a soft chair. She poured wine for herself and took a seat across from him.

After taking a hefty slug, he smiled. "Ah, perfect." He lifted his glass. "You must be tired. Please, rest if you like. Tomorrow's going to be a long day."

"I plan on doing that. But first, I think we need to talk more about Raine. I've been doing a lot of research, and I have some interesting updates."

"Yes, absolutely." Sean rubbed his eyes with the heels of his hands. As much as he tried to think positively, a tiny bell of alarm gave him pause. "You talk, I'll listen."

"Okay, but feel free to ask questions as I go along." She gracefully lifted and folded those beautiful legs under her. "For lack of a better term, let's attribute the unusual talent Raine displays to the results of a 'hybrid ESP.'" She held fingers in quotes. "There's a few technical terms that might apply, but for our purposes, and from what I've witnessed, in addition to what you've told me, she doesn't quite fit any of the conditions or specific clinical categories—"

"Conditions?" he asked. "Is this some sort of disease?"

"No, not at all. And it's not the same connotation

you might apply to a medical or psychological anomaly. We should probably term it something else. Let's call her situation…well, simply a gift. I know we've thrown that word around a lot, but it really does fit. Because from all I have researched and can determine, this is not a disease of any kind and therefore offers very little, if any, downside. It's something she has that only a very few others possess. Basically, as in most situations where an anomaly of intelligence is involved, most studies indicate her gift is enhanced by certain chemical reactions in the brain."

Sean frowned and shifted in his chair.

"Don't be alarmed at that; it's not something to worry about. The better news is it doesn't come with any known side effects or conditions one might expect from, say, a savant or high-functioning autistic child. I mean like social issues, self-destructive behavior, and the like. What Raine has been blessed with is very rare."

"Are there others with this condition?"

"It's something only a handful of people currently or in the past have experienced, as far as we know.

"But let's get back to the chemical part. We don't know what causes her brain to produce the chemicals that enhance her ability of keen perception, or what regulates the level of the chemicals and causes them to increase or dissipate. So, the ESP she exhibits can come and go, depending on the level of the stimulating chemicals. Without getting too technical, there are literally hundreds of thousands of chemical reactions that occur every second in the brain. Most everyone has heard of two of the main chemicals—the ones that get a lot of press. Dopamine and serotonin are the most common. They are the *happy* and *mood* chemicals. But there is also a hormone called norepinephrine, which is secreted by the adrenal glands. This is the *fight or flight* chemical the brain produces when we're faced with fear or danger. The brain can respond in literally hundreds of ways, depending on the mix of this hormone with the other brain chemicals."

"I have to admit, this is Greek to me."

"Not to worry; it's Greek to a lot of people. But think of it like this. The level of chemicals her brain produces varies—when and why, we don't know, but it serves to dictate how strongly or how weakly her brain will react or in her case, dictate the strength of her extrasensory perception."

"You said there were a few others with this gift. How does her case compare to the others with similar ESP?"

She took a few seconds to formulate her next statement and looked gorgeous in the process. He was reminded of her at her office, and she was quite sexy in her element.

"Well, to start with, the other cases display this ability rarely, not frequently, as Raine does. I mean—and this is going to sound very strange to you—she has a nearly *constant* ability to know certain things before they happen. And unlike others with the gift, hers appears consistently accurate, not in the sense that she can predict the future and not even in the purest sense of the word predict. Now this is going to sound even stranger, but hear me out."

Sean leaned forward in his chair.

"It is more a situation where she can give you an answer to a question because her mind perceives that the question will be asked of her and an answer given to her in the future. The anomaly is that the question she will be asked—for the answer she can give—can be asked either in the following few seconds or minutes, or even an infinite time later. It seems this time frame varies greatly with her. This whole process is a rare type of extra-sensory perception, a super-advanced version of it, if you will. But what makes Raine very different from the others is that because she has this ability to have *extended* beforehand knowledge of a question, she can look for the answer to a question well in advance to prepare for the time she will be confronted with it."

She paused. "Does that make any sense at all to you? When I hear my own words, it makes me wonder if *I* understand it. When you first mentioned this particular aspect of her gift, my first reaction was to have her tested further. But there aren't any known studies or level of testing that would tell us much, given the rarity and extent of her perception. This type of testing needs to be developed, but it's hard to justify the cost of research when such a small number of people display this type of perception."

"Look," he said. "I don't pretend to understand this at all. I try to keep it as simple as possible. And thank you, you've done a good job at keeping it that way for me. I try to equate it to an event that's happened with her. Like when she knew that Chinese custom before I told her. I assume I am correct in making that comparison?"

"Yes, exactly."

She sipped her wine and took a deep breath. Listening to Noelle and seeing how intently she spoke was having an effect on Sean he couldn't fully put into words.

"A few days ago I was reading in a journal about a man in Mississippi—no, Alabama—who had a gift that was somewhat similar to Raine's." She paused, shook her head, smiled, and then continued. "No, not really nearly the same, but at least related to the same concept. This gentleman was a farmer, uneducated, not as intelligent as Raine—not even close, for that matter. But this man, I think his name was Randolph, had an uncanny ability to *simultaneously* verbally simulate words and sounds of other people and even the sounds of animals. Not in the sense of being an impressionist. What I mean is he could mimic anyone or any sound— not after it was spoken or after he heard it, as a parrot learns to do, but *as* it was spoken and *as* the sound was made, simultaneously. And in the same volume, inflection, and tone."

"I'm not following you," Sean confessed through a yawn.

"What I mean is he could, as I am talking to you right at this moment for example, say the words I am saying along with me at the time I say them, speaking simultaneously with my words, and in fact, with any sound that comes out of my mouth, with every volume and inflection of my voice.

"I remember seeing a clip from the research where Randolph was invited as a guest to a late-night show on the same night when Jerry Lewis, the comedian, was also a guest. I think it was on Johnny Carson, or...or who was another late-show host? Further back?"

"During the research for one of my books, I studied some of the older hosts. Was it Dick Cavett?"

"No—"

"Jack Paar?"

"Yes, maybe him. Anyway, you know how Jerry Lewis can make those funny, goofy sounds—not words you know, but sounds and gestures only he can make?"

Sean smiled. He thought of Friday night movie time with Raine. "Yeah, I seem to remember some of his routines. One of Raine's favorites is *The Absent-Minded Professor.*"

"Yes, I love that movie also. Well, this Randolph man could duplicate every nuance, every sound, and every word Jerry was saying at the exact same time Jerry said them. Not a split second after, but at precisely the same time. Jerry freaked out and tried everything in his power to trip Randolph up, but he never succeeded. No one could have scripted this or memorized the routine. It was, frankly, amazing. I've never seen anything like it."

"Until now?"

"Yes, in a way, but not in the exact way. At any rate, the same concept applies." She yawned and shook her head. "Where Raine differs is that she knows the outcome of events because at some time in her future she will be exposed to knowledge of them—as odd as that sounds. But unlike this other guy, and based on what you've said and my own observations, she seems to know what will be said days, weeks, months, even longer in advance. I don't think she could simulate the sounds, like this other man did—at least the tests didn't indicate that ability—and I don't think she can foresee the future, unless of course it is to be later verbalized to her in some way. But it is an extremely powerful gift."

"My God, Noelle." Sean shook his head. "That

means some of the stuff she knows today might not be known to anyone else for years. Look, I don't get it. How? Why did this happen to Raine?"

"I don't know. Believe me, I wish I did. This is another example of how little we do know concerning the human mind and condition, in general. You hear all the time how we use a small fraction of our brain and its capabilities. Maybe, for some genetic reason, the part of the brain that is capable of these kinds of special gifts is being chemically stimulated in some manner. We don't know the answers or even a fraction of the answers.

"But now you know what's been keeping me up at night lately."

There was a long silence.

"Let's pray no one ever gets in a position to exploit her condition for the wrong reasons," Sean said. Noelle shook her head.

"Exactly. We can't let that happen. Sean, we have to protect her."

"Should we be doing this interview in the morning?"

Noelle sat quietly for a while.

"I've given it all a lot of thought. I don't think Raine's gift can be hidden away forever. I think it's better if we control her 'coming out,' instead of allowing rampant speculation concerning what she can and cannot do. Maybe this way, she can have her fifteen minutes of fame and then things will settle down. If the public can see her as just a darling little girl, maybe they won't make her out to be some sort of myth—or monster. Hopefully, she will become old news quickly, and you and she can get on with your lives."

He walked toward her, motioning to his empty glass. He looked at her empty glass.

"Yes, please." She handed him the glass.

At the bar, he stopped and turned to Noelle.

"I'm trusting you on this, Noelle. I think it goes without saying I am not comfortable with any of it."

After an uneasy smile, she looked at her folded hands but didn't offer the reassurance he needed to hear.

****

It was an unseasonably cool May morning in the city. They stood on the sidewalk, trying to stay warm. Sean fidgeted against the cool breeze, waiting for the limousine that would take them to the studio. Raine circled him, playing the dizzy game, laughing and humming some new, unknown tune. He breathed a sigh of relief. It was good to see her behaving as if she hadn't a worry in the world. In less than an hour, they were scheduled to go before millions of people all over the world for three minutes, which to him seemed more like three hours. And yet she skipped happily around him, humming and getting dizzy. It did little to ease his anxiety to look at Noelle. Her arms were folded against the chill, and she was in constant motion.

She turned toward Raine. "What's that tune you're humming, little one?"

"I don't know." Raine continued circling and humming.

Sean, like Noelle, had managed only to pick at breakfast. Raine had eaten like a wolf, as if she hadn't eaten in weeks. He only hoped she wouldn't "beep" on national television.

The limo arrived, right on time. Charles, the driver

from the day before, walked around, opened the door, and tipped his hat. He had another big smile on his face. Good mornings were exchanged.

"Daddy, how many more hours until we go to the play?" Raine stepped into the limo, holding Noelle's hand. He followed the ladies, averting his eyes from the doctor's superbly shaped posterior. Her sleek business suit looked as if it was sculpted around her.

"Twelve hours, sweetie." He held out his watch, but little Miss Jumping Jack was distracted by the interior of the limo, as Charles entered the vehicle.

"I trust you all slept well?"

"Yes." They all responded at once, causing Raine to giggle.

"I slept with my lion last night. Man-oh-man," she whispered, her mouth flying open. "This is a big car."

"Yes, it is, Miss Raine. And I'm so glad you are enjoying Mr. Lion," Charles said and moved the limo effortlessly through the traffic.

A dozen people could have fit quite comfortably in the luxuriously appointed white limo. Before they could take it all in, they arrived at Global Studios, no further away than a couple of blocks. The whole trip took less than two minutes. The bright red news ticker, outside the entrance to the studio, reminded the populace of tension in the Middle East and the arrival in New York of an Israeli diplomat. The driver opened the door and helped the ladies out, then pointed to a door where a young woman stood. The woman approached and then hurried them to the door. She introduced herself as Paula. Sean missed her last name. She greeted each one of them by name and welcomed them to New York.

Inside, Paula led them down several halls past

offices and equipment rooms, by a break room with tables and vending machines and into a room lined with comfortable-looking chairs, two loveseats and a sofa.

"This is the Green Room." She indicated fresh coffee and pastries, as well as a refrigerator she said contained soft drinks and juice.

Sean couldn't imagine eating or drinking anything at the moment. Noelle looked as if she might throw up. Raine asked if she could have a doughnut and a Coke.

"I think that might be too much, sweetie," he answered. "Let's wait a while."

"Okay," Raine whined but never lost her smile.

Paula asked if there were any questions. When none were offered, she stepped to the door and looked at her watch.

"We're running a few minutes behind. The segment for Senator Blane, which is right before yours, hasn't started yet. He's running late. He should—" Before she could finish her sentence the door swung open and a rotund man in a dark suit, white shirt, and red tie strutted in. Behind him was a young woman with thick, horn-rimmed glasses, dressed in a business suit. She held a notebook close to her face and spoke to the senator as they entered the room.

"You have Representative Mullens at ten, Senator Wiggins at eleven before lunch with—"

"Excuse me, Senator," Paula interrupted, again looking at her watch. "You're on in three minutes." She then turned to Sean. "And Miss Sampson is on in eight minutes." With that she turned and disappeared through the door.

"Thank you, Miss Weinguarden." The senator flashed pearly whites. Sean found it amusing the senator remembered Paula's last name with little difficulty. The senator shushed his assistant's regurgitation of schedule and walked over to the loveseat where Sean and Noelle sat. Raine fluttered around the room. The senator introduced himself and shook hands as if campaigning. When told they were from Alabama and Florida and not constituents, the senator lost interest and found a seat across the room. Sean turned to Noelle as Miss Bouncy tracked the senator down and struck up a conversation. The senator seemed pleased at the attention and asked Raine questions that were lost across the room.

"Are we ready?" Noelle asked.

"I think so." He focused his attention on his daughter, while she continued jabbering with the senator, before turning back to Noelle. "It certainly appears that Raine is. Doesn't seem like she's worried much at all. Never a stranger, huh?"

Noelle looked toward Raine, and the smile left her face. Sean followed her stare across the room. The senator paled. His mouth flew open, and his arms were animated. He stared at Raine as if she were a ghost instead of a three-year-old. Sean thought the man might be having a heart attack.

"Young lady." The senator's tone darkened. He stood and moved away from her, as if she were the plague. "How did you—where did you hear that?"

At that moment, Paula leaned inside the door. "Senator, you're on…sir, are you all right?"

Sean quickly retrieved his daughter. The senator's aide had not moved from her seat. She stared at her boss, her mouth agape. After a moment, the flustered man regained his composure.

"Give me a moment," he snapped at Paula, then turned to Sean. His voice was low and threatening. "I don't know where you got your information, sir, or why you have poisoned this young child's mind with such fiction, but I don't appreciate this outrage at all. I *will* be in touch with you, sir. This conversation is not over."

"What the hell does that mean?" Sean demanded, tightening his grip on Raine, who clung to him like glue. He made a move toward the senator, but the man quickly stepped away toward the door. Before leaving the room, the senator pointed to his aide. She continued to look at him as if seeing him for the first time. Tears streamed down her cheeks.

"Not a word of this to anyone, Susan. I mean it." He then looked first at Raine and then Sean and wagged his finger at them. "And get these people's names."

****

The next minutes were some of the longest of Sean's life. A few moments after the senator left, the aide sat dumbfounded, ignoring the senator's instructions to collect names. Instead, she pulled a cell phone from her purse. Her hands trembled as she exited the Green Room and punched numbers as she left. Raine's lip trembled as if she might cry.

"Honey, are you all right?"

"I don't know."

"What happened, sweetie?"

"I don't know," Raine muttered, and lowered her chin.

"Honey, you're not in trouble. Daddy's just curious why the senator was so upset. Quite honestly, sweetie, I've never trusted that guy anyway. He seems like a shady character to me. What did you two talk about?"

After a long silence Raine looked up at him with tears in her eyes. "He's a bad man, Daddy."

"What do you mean, sweetie?" Noelle asked.

"He—"

At that moment, Paula opened the door again. "You guys are up." She waved her hand frantically for them to hurry. "The senator had an emergency and couldn't do the interview. We have a minute and a half to get you into place before the break is over. Is everyone ready?"

Paula forced a smile and ushered the trio hurriedly out the door, between cameras and over thick cords and wires, to their places on what she referred to as the curvy couch. In a few seconds, they were joined by the three hosts of *Global This Morning*, who were introduced simply as Margie, John, and Bret, before going live. A man with a clipboard walked out onto the set and began a countdown.

"Eight, seven, six, five." The rest of the countdown was silent, indicated by his diminishing fingers. Everyone became still except for Raine, who dangled her legs against the couch front. The man with the clipboard and headphones pointed to Bret.

"Welcome back." Bret smiled into the camera. "And now as promised, this morning we have some special guests with us, all the way from Ono Island, Alabama. And one of these guests is a very, very special little girl from China. And let's see if she'll tell us her name. Wait, let me guess. Is it going to *rain* today?"

The camera zoomed in on Raine, who smiled, waved, and then giggled. There was no sign of the tension from the events of the last several minutes. Sean glanced at a monitor. His little ham was back, and a natural on camera.

"Bret, you have to like this little one already," Margie Mason retorted and smiled at Raine. "She's the only one I know who actually laughs at your jokes."

"I *do* like her." Bret turned back to Raine, then to the camera. "This, ladies and gentlemen, is the young lady you've been hearing about all morning. Miss Raine Sampson. Raine, how old are you?"

"Three."

"Three years old?" John Jackson echoed.

"Well…" Raine rocked in her seat. "Three years, two months. and six days."

"My, my, you seem to have your age down to a science. I guess what they say about you is true." Bret raised his eyebrows. "Raine, they tell me you're good at tests, too."

"I guess." Raine shrugged toward Noelle.

Noelle licked her lips.

"And who are these guys with you?" Bret asked.

Before Raine could speak, Margie chimed in. "I can tell you who the good-looking gentleman sitting next to this lovely lady and darling little girl is." She smiled warmly. "That is Sean Sampson. Sean is the author of several best-selling novels. Isn't that true, Sean?"

On the monitor a graphic displayed front covers of two of his biggest sellers, with his name inscribed across the bottom.

"Well, yes." He picked imaginary lint off his pants, buying a few seconds to think through a response that would shift the focus back to Raine. "But I'm also this little girl's dad. And I'm very, very proud of her."

"And we've all heard a lot about this little girl," acknowledged John. "And everything points to this cutie pie being a very smart child."

"We truly have heard a lot. And apparently she is a smarty-pants," Bret said. He then directed his attention to Noelle. "With Sean and Raine is Dr. Noelle Victor, a well-regarded child psychologist who has a practice in Pensacola, one of my favorite towns in the great state of Florida. Dr. Victor, I understand Raine did well on some tests you gave her down there in the sunshine state recently?"

"Yes." Noelle's voice was strong and calm. Another glance at the monitor verified that the camera loved her as well. "In fact, her scores were near perfect on every section of the tests, something that hasn't been done previously by any child."

"What are your favorite subjects in school, Raine?" asked John.

Raine giggled. "I don't go to school, silly."

A laugh from off-camera caught his attention.

"Of course," John said. He smiled. "And most will agree with you, little one. I am a silly man. Well then, tell us what you *think* your favorite subjects will be when you get to go to school? What are your ambitions?"

Without missing a beat, Raine gave her answer. "Quantum physics, I think, and maybe calculus. But I like chemistry, too. I want to be a doctor."

A feather could have knocked Sean over. Noelle's mouth fell open. This was the first he had heard of his daughter's ambitions. He immediately thought of the nine-letter word on the crossword puzzle. *A-m-b-i-t-i-o-*

u-s.

At first, a few light laughs tittered around the couch. The look of determination on Raine's face didn't change. She was dead serious. John was fast on the reply.

"And something tells me you will be a *good* doctor. Speaking of calculus, Raine, do you want to play a math game?" He reached into his pocket and held up a calculator. The camera zoomed in on it. "Are you fast at multiplication?"

"I don't know." Raine shrugged her small shoulders.

"Well, we're going to find out. Okay, here we go." John punched numbers in the calculator as he spoke them. "What's twenty-five times thirteen?"

"Three hundred twenty-five?"

John held the calculator up to the camera and the numbers flashed on the screen.

"Wow," Margie cried. "That's wonderful. And fast."

John didn't seem overly impressed, but carried a sly smile. "Okay, now for an all-expenses paid trip for you, Dad, and a guest to Walt Disney World in Orlando, what's five thousand six hundred and fourteen times seven hundred and eighty-nine?" Again, he punched the numbers in as he said them. "You have ten seconds for the—"

"Four million, four hundred twenty-nine thousand, four hundred forty-six." She giggled. "That's a lot of fours. And at my next birthday, I'll be four, too."

John's face paled as he stared at the calculator and silently mouthed the numbers. His hand shook as he held it up for the camera. Several *oohs* and *ahhs* were heard on and off camera as the exact string of numbers filled the screen. Raine looked at the monitor again and smiled. For a moment, the set was quiet.

Bret shook his head in disbelief. "Absolutely amazing. Folks, I can tell you this was not rehearsed. After this amazing display, we're going to have to spend a couple of more minutes with Miss Raine. That is, if Dad and the doc don't mind?"

The camera framed both Sean and Noelle.

"Well, ladies and gentlemen, the doc is nodding, and the dad is shaking his head. I'm going to take that as an affirmative. When we come back, we're going to talk more to Miss Raine and talk with her father about the adoption program in China and across the world."

Sean could not remember being more proud of his daughter.

Or more scared.

The music was cued, and the cameras faded. Sean listened absently to the *Global This Morning* theme-song music. He looked at Noelle precisely as she found his gaze.

"The music." Her eyes widened.

"I know," Sean whispered. "It's the song Raine hummed while waiting for the limo."

"Do you watch—?"

Sean shook his head. "We don't do a lot of TV, especially in the morning."

"Then where did she hear—?"

A chill traversed his body.

Chapter Ten

It was a big morning for Raine. After her extended segment on *Global This Morning*, one of the staff from the show—Sean remembered he had introduced himself simply as Warren—invited them to meet in his office briefly before returning to the hotel.

"Please follow me," Warren said, as the network broke for commercials. He gave them only seconds to say their goodbyes to the hosts, before whisking them away down a long hall. "Right this way."

Several people looked out from offices along the hall. Others stood in doorways. A few were smiling. Others patted Raine on her head and congratulated her for her performance on live television. Raine laughed and gave high fives and seemed much more comfortable with the attention than was Sean.

The sparsely appointed office gave no hint as to Warren's capacity with the network; maybe an associate producer or a security staff person? In the aftermath of Raine's amazing performance on live television, the entire aura on the set and elsewhere in the studio changed to one of uncertainty or even shock. Everything seemed to take a back seat to the fact that the world had just been introduced to something seldom seen, someone very special, all in living color and on live TV.

Sean was surprised to discover the reason behind

the short meeting was to ensure the security of "Miss Sampson's party," as Warren put it. He explained a lengthy procedure concerning how the rest of the day would be handled—as he put it—beginning with the return to the Hilton. Instead of the limo picking them up curbside, the three of them were escorted through a maze of halls, corridors, and elevators until they reached a parking garage. There, two men dressed in dark suits loaded them into a dark-colored SUV with tinted windows. They were whisked into another parking garage attached to the Hilton, where they were escorted via a service elevator to a different suite. At first, Sean was amused at the cloak and dagger procedure, until one of the men who stood outside their waiting suite delivered the rest of the instructions.

"Mr. Sampson, *Global News* has taken the liberty of arranging an escorted tour of the Empire State Building at four p.m., followed by a private dining room for your party at Ellen's Stardust Diner in Times Square at six thirty p.m. this evening. This all, of course, is complimentary, and Global will provide the transportation to and from your tour, dinner, and the play. We have taken further liberty to upgrade your theater tickets to a stage-side balcony section, which affords privacy and outstanding close-up action of the play."

A couple of bell hops arrived with their luggage. For a moment Sean was astounded by the reality of the situation. He looked at Noelle, then Raine. His daughter's mouth dropped open, and her eyes widened. It might be difficult to enforce the required nap that was on the agenda for early afternoon.

"Daddy, did you see all the wires and stuff and

cameras in the studio?"

"Yes, sweetie," Sean said. He never took his eyes from the man in the suit.

"Noelle, would you take Raine in the suite and check out the room-service menu?" He smiled at the two ladies. "I would like a word with our friend here. Then, my little celebrity, I want to hear everything you have to say about your first time on camera."

"Of course." Noelle took Raine's hand.

After the door closed behind them, he addressed the escort. "We're only blocks from all the events you mentioned. What if we walked? The weather is great. I was thinking of maybe taking my daughter and the doctor to a few other stops along the way. I wanted to buy my daughter an American Girl doll, and take her on the carousel at the Toys R Us."

Without so much as an acknowledgement of Sean's statements, the escort pushed the button on a device attached to his left shoulder and leaned toward it.

"Chuck, can you get Paula for me?" He smiled at Sean while he waited for an answer. "Mr. Sampson, I hope you will forgive our cautious behavior. Your daughter's appearance this morning has created quite a stir among the media. Because *Global This Morning* has consistently rated the top spot on morning shows, several million people witnessed her segment this morning. No doubt, she will become an instant celebrity. We at the network take responsibility for this notoriety and are obligated to assist you in retaining your privacy for the duration of your stay in the city. That's why we moved you to this suite and changed the registration to a random name. When is your return flight, Mr. Sampson?"

"It's not until late tomorrow, but—"

"Allow me to schedule an escort for you tomorrow morning, say around ten, for a walking tour to the attractions of your choice, in addition to today's planned events?"

"Well, sure, that would be nice—"

The man held up a hand and pressed a finger to his ear. He nodded as he listened, mumbled something, smiled, and turned to Sean.

"Everything has been taken care of. Your shopping tour is scheduled for ten a.m."

Sean nodded. The man thanked him, and Sean started toward the room. He stepped toward the door and then turned to thank the man.

The suit with shades was gone.

Inside the suite, Raine had cornered Noelle at the small table in the dining area. She looked up as Sean entered.

"Daddy, did you see all those TV sets this morning?" Her eyes were wide, matching the smile on Noelle's face. A more delightful sight Sean could not remember. They looked so natural together. "I bet there was a hundred of them."

Sean's thoughts meandered to the senator. He had to broach the subject with Raine, but now wasn't the time. He resolved to keep things light.

"And you were a natural on every one of those screens." He pulled a chair out and sat.

"Would you like something to drink?" Noelle pushed away from the table.

"No, please, sit," he said. "I'm fine."

From the corner of his eye, he could see the look from Noelle. It gave him a funny feeling in the pit of his stomach. Raine continued her rhetorical recital of the morning's event, but he felt the heat from Noelle's gaze. He glanced quickly over to her, and she looked away, back toward Raine.

"And all those people at the TV station were so nice." Raine's eyes beamed as she hesitated. "That was really fun."

"You did so well on your interview," Noelle chimed in. "You looked so pretty on television. I think your daddy is right—you are a natural on the camera. You could be sitting on that couch some years from now, hosting the show."

"I think maybe she'll be sitting on that couch again one day, but maybe as a quantum physicist?" Sean said. He reached across the table and squeezed Raine's hand. "When did you decide that was what you wanted to be? You never said anything to Daddy about that."

The smile vanished from her face and she withdrew. "I don't know."

Sean realized his err. "Honey, it's okay if that's what you want to be."

"Are you mad because I didn't tell you?"

Sean walked around the table. He lifted her into his arms and sat. "Of course not, sweetie. I'll be very proud of you no matter what you decide to be. It's okay you didn't tell Daddy."

"Are you sure?"

"Of course." He held her close. "Daddy was surprised, not unhappy. I think it's great to know what you want to do, even at three years old. But if that changes someday, it's okay also. Isn't that right, Miss Noelle?"

Sean glanced to Noelle, who quickly wiped a tear

from her eye.

"Are you okay, Miss Noelle?" Raine jumped down and held her arms out to Noelle, who lifted her onto her lap.

"Yes, sweetie, of course." She glanced at Sean. "I'm better than okay, little lady. I'm very happy you did so well today and that you know what you want to do."

Noelle never took her eyes from Sean. "In fact, I can't remember ever being so happy."

****

"What the—?" James looked at the others and shrugged his shoulders.

"What happened to the senator?" One of his friends stood from the table of eight, as if his action might change the programming for the popular morning news program. "Didn't they just say Blane would be on next?"

The others looked at him as if he were to blame that the senator hadn't shown. Instead a little Chinese kid's face had filled the screen.

"Just like them TV people to bring in foreigners instead of one of greatest men what ever lived." Another stood and for a moment James thought he might walk over to the counter of the small diner and bust the old RCA set that was mounted above it.

James looked around at the angry faces. "Wonder where the hell he went? Ain't like him to take no second place to no chink."

Yet another of his friends motioned for the waitress and pushed away from the half eaten plate of eggs, sausage, and biscuits. "I'm going out for a smoke before heading to the work site."

"I'm with you," said another.

James stood and retrieved his wallet. He flipped a five and two ones on the counter for the dark-skinned server. A dollar is about all the work she did. Most of the time, she avoided the table altogether. Can't find good help anymore.

He was not happy with World Cable News. Putting on a foreigner in place of the great Senator Blane on *Global This Morning*. What was that all about? He made a mental note to see if he could find out what happened to the senator.

The country was messed up enough. They sure didn't need any more foreigners coming in, taking all their jobs and benefits. That network better get it together, or they were going to lose him and his friends fast.

Chapter Eleven

Life can sometimes be defined by one moment in time. Noelle found this to be true countless times during her six years of treating troubled children. A harsh word, a hateful slap, something as simple as a parent's failure to show up for an important event, can often change the course of a child's life. The human condition is fragile. One moment can alter a life forever—many times for the worse. A child's life can be virtually destroyed by thoughtless actions, sending him into a spiral that hurls him into failure, or worse causes him to make foolish decisions, even as far as ending his own life or taking someone else's. She often felt helpless, unable to reach a child buried far too deep in despair.

Conversely, children on the verge of self-destruction could be set on the right track by a kind gesture, a loving touch, or a thoughtful act. She had played a part in several success stories, which made her life as a psychologist rewarding.

As a child she had been one of the lucky ones. Growing up was easy for her. She had parents who cared deeply for her and were always there for her. It was easy for her to determine what constituted a good father—she grew up with one of the best. She remained close to her parents, now more than ever. They lived in New England, but she spoke to them at least once a week. One day she would find a man to love, a man like her father. He would be a man who loved her and cared for her, as her own father had.

Such a man was a few steps away from her at that moment. But was he really a man she could trust? As much as she tried to keep things in perspective—after all, she had known him for only a matter of months—she was losing a battle between her logic and her heart.

She looked at herself in the bathroom mirror, and it all became so clear. The moment that would perhaps become the defining moment in her life happened earlier in the day, while sitting on the curvy couch at the studio. It happened in front of millions of people across the country and the world. It was the instant she looked at Sean looking at his daughter as she dazzled the world on live television. At that precise moment, Noelle knew she was falling foolishly in love with Sean Sampson.

Yet, if she were totally honest with herself, there could have been other moments that came very close. She peered into the blue eyes of her reflection and could recount several. Watching him set up the tarp on the beach. When he lovingly wipe the blood from his daughter's lips after she fell at her birthday party. His expression during any number of occasions when Raine smiled at him. Oh, she had tried to convince herself otherwise, but there had been another very special moment—when he kissed her. Whether he knew it or not, he took possession of her heart that day in his kitchen at the moment he took her face in his hands and claimed her lips. He might as well have held her heart in those strong hands. At that instant, as much as she denied the truth, she became his to do with as he desired.

The circumstances around that unforgettable day in the kitchen had not allowed things to progress. In retrospect, this was good. Otherwise, she would have been helpless to stop any intentions he held. She would have been unable to stop him. It would have been a done deal. She had fantasized a thousand times about his body against hers. Even a passing thought of him or that kiss had her juices flowing.

She remembered thinking, hoping a time would follow when he might have designs to finish what he started. Instead, nothing was finished or resolved. Discussions concerning the kiss remained taboo.

Noelle knew it was up to her to make something happen to resolve—one way or another—the feelings that were aroused by the kiss. But was that what she truly wanted, to put herself out there to be hurt again? Had he given her any reason to believe he had similar feelings? Surely he also wanted to see where the kiss might take them, didn't he? She was aware of it when he looked at her. She was sure of it when he touched her hand, as he had while helping her from the limo.

She finished putting on light makeup and brushing her hair and wondered if she was kidding herself. What made her think she had a chance with this man? It was hard enough competing with the situation surrounding meeting him. She also had to compete with the memory of his wife. The thought of his losing his wife still made her want to cry. It is so hard to fight a foe you cannot see, but one you know is still very much there.

She slipped the cocktail dress over her sleek body. All was fair in love and war, right? She turned in front of the mirror and smoothed the navy blue fabric against her slender body. The dress and jewelry she had chosen were exactly what she wanted. She liked what she saw.

She prayed he would feel the same.

****

"Damn it!" Sean looked outside the bathroom toward the king-size bed where Raine rested. She didn't stir.

He hated neckties. He struggled to get the length correct. His hands trembled, no doubt some leftover adrenaline from the brief but intense encounter with the senator. He tried to forget the flustered lawmaker's words, but the scene played over and over in his mind. He had read once that the senator had suspected links to white-supremacy organizations and others of less savory character. Did the incident have anything to do with Raine being Asian? There had always been, lurking in the back of his mind, a fear that one day she would be faced with racism. He hoped and prayed he would be equipped to help her deal with that issue. Because Raine refused to talk about it, he might never know exactly what transpired between her and the senator. He refused to press the issue, not in the near future. Today was such a joy for her, so he wasn't going to spoil it by pressuring her to fill in some blanks. There would be a better time for that.

Raine had continued the banter nonstop, right up until nap time, fluttering between him and Noelle, talking about the planned events. She was particularly excited about the play, having read the book and seen the animated movie at least a dozen times in the week prior to the trip. *The Lion King's* villain's sultry accent and sarcasm played like a broken record in Sean's mind.

He had to put the morning's events behind him. He could think of no better way to accomplish that than to change his thoughts to Noelle. He had studied her earlier, on the set. Try as he might to keep it all in perspective, it would be hard to deny the affection she showed for his daughter. Yet he was having difficulty determining where this relationship with Noelle might be headed, if anywhere. Most of the time she was all work and never deviated from the professionalism that had distinguished her as one of the best in her field. Noelle always seems to know what to say to Raine and how to react to what his daughter said. At other times, she loosened up and joined them in the banter and fun, as if she was part of the family. This behavior both warmed his heart and gave him cause for alarm.

What exactly were her intentions, outside the evaluation of Raine's gift? Or did she harbor any? Was Sean trying to read something into Noelle that wasn't there? The dynamics of the situation confused him.

Then there was guilt. There was no denying that it was there, rearing its ugly head. Adding to the mix was that she was such a beautiful woman. Not only physically, but in every sense of the word. He wasn't going to kid himself; he was physically attracted to her as well, to the point of staying on edge when she was around. Lately, she was around quite a lot.

He continued the battle with his tie, made more difficult with a keen awareness she was merely steps away in the connecting suite. He subconsciously listened for the door between the main room of the suite and her room, waiting for it to open, breaking the silence. Was she sleeping? Was she reading? Was she watching TV? He thought about her constantly. He was excited about the events that afternoon, as if he were about to go out on a date. Was that what the rest of the day would be? One long date with her?

He gave himself one final once-over in front of the mirror, took a deep breathm and checked his watch. The escort would be at the door in about an hour and a half. He straightened his coat, rechecked his collar and tie, and took another deep breath. He splashed a light portion of cologne onto his hands and then his face, and walked out into the bedroom to check on Raine. She needed to be rested, so she wouldn't be bouncing off the walls, as she often did when she was tired. She stirred as he walked the bed. He tiptoed past and into the main suite, quietly closing the door behind him.

He stood at the bar, and the door to Noelle's suite opened. Their eyes met, but words evaded him. She walked slowly across the room toward him, and never looked away. There was something different, something new and predatory in her expression. She was dressed to kill. He couldn't quite put his finger on exactly what was different about her.

He forced himself to breathe.

She smiled, and his legs felt weak.

His heart was in trouble. He was in way over his head.

****

Noelle had never seen a more beautiful man. He stood across the room like a deer in headlights, gorgeous. He wore a navy sport coat, khaki slacks, bright white shirt, and peach tie. Each piece of clothing seemed designed and tailored perfectly for those broad shoulders and slim hips. Time stood still as she walked slowly toward him. His eyes fixed on her advance. The closer she got, the more her heart hammered. She stopped a few feet from him and smiled.

"You look…stunning," he said.

"I was about to say the same about you."

He moved ever so slowly toward her, stalking her, drinking her in with his eyes. She willed her legs to take her closer. She thought she might keel over, yet strangely, she had no fear. If she did faint, she hoped she would fall into his arms. He licked his lips and leaned closer still.

If he doesn't kiss me right now, right here on this spot, I will die.

"Daddy?"

The sleepy sound came from behind them.

The spell was broken. A different Sean Sampson appeared before her eyes. The passion in his eyes faded. Noelle found humor in the moment and laughed. From the look on his face, he did not.

"Hold that thought." He turned toward the door behind him. "And yes, I would like a drink, if you would be so kind as to make one for me, please."

"It would be my pleasure." She moved toward the bar, walking in his wake. The subtle scent of his cologne was dizzying.

He groaned, took a deep breath, and knelt to Raine. He lifted the child into his arms and made his way to a chair.

He took the drink she offered and drained it quickly. She sat across from him and found her glass of Chablis quite tasty as well. Raine asked for a rare cola. When Sean approved, Noelle brought it to her. After all, everyone needs a bite of the forbidden apple once in a while, especially while visiting the biggest apple of all. She sat again and gazed at Sean. In spite of the opportunity lost, she was at peace.

Where would we be now if Raine were still asleep? Seconds ago, we were in another world.

The little girl's timing was impeccable—just in time to bring Noelle back to reality.

"I can't wait to get my dolly Felicity. She lived during the times the colonies gained their independence from England. Did you know that, Daddy? And she had a friend named Elizabeth. I want to get them both, since they were friends, but I know we can't afford *two* dolls. Anyway, I know I'll just love her. Did a lot of girls back then have red hair? Elizabeth's hair is blonde. I wonder how I would look with blonde hair, Miss Noelle."

She rambled on and was soon wide awake. She jumped from chair to sofa, sofa to stool, stool to chair, not pausing for answers to her own questions. Noelle wondered if the planned events could ever live up to her excitement and expectations.

A loud knock on the door reverberated around the room.

Chapter Twelve

Raine stopped in her tracks and looked toward the suite door. She wore a strange expression.

"We'll be right with you, guys." Sean opened the door but never looked away from Raine. "My little comedian, I want you to hit the potty before we leave."

"Mr. Sampson?" A man in dark suit and dark tie moved inside the room and produced a badge. "I'm Special Agent Storm, FBI." He turned quickly to another suit, who stood behind him. "This is Special Agent Pete Willis. May we come in, please?"

"What's this about?" Sean looked again to Raine, who scurried over to Noelle.

"Just a few quick questions, Mr. Sampson." The agent turned toward Raine and then smiled innocuously to his partner. Before Sean could object, the second agent moved inside the room and stood beside his partner. Storm closed the door behind him.

"Let's wait in your bedroom while Daddy talks to these gentlemen," Noelle said to Raine while Sean examined the identification badges.

"Ma'am," Willis said. "Please remain where you are. We have a few questions we want to ask the young lady."

"Like hell you do." Sean felt a surge of adrenaline. "Noelle, take Raine to her room, please."

Willis glanced to Storm, who nodded,

imperceptibly. When the ladies were gone, Sean approached the agents. "Now, what is this all about?"

"Mr. Sampson, there is no need for hostility. We don't mean to cause any alarm." Storm flashed a smile that did little to reassure Sean.

"It's a little late for that," Sean said.

"Mr. Sampson…" Willis indicated a chair. "May we sit?"

"Do I have a choice?" He nodded to both men, and they sat. He remained standing.

"Please, Mr. Sampson." Storm nodded to the sofa across from them. "Please sit."

Sean hesitated for a long moment before taking a seat. "This better be quick. We have plans."

"Mr. Sampson, your plans won't be compromised," Storm said.

"We've detained your escort for a few minutes while we get some answers," Willis said.

Storm gave Willis a poisonous glance. "What my colleague means is that your escorts have agreed to give us a few minutes to ask you some quick questions." Storm's statement seemed directed more to his partner than to Sean.

"About what?" Sean felt the heat rise in his face.

Storm spoke in a low volume, and calmly. "Mr. Sampson, this morning at eight fifty-four a.m., the FBI was contacted by and subsequently interviewed a young lady by the name of Susan Feldon, personal aide for Senator Charles Blane—I believe you met her and the senator in the Green Room at Global Studios earlier?"

"And?"

"Ms. Feldon was quite upset and offered up certain information she supposedly obtained from your daughter that might directly implicate the senator in some possibly unlawful activities relative to the misuse of federal and state funds." Willis's tone was more accusing, and he spoke as if reading Miranda rights. "Stop me, Mr. Sampson, when I get to a point that sounds familiar to you."

"And what the hell does that mean, Willis?" Sean stood.

"Sit down please, Mr. Sampson." Storm held his hand out. "Pete, there's no need for that kind of tone here."

Sean stared Willis down before he settled onto a chair.

Storm continued, "Mr. Sampson, as my partner was saying, Ms. Feldon stated that, during a casual conversation between the senator and your daughter, she, your daughter that is, asked the senator—" He took a small notebook from his jacket pocket. "She asked the senator why he took the money and hid it in a far away bank."

Storm looked up from his notes. "When the senator scoffed at the statement, your daughter looked to Ms. Feldon and asked her to write something down. She subsequently gave the aide information concerning a bill recently passed in Congress. Your daughter told her to take the information to the ethics committee, and they would understand what the information meant."

The blood drained from Sean's head. He quickly regained his composure.

Willis chimed in. "Mr. Sampson, the information your daughter gave Ms. Feldon included government form numbers relative to a recent congressional appropriation. The ethics committee reviewed those forms thoroughly and noted some discrepancies, including transactions linked to a questionable organization. They subsequently issued a directive to further investigate the transactions and the senator, and your daughter's knowledge of said transactions."

Sean had had enough of Willis's innuendoes. The action he wanted to take—namely knocking Willis down a few notches—was not feasible, so he took the second best course and remained seated, directing his voice toward Willis. "I know you have the authority to be here, and you're probably just doing your job, but if you imply again any wrongdoing whatsoever by my daughter, I will kick your ass six ways from Sunday—Special Agent or not. Do you understand?"

Willis swallowed hard and sat motionless.

Storm stifled a laugh. "Mr. Sampson, please," he pleaded, holding his arms out. "We're curious to know how your daughter came by this information. That's all. We aren't stupid; we know your daughter could in no way be assumed to be dishonest or involved in any fraudulent activity. And I think Willis would agree after having this little chat with you that you are most probably not involved in any wrongdoing either. We just need to get a clear understanding how your daughter came to have the information she presented to the senator and his aide."

Sean rubbed his eyes and ran his hand through his hair. "I think you need to talk with Dr. Victor."

****

If Sean had any doubt Noelle Victor knew what she was talking about, in relation to Raine and the gifts with which the child had been blessed or cursed, depending on how one might view the situation, it dissipated as quickly as mist in the desert during her short talk with the agents. Although Sean was in the middle of a word game with Raine on his smartphone, one he was losing miserably, he listened through the open door to the bedroom. She had them eating out of her hand. If what she said was even soaking in. *He* would find it hard to concentrate on the message, given how she looked in that sexy dress.

After a few more minutes, which unfortunately ran twenty minutes into the planned events of the day, Willis smiled and asked Sean nicely if he would come back into the room. Noelle said it was okay if Raine came back also, although the child protested and wanted to stay and finish her father off with a word she said would net eighty-seven points.

"Sean, I think it's all right for these gentlemen to ask Raine a couple of questions." Noelle gave him a nod. "Providing, of course, they stay within the agreed-upon parameters."

Sean's protective instincts kicked in, but he relented.

Raine sat between him and Noelle on the couch, holding hands with them both. She had a death grip on his hand. Storm took the lead. He knelt in front of Raine and smiled.

"Hi, Raine, my name is Sam Storm and I work for the United States Federal Bureau of Investigation. Doctor—I mean, Miss Noelle—thought it would be all right if I asked you a couple of questions. Is that okay with you?"

"I saw the forms online," Raine said.

Sean smiled, not the least bit surprised she had cut to the chase.

Storm looked taken aback, and he tried to shake it off with another strained smile. "You saw the forms online?"

"Yes, sir. Well, I had to go to several government websites before I could figure it out, but yes, sir, I figured out what was going on by looking at the forms online."

"Okay, sweetie." Storm looked more confused than ever. "Let's back up for a minute, and then we'll have you guys on your way to your tour in no time."

"We're going to the Empire State Building." Raine's eyes lit up.

"I see. That sounds like fun." He forced another uneasy smile. Storm was clearly not in control of the inquisition but forged ahead anyway.

"First of all, can you tell me what you meant when you said you figured out what was going on? Can you tell me what you saw that clued you?"

"Duh," Raine said.

Noelle lost it, laughing out loud. Sean couldn't stop a smile.

"It's a mathematical equation," Raine continued. "A statement of funds disbursement and things. Ouch, Miss Noelle, you're squeezing my hand!"

"Oh, I'm sorry, sweetie." Noelle patted Raine's fingers.

"That's okay." Raine took a moment to get back on track. "It's a compilation of debits and credits, in relation to the appropriation and resulting expenditures. I see why nobody found it, because at first look I almost missed it, too, even though it's a matter of public record. Somebody really worked hard to cover it all up."

"Cover what up, Miss Raine?" Willis asked. His subdued tone seemed to surprise even Storm.

"Hang, on, Pete." Storm turned back to Raine. "Continue, please?"

"Well, when you look at the numbers, at first glance, it looks like everything's okay. But I saw the line adjustments, and then saw some of the numbers were misstated. I needed to go to another link to see what those adjustments were supposed to be. And that's when I found out it was a circular monetary anomaly."

"A circular monetary what?" Storm rubbed his face.

Raine giggled and pointed to Storm. "Gotcha. I was just kidding, mister. I made those last words up."

Storm seemed to be trying to find some humor in her gotcha but didn't crack a smile. Raine picked up on the agent's irritation and stopped smiling.

"The numbers didn't add up. There was about a million dollars missing."

"I see." Storm took out a handkerchief and wiped his brow. His forehead furrowed into a frown. "But doesn't this happen every day? I mean, appropriations aren't always spent, are they?" He looked around at the others with a look of confusion on his face. "Doesn't some of the unspent or unaccounted-for money from any appropriation eventually come back to the treasury?"

Sean found it amusing that his three-year-old daughter seemed to be giving a fiduciary lesson to federal agents. He struggled to wrap his mind around this concept.

"Yes, sir." Raine yawned. "But the money never came back to the treasury. Some went to an organization that hates people who aren't white and some went somewhere else. I found some brokerage records where that bad senator bought 21,600 shares of OneCom a week before. The buy was not in his name; it was in a corporation's name. But after digging deeper, I found out he was involved. He had me fooled, but I traced the shares purchase back to a company he indirectly controls."

"OneCom?" Willis asked, so softly Sean could barely hear him. Sean braced for another *Duh.*

Raine hesitated but passed. "OneCom is one of the companies that got the money from the bill the senator pushed through the appropriations committee, the same one he silently controlled. When that bad senator's company bought the shares a week ago using the missing money, they were worth fifty-one dollars each. I bet today OneCom is worth a lot more after announcing the expansion plans made possible from the money they got from the bill."

Willis studied his cell during Raine's statement. He shook his head in disbelief and in a whisper admitted, "She's right. OneCom closed at sixty-five yesterday. It's at seventy-two today."

This revelation rendered the agents quiet. For the next few minutes, Willis and Storm frantically scribbled on their notepads. As if in a trance, Storm shook Raine's hand and thanked her for her answers and the great service she had done for her country. And for the time her explanations would save the ethics committee in its investigation.

Raine was unimpressed. "Daddy, when can we go to the Empire State Building?"

"I'll send your driver up right away," Willis said

absently.

"Wait, wait, wait a minute, gentlemen." Noelle stood. The agents' gaze followed the movement of her legs. "What about us? Surely you can see this might…afford us some special attention?" Her quick glance toward Raine told Sean her choice of words was meant to prevent issues. One look at Raine, who had found a tour book, and Sean knew Noelle had been successful in avoiding any panic.

"Oh, no, ma'am," said Storm. "You don't have anything to worry about. And perhaps I should have formally appealed to you to please keep all this confidential. No, no, you'll be perfectly safe for the duration of your trip. With any luck, news of this possible scandal won't hit the airwaves for another week or so. About the only problem you might encounter tonight is this little one's popularity that will surely come as a result of her interview this morning. My wife loved her. Talked about her all day long. Raine this, Raine that. And when she found out I might be on my way here—not sure exactly how she knew that— well, she put two and two together and wanted to come along, just to meet the little girl."

There was another knock on the door.

Sean hoped it was only the escort, and not Storm's wife. Or the CIA.

****

Noelle was touched by how Sean had gone after the FBI agents when he felt Raine was threatened. She had listened to it all from Raine's room. It was a side of Sean she hadn't seen, and she found it quite erotic.

The agents left with enough scribbled on their notepads to keep them busy for some time, allowing the afternoon's events to get underway.

The black SUV moved deftly through the traffic to the Empire State Building. There were hordes of people at the entrance to the building when they arrived. Noelle wondered if they were tourists waiting to take the elevator to the top, or if they were fans of Raine and had somehow word had gotten out about their plans. A couple of large gentlemen were waiting, in the familiar dark suits and shades, and opened the rear doors to the vehicle.

"Okay, ladies and gentleman, we're here." The driver turned toward the back seat. "Follow these guys to the doors and catch the elevator to the top. One of your escorts will notify me when you're ready to leave, and I'll be waiting right here when you get down."

Noelle glanced at Sean, who wore a worried look. He held tight to Raine's hand. In single file, they stepped out onto the curb and fell in behind the escorts. Halfway to the doors, the crowd surrounded them.

"There she is," one woman shouted.

"It's the little girl who was on television this morning," said another.

Sean swept Raine up with one arm. With the other, he pulled Noelle closer. Her apprehension melted at the strength of his touch. She could feel his breath on the top of her head. The smell of his new shirt and a hint of cologne were intoxicating.

"Hey, little girl, what's three thousand one hundred and twelve times four hundred eighty-six?" asked a man holding a small calculator.

"One million, five hundred twelve thousand—"

"It's okay, sweetheart, you don't have to answer." Sean turned Raine away from the man.

Once inside the building, the escorts walked them directly into the elevator. A few others from a line joined them. When the door closed, the silence was deafening.

"So cute," an elderly lady said and held fast to an older gentleman.

A trio of young girls seemed more interested in Sean. Noelle watched them watching him, although he never noticed. He seemed intently focused on protecting her and Raine. She moved closer, causing the young girls to glare at her. She smiled in return and held fast to Sean.

"Mr. Sampson, I'm Steve Chandler with the *New York Times*." The voice came from a man in the corner of the elevator. He extracted a small recorder from his pocket and pushed it above the others. "I wonder if you could answer a few questions?"

Sean turned toward the man. "Not now, please."

"Only a couple of questions," the man insisted. "Can you tell me—?"

The smile slid from Sean's face, and Noelle felt his grip tighten on her shoulder. The tone in his voice changed instantly. "I said, not now."

This seemed adequate discouragement for the man and he backed away.

There were only a dozen or so people on the observation deck. To her disappointment, Sean let Noelle go but held fast to Raine. During the entire time at the top, in fact, he let go of Raine only once—when she wanted to look through a telescope. Even then his arm was around her waist. People were less inquisitive at the top, so Noelle forced herself to enjoy the scenery. Sean remained guarded.

Once back in the elevator and on the way down, Noelle prepared for the worst. Before the door opened Sean gathered her and Raine in again in preparation for a renewed crowd of curiosity seekers. The numbers had increased. The SUV waited at the curb as promised. The escorts were able to get them back into the vehicle with little resistance.

Next stop was Ellen's Diner.

"I hope you don't mind." The driver pulled the vehicle to the curb in front of the famous eatery. "We were able to arrange a small private dining area for your party. From what I understand, it's situated away from the main dining area but in full view of the stage, so you can catch all the entertainment."

"That would be fine," Sean said and seemed relieved.

They arrived soon to their table, where a server waited. He was a young man, tall and muscular with a baby face. His eyes were large and brown, and his face alive with excitement. He greeted them warmly and seated Raine first before making his way around the table to seat Noelle. He stepped back to Raine. She wasted no time in burying her face behind the menu.

"Miss Raine, may I have the honor of your autograph on my apron?" His smile was wide. "I never miss *Global This Morning*, and I did so enjoy seeing you on television this morning."

Raine's mouth flew open. She looked excited and embarrassed as she glanced toward Sean. "Autograph? On his apron?"

Sean nodded.

"Okay." She took a pen the young man offered. When she struggled with how and where to sign, the young man lifted a foot onto the edge of her chair and smoothed the apron over his knee.

"Right here," he said and Raine carefully wrote her name in big letters across the fabric. "Thank you so much. Now, what may I bring you to drink?"

Raine once again looked at her father. "Can I have a Coke, Daddy?"

Sean looked over to Noelle. "I think, Miss Noelle, that anyone big enough to sign autographs should be allowed a second Coke of the day every once in a while, don't you?"

A funny feeling washed across Noelle, and she couldn't find words. For a fleeting moment, she felt more like family than the doctor. She willed the lump in her throat away and nodded. "I would agree wholeheartedly, Daddy."

"Goody!"

Sean ordered the same, and Noelle dittoed, only diet.

During the meal, the server earned his autograph. Accompanied at times by two other servers, he serenaded Raine with a '60's love song. Noelle recognized the tune, although she doubted Raine did, but it didn't matter. The little girl blushed. A huge smile remained plastered across her face during the entire performance.

Noelle couldn't remember having so much fun, or being so happy, albeit with a degree of caution. In spite of the royal treatment, there remained a part of her that feared it would all go away in the blink of an eye. Were her excitement and caution due to the overwhelming atmosphere of the city and the events, or the anticipation of perhaps eventually being alone with

Sean? The latter, in fact, consumed her thoughts the entire evening.

****

The seats at the theatre were choice. Noelle watched the excitement bubble for Raine as they waited for the play to begin but had her doubts the child could stay awake for the entirety of the show.

The house lights dimmed, and the crowd became quiet. Raine's eyes blinked, and her head bobbed. Then the show began with the trademark chants that echoed throughout the theater. The animal characters filed down the aisles. Sean's arm instinctively pushed in front of Raine as she sprang from her seat to the balcony rail to watch the characters below. From that point on, Raine was wide awake and barely blinked throughout the entire show.

On the way back to the hotel, Raine fell asleep. Sean stretched her out and placed her head in his lap and her legs across Noelle. Her heart fluttered as he gazed at her during the short ride.

A peace settled over her. No words were spoken.

None seemed necessary.

****

"Would you make us a drink?" Sean guided a sleepy Raine toward the bath.

"It would be my pleasure," Noelle said. She knelt and kissed Raine on her forehead. "I had a great time with you tonight, sweetie."

"Me too." Raine smiled. Heavy eyelids blinked.

Tonight had been one of the best nights, if not *the* best night of Noelle's life. She wanted to pinch herself, but refused, afraid it might be a dream. It would be easy to believe this man was real and not like the others.

She finished making drinks as Sean returned. He quietly closed the door to Raine's room. He stood for a moment looking at her from across the room. Just like that, the nerves were back. Her heart raced. She lifted his drink, met him in the middle of the room and handed it to him. He held his scotch glass out and clicked the rim of her glass of wine.

"Thank you for a wonderful day and night." He sipped his drink.

"You're going to have to stop doing that."

"What?"

"Reading my mind, and saying my lines." She sipped her wine. It was chilled to perfection. She took his arm and guided him to the couch. "Tonight was like a dream. Thank you."

"Wait." He made his way to the entertainment center, never letting loose her hand. Soft music soon played. "May I have this dance?"

"You may."

He took her hand, and slipped his arm around the small of her waist. The simple act took her breath away. He moved with her to the slow rhythm of the music. She felt weightless, steadied by strong arms and powerful shoulders. Once again his breath tickled her ear. Time seemed to stand still. The music stopped, but they continued to dance. She looked up into his eyes. His dark eyes seemed to look into her soul as his gaze darted back and forth.

"I'm not sure I know how to do this," He sighed, and his cheek brushed hers. "It's been a very long time."

"Well, you did it again. You stole my line. Why don't we start here?" She tiptoed, raised her lips, and met his. He teased and lightly nipped at her lips. His actions stirred the hidden desires of her body. His body responded, and she moved closer. His lips played with her mouth until his tongue found hers. She cooed as he explored her mouth.

He stopped suddenly and lifted her into his arms. He kissed her and moved slowly toward his room. Once inside, he managed to close the door behind them without a sound, and quickly lock it with so little effort she wondered if he had rehearsed it. He placed her gently on his bed and switched the lamp to the lowest level of light. The room was cast into shadows. Nothing had ever felt so right. She opened her heart to him and allowed him into the depths of her soul.

****

She had forgotten how it felt to be so content. It wasn't just the lovemaking—although that was nothing short of fantastic—it was the comfortable silence between them as she lay with her head on his chest, snuggling with his strong arms around her.

"Thank you," he said softly and pulled her closer.

"For what?" She lifted her head and looked through the dim light into his eyes.

"Thank you for being you. This wasn't easy for me. If you hadn't come along, I wonder if I would've ever gotten past the memories. I couldn't imagine ever becoming close, in this way, to anyone before now."

"Why?"

He shifted, but didn't loosen his hold on her. "Guilt, I guess. I had always thought Patty would be it for me."

She lifted her head again and kissed his cheek. "I understand. I can't imagine how difficult this was for you."

"I'm sorry, I know this is not something you want to hear especially after—well, at this moment. There is so much about the circumstances around her passing that I've struggled with."

"Sean, you have nothing to be sorry about," she said and snuggled close to him again. "You can always talk to me about Patty, anytime you want. I'm not so naïve as to think you didn't have a life before I met you. Please don't ever think it bothers me to hear about her. She will always be a part of you and of Raine." Noelle hesitated, wondering if saying more might do more damage than good. She followed her heart. "What circumstances do you mean?"

"Some things I would've done differently."

She knew the subject was hard for him, and she needed to tread lightly. She opted for silence to see if he would continue.

"I guess I will always wonder what would have happened if I had insisted she start treatment and put off the trip to get Raine."

Noelle again hesitated, carefully thinking through what she wanted to say.

"Was she sick for long?"

Sean hesitated enough to give Noelle worry that she had gone too far. His chest rose with a deep breath. "Stage four by the time the cancer was detected."

Noelle searched her mind for a way to suggest that getting immediate treatment would have made little to no difference in the progression of her disease.

"The adoption process was lengthy. We had our medical exams early on, months before the dossier was sent to the authorities in China. She must have started getting sick after that point, or else the cancer would have been detected then. It was eight months from that point until we traveled to get Raine. The disease must have progressed rapidly, and you would think she would have symptoms during some of that time."

"Maybe she did."

Sean head jerked around toward Noelle, and her heart sank. Had she gone too far? Had she crossed a line with the comment?

"You know, I never thought about that," he said. Noelle finally breathed. "Now that you mention it, it would be like her to keep it from me. She really wanted to stay on track in going to get Raine."

Noelle remained quiet. She wanted his own admission to sink in. If he really listened to what he had said, he would surely see there was nothing he could have done to change the way the events unfolded. After a few moments of silence, he gathered her closer. He lifted her chin and kissed her lightly on her lips.

She laid her head against his chest. It was strange how safe and content she felt, soothed by the strong heartbeat of the first man with whom she had ever been in love.

Chapter Thirteen

As morning approached, Noelle gently kissed Sean and moved silently through the dim light back to her room. She wasn't sleepy but instead messed the covers of her bed in case Raine happened in. At first light, she took a long luscious bath in the large tub filled to the brim with hot water and therapeutic bubbles. She washed her hair, dressed and had time to start one of his books she had stowed away in her luggage. His writing was very good. It made her sad there hadn't been anything new from him in a while.

She didn't hear from Raine until eight o'clock, much later than she had expected. After a quick hug and "Good morning, Miss Noelle," she asked if she could order room service. The two of them sat on her bed while Raine dialed the numbers. She opened the menu to precisely what she wanted; she didn't need to read through it. She placed a seemingly endless order, enough food to feed an entire floor of the Hilton. Noelle added a large pot of coffee and a plate of fresh fruit. The food arrived before nine.

A few minutes later, Sean came yawning and staggering into the kitchen area. He smiled, blew a kiss to his daughter, who was chomping on a stack of French toast, and headed straight to the coffee.

Oh my God. Messed-up hair, bare feet, T-shirt, and blue-striped pajama bottoms—did this man ever *not* look luscious?

He pulled up a chair, sat down, and sipped his hot coffee. He gazed around the table to the mountain of food in front of him and picked up a piece of toast. He searched out and located strawberry jam and frowned at Raine. She was eating as if there were no tomorrow. "Thanks for leaving me a piece of toast."

She giggled and pointed to the array of food. "There's more food, Daddy. You're teasing me again, aren't you?"

He seemed cocky, she thought, and for a moment she felt slighted. He must have read her mind. His sultry look in her direction made her tingle.

"And good morning to you, Miss Noelle." He took a bite of the toast. "Sleep well?"

"Like a kitten." She spoke in a low and raspy voice, and she thought he might choke. "My bed was big and comfy. How was yours?"

He looked at his daughter and made a funny face. "Hmm, my bed was big and comfy, too." Then back to Noelle. "Is your bed like mine, or did you sneak in and sleep in my bed?"

She covered her mouth as coffee spilled down her chin. She wiped it from her face with a napkin and coughed. This was enough to set Raine off. Milk squirted from her mouth, and she let go a deep belly laugh.

"Mine was big and comfy, too," Raine said in a deep daddy voice. "Did you both come in and sleep in my room?" The little girl laughed so hard, a posterior beep rattled her chair. She covered her mouth with her hand and managed to say "Excuse me" between laughs. The contagious laughter spread around the table.

"I doubt that was a compliment about the food," Sean said dryly, setting the laughter off again.

Noelle was sure all of them had lost their minds. She wondered if it was because they felt the same comfortable peace she did. Never had she been more at ease around anyone. She needed to pinch herself. It all seemed too good to be true.

"Penny for your thoughts," Sean said.

"I was thinking about what a fun day we have in store." She winked at Raine. The little girl's eyes grew big, and a smile swept over her face. She got down from her chair and hopped onto Noelle's lap.

In a whisper loud enough to be heard across the table, Raine shielded her mouth and whispered into Noelle's ear. "Can we buy something nice for Daddy? For taking us on this trip?"

"I think that is a great idea," Noelle whispered back.

"Okay, you two." He shook his finger at them. "What are you up to? There will be no secrets from the daddy."

Raine hunched her shoulders and put her hands palm up in front of her. "What?"

"I'll never tell." Noelle shook her head.

"Okay, young lady," Sean said. "If you're done with your breakfast, scoot and brush your teeth. And floss. When was the last time we flossed your teeth?"

"Don't you remember, Daddy? You did last night."

"Oh yeah, I guess I did, didn't I? Well, let's do it again this morning."

She was off, skipping and humming.

He looked across the table at her. Nothing needed to be said.

"Last night was terrific," he whispered and reached across the table for her. As their hands touched, the electricity tingled. His warm, strong hands made her more certain she was exactly where she wanted to be.

****

The morning passed quickly. Much of it was spent shopping in toy and doll stores that the city was famous for. After checking in with her office and speaking with Connie for a short while, Noelle excused herself near FAO Swartz, claiming business to take care of. He used the time for a quick call to Derek.

"Hey buddy," Derek answered. "I was thinking about calling you. I spoke to your editor, and she's asking a lot of questions. The whole publishing house watched Raine's interview and are excited about the publicity it brought. She thought this might be a good time to think about another story."

"Well, as a matter of fact, I have been toying with an idea. Don't be setting up any book signings yet, buddy. I need to get back to writing at my own pace. I don't need anyone pushing me, okay?"

"Of course. You know me better than that. But I think it's great you're considering it. Buddy, I have to say you sound so much different today from the last time we spoke. The Big Apple must be good for you."

"It's been a great trip," he said as he and Raine arrived at the American Doll beauty salon. "Look, I'll call you later, we have to see about a perm for Raine's new doll. I would let you talk to her, but she's struck up a conversation with one of the beauty technicians. Neither looks like they want to be interrupted. Serious stuff."

"Not to worry, I'll catch her later. You guys enjoy

your trip, and we'll talk when you get back to Ono. Oh, by the way, your book sales have skyrocketed since your appearance. Go figure, never seen that happen before on books that were released so long ago."

Sean ignored the good news. Something else was on his mind that he needed to run by his friend.

"Derek," he said, lowering his voice and taking advantage of being out of hearing distance of anyone. "I want to tell you something."

"I'm all ears, buddy. What's up?"

"Sometimes, lately, I can't remember her face." His friend remained quiet. "And you want to know the strange part?"

"What's that, my friend?"

"That doesn't bother me a lot. Should it?"

"Not at all, big guy," Derek said softly. "You deserve to be happy, Sean. Don't question that. Just go with it."

Sean ended the call. Noelle returned with some sort of secret package she held close for the rest of the day. She caught up with Raine as the technician strapped her doll into the chair to begin her treatment.

"We have to hurry, Miss Lucy," Raine explained. "I'm having lunch with her, Daddy, and Miss Noelle in a little while. Can you make my dolly real pretty for that?"

"Of course I can," answered Lucy. "Let's start with some makeup, shall we?"

It was hard to determine which lady was having more fun, the little one or the doctor.

Sean and Noelle agreed to stay another night. The producer from Global had extended the invitation, and neither could think of any reason to refuse. Congress would have to wait. The episode with the senator had clouded the viability of that leg of the trip anyway. This helped to make the rest of the day seem less hurried. Most of the afternoon was spent shopping. Later, they took a tour on the Hudson River. The view of the city's skyline exceeded Sean's wildest expectations.

"How are you doing?"

He turned to Noelle and smiled. "Couldn't be better."

They reached the dock, and on the way to dinner, he thought about what a perfect day it had been.

The entire day Raine was between them, holding hands with both him and Noelle. Without warning she took Noelle's hand and placed it in his. She looked up at him, then at Noelle, and smiled. She then lifted her arms toward him, making sure when he picked her up, he didn't let loose of Noelle's hand.

Sean heard the ring tone as they arrived at the restaurant. At first, he thought it was his own cell phone, but soon Noelle pulled hers from her purse.

"Hello?"

He watched her expression change while she listened, and he knew something was wrong.

****

"I'm so sorry." Noelle was upset as she packed her bags. Sean and Raine sat on her bed, both with somber expressions. "I'm so sorry I made us rush through dinner. If Connie hadn't booked me on the late flight, it would be midday tomorrow before I could get out of the city."

"Don't worry about it," Sean touched her shoulder. "I'm glad she was able to get you back home before midnight."

C. Barry Denham

"Why do you have to go, Miss Noelle?" Raine's expression of sadness said it all.

Noelle paused for a moment and sat next to her. "Honey, I'm sorry." She couldn't keep her voice steady. "Sweetie, I have another patient who needs me right now."

Raine's head drooped. "Miss Noelle, I have to go potty. You won't leave before I get back, will you?"

"Of course not, honey." Noelle smiled. "I'll be right here when you get back."

When Raine closed the bathroom door, Sean moved closer. "I know you have to go, but first, there's something I want to say." He reached for her hand. "I've been thinking about holding you all day. Just holding you. I couldn't wait to get you alone again, to kiss you."

Noelle's pulse quickened. He had said this with such urgent sincerity, it made her heart melt. No one had touched her with words as much as he had. There was sadness in his voice. She kissed him gently on the lips.

"I don't want to go, either," she said quietly. "I have been looking forward to tonight all day long. But I have to go."

"I know, I didn't mean to make you feel bad about having to leave." He tightened his grip on her hand. "Tell me about your patient—as much as you can, I mean."

"She just turned fifteen." Noelle fought to control her voice. "I've been seeing her for a short time, but we were beginning to make progress. And now the overdose. She's been admitted to Children's Heart Hospital in Pensacola. For the most part, she's physically okay. But she is mentally and emotionally fragile. She's asked for me, and I have to go to her."

"I completely understand. And I'm sorry if we have monopolized you so much lately."

"No, no," she replied. "She may well have decided to take her life in any case, with or without me there. I gave her my cell phone number before I left and made her promise—" She lost her voice again in spite of efforts to remain in control of it. He put his arm around her and drew her closer.

The door to the bathroom opened, and Sean moved away as Raine entered the room, her lower lip still protruding.

Within minutes, a bellboy would be arriving for Noelle's luggage. It was time for saying goodbye, and she couldn't shake the emptiness this brought her. It was hard to tell who was taking her leaving harder. The door chime rang out.

"Can we have a hug?" Raine reached out for Noelle. When she picked her up, Raine looked to her daddy. "You too, Daddy?"

Sean gladly obliged.

Sean answered the door and the bellboy stepped inside. Noelle looked toward Raine and nodded. The child's eyes lit up, and she darted from the room, across the suite to her own room.

"Where is she going?" he asked.

"You'll see." Noelle was more excited than she thought she would be. "We've gotten you something to say thanks for treating us girls to such a great time."

He gave her a sly look as the little girl returned with a small wrapped gift.

"Here, Daddy." She handed the box to Sean.

"What—"

"Just open it." Noelle folded her hands nervously. "We thought you might need this."

He smiled and tore the wrapping away. When he opened the box, the smile was replaced by an awkward look, one Noelle wasn't prepared for and couldn't label.

He seemed to rebound quickly but gave only a weak smile. "It's very nice," he said and gave hugs, first to Raine and then to Noelle. The bellboy cleared his throat, and Sean moved in that direction. "You'd better go."

Noelle swallowed a disappointed sigh. The gift to which she had given so much thought had not been well received.

The ride to Kennedy seemed endless. Noelle thought long and hard about Sean's reaction to the gift she thought he would have loved to receive. Yet he had seemed uneasy, even shocked when he opened it. It wasn't the cost; she had thought it appropriate for an author. An engraved gold pen for book signings seemed to be the perfect gift. Yet she might as well have given him a poisonous snake, judging from his reaction. Why had he reacted as he had? Had Patty given him a similar gift?

She wiped away a tear, sitting in the back of the cab. She had never felt so confused. It wasn't only his reaction to the gift, even though that contributed to the horrible send-off. She wanted to leave them on a high note, and yet the whole gift presentation was one huge downer. Not the fairy-tale ending she had imagined, given the last couple of wonderful days. It had done little to instill the trust she had worked so hard to build.

What was she thinking, falling so fast and so hard

for someone whom she barely knew? What made her think she could trust this man? And what made her think she could compete with his past and his hidden agendas?

She was such a fool. What was he keeping from her? There were things she might never know about him. She had to step back and put things in perspective. This had gotten way out of control.

Yet, with every mile that separated them, an emptiness invaded her. She rubbed her arms against a sudden chill.

Dr. Noelle Victor, the island. She had always prided herself in being a strong and independent woman who knew exactly what she wanted out of life. Prior to meeting Sean, that desire had been to continue gaining prominence in her profession and to simply be the best of the best at what she did. How had she lost sight of that?

She had to get a grip and come down from the pedestal Sean had lifted her to. There were other patients. She had a life and a profession she couldn't turn her back on. Many others depended on her. There were eight people on her staff for whom she signed paychecks each week. If nothing else, they needed her to stay focused. There were some eighty or so children and adolescents who needed her. She couldn't just walk away from them, yet she would probably do it if he asked.

There was no doubt he cared for her. Yet she had seen the way other women looked at him, the way he turned so many heads. What did she have that other women didn't? Truth be told, probably nothing. Was he an "out of sight, out of mind" person? Or was he the "absence makes the heart grow fonder" type? She knew so little about him, yet she could describe some of his attributes in erotic detail. She had fanatisized about having a future with this man, even having more children with him. But there was more to Sean Sampson than he was showing. That scared her.

She shook her head and turned to see the city grow smaller behind her. In a few hours, she would be back in Pensacola at the hospital with her troubled patient. The taxi pulled up to the curbside at the airport. She took money from her purse and stepped out as the driver opened the door.

Time to get back to the real world. Time to put a stop to all the confusion. She reached the line at the ticket counter. Her cell phone chimed, and she looked at the text displayed on the face of her phone.

It was from Sean.—*I miss you already.*—

Why did he have to go and make it harder for her to walk away? Without hesitation she responded.

—*Miss U 2.*—

****

Sean smiled when he received the reply. Knowing she missed him as much as he missed her would make the hours pass more quickly until the next time they were together. He resolved to make the best of the day and give his undivided attention to Raine. She had been such a trooper throughout all that had transpired. During the one-on-one time, he would find a way to delve deeper into the episode with the senator.

He made his way to Raine's bathroom to make sure she had brushed her teeth as instructed. He glanced at his watch. It was still early. He knelt beside where she stood on a stool at the sink and shook his head.

"What is it, Daddy?" She had a concerned look on her face. "Did I not brush good?"

"You did fine, sweetie. I'm sorry you'll have to do it all over again later."

"Huh?"

"Well, you can't go to bed with all those sugar bugs in your mouth."

"Are you teasing me, Daddy?"

"No, not at all." He took her in his arms. "It's just you should always brush your teeth after ice cream."

Her eyes grew wide. "We're going to get ice cream? At night?"

"Well, I would hope we could find some somewhere in this big city."

"Yippee!" She dragged him all the way to the hotel door. Sean checked his pocket for his wallet and opened the door. Two men in suits approached from down the hall. Sean closed the door behind them and turned toward the elevator.

"Mr. Sampson?" One of the men called out.

Now what?

He stood silently as they approached. Raine moved behind him and held onto his pant leg.

More badges. The other man spoke.

"Mr. Sampson, we're from the National Security Agency. You and your daughter will have to come with us."

"Like hell," Sean said. Raine tightened her grip.

"Mr. Sampson, this is not a request," the first man said.

Sean had no options. Little eyes and ears were watching and listening. Resisting would only make matters worse. He took a deep breath and patted his daughter's shoulder. He looked at first one, then the other of the men.

"Gentlemen, can you give us a second?"

The agents glanced at each other, and one looked at his watch.

"Two minutes," the agent said and folded his hands over the front of his suit. When he didn't move, Sean felt the heat rising on the back of his neck.

"I'd like to talk to my daughter alone."

The agents backed away slowly. Neither seemed quite sure what to do next.

"Can you guys wait for us at the elevator?"

They complied. It was only steps away from where he and Raine stood, but it would give him at least a small measure of privacy. When they were gone, he knelt in front of Raine.

"Sweetie, Daddy wants more than ever to have some ice cream, then pile up on the couch and watch a movie, you know, like we always do at home?"

She stood attentively, frozen before him, and nodded her head. "It's okay, Daddy. I know we have to go with them. I had my heart set on some ice cream, though."

Sean drew her near and hugged her. He whispered in her ear, "I think maybe I can talk these guys into a compromise."

He stood and took hold of her hand.

"Okay, guys," he said, lowering his voice. "I'll make a deal with you. We'll come with you, no problems. But wherever it is we're going will have to wait until we find some ice cream. Gentlemen, I'm sure you will agree that a promise is a promise. And I promised this little girl some ice cream. Do you have an issue with that?"

The agents looked at each other. One smiled and turned to Sean. "I think we can accommodate your request, Mr. Sampson. I happen to know a great little ice cream shop a block or so from here. We'll be happy to call ahead and inform our plane of the delay."

"And where might this plane be going, gentlemen?"

"Washington, D.C."

"Why does that not surprise me?" He reached behind him and lifted Raine into his arms. "Sweetie, looks like we get to visit the Capitol after all."

One look in her eyes told him she wasn't as excited about it as she once had been.

Chapter Fourteen

The revised plan was to meet Sean and Raine in Atlanta for the *World News* interview. They had opted for the extra day in New York, courtesy of the extra time afforded by cancelling the Washington leg of the trip. Having to return to Pensacola was a blessing in disguise. The revised schedule gave her the time she needed to understand why Sean had reacted to the gift in the manner he did. Maybe by the time they were together again in Atlanta, she could have it all figured out. First and foremost, she needed to slow down the relationship. That might not be easy at all, so the extra time was a blessing in that regard.

Was the gift reaction about his feeling pressure to write? Maybe losing his wife had taken an even deeper toll on his inspiration to write than she had imagined. Given the chance, she would use all her expertise to help him through this. And maybe that would distract her from being so attracted to him.

On the day she was scheduled to leave for Atlanta, she arrived early at the office and found not only Connie at the reception desk, but a man in a dark suit sitting in the waiting room. In spite of his disarming smile, uneasiness surged as he stood to greet her. He approached with extended hand. Noelle glanced at Connie, who simply shrugged.

"Dr. Victor, my name is Sanders. May I have a few

moments of your time before your patients arrive?"

"And this would be concerning…?"

Sanders looked at her, then Connie, and plastered another smile on his face. "It's a private matter."

"Then you'll have to make an appointment." Noelle moved toward her office.

"Dr. Victor, I'm not selling anything, and I'm not in need of a psychologist—well, at least not for treatment." He shook his head. "Although my wife might question the latter claim. Let's just say this is a matter of utmost importance concerning your recent visit to New York."

Was something wrong with Sean or Raine? "What do mean, my visit to New York?"

"Dr. Victor, there's no need for alarm. If you would allow me a few minutes of your time, I am sure you will understand why I'm here."

Noelle hesitated for a moment and then pointed to the door to her office.

She followed him in, closed the door, and indicated a seat. Sanders stood in front of it and waited for her to walk around her desk to her chair before sitting. She took a deep breath and gave him her full attention.

"Dr. Victor, I am with the National Security Agency in Washington, DC. Yesterday our office was made aware of an incident that occurred at Global Studios, an incident between one of your patients and Senator Charles Blane, the Chairman of the Committee on Appropriations. I understand you were also present later that day, when FBI agents interviewed your patient?"

"Mr. Sanders, as you must be aware, I am not at liberty to discuss anything to do with any of my patients."

"Dr. Victor, let's cut to the chase, shall we? As you may or may not be aware, I have the authority under legislative law to exempt you and me from patient privilege or any other HIPAA requirement you are referring to in matters concerning national security."

"National security? What are you talking about?"

"Dr. Victor, I assure you that it is essential you cooperate with me concerning—"

"And I can assure *you*, Mr. Sanders, I am not discussing this matter for a minute more without first talking with my patient's father and an attorney." She reached for her intercom button.

"Dr. Victor, you will most definitely get your chance to speak with Mr. Sampson. And an attorney, if you so desire."

Noelle froze. She frowned and gave Sanders an inquisitive look.

"Please forgive me. I should have clarified my intentions. I am here today to escort you to Washington. As we speak there is a plane waiting for us. Mr. Sampson and Raine are in Washington, awaiting your arrival. Mr. Sampson specifically asked for your presence during our further interrogation—"

"Interrogation?"

Sanders's face reddened. He took out a handkerchief and wiped sweat from his brow. He took a deep breath and stuffed the handkerchief back into his jacket pocket. "Dr. Victor, I have spent the last thirty-six hours with a team of financial experts and mathematical statisticians—some of the best in the nation—trying to reconstruct the logic your three-year-old patient gave to the FBI agents in her attempts to explain how Senator Blane allegedly pulled off the most intricate scam of taxpayer dollars in the history of Washington. And quite candidly, Doctor, in spite of all you may have heard about layers of oversight in Washington, to supposedly be able to pull something like this off is quite a feat in itself. A few hours ago this team was able to figure out what your young patient learned after mere minutes of research on the web and her review of intricate government forms. The fact she was able to access those forms, in itself, is an intriguing mystery to a lot of people, including myself."

"Look, Mr. Sanders. I'm glad they figured it all out. But I fail to see what this has to do with me or my patient, and why the urgency to disrupt my schedule as well as the schedule of my patients, not to mention her father's life? Soon, I will have a waiting room full of other patients."

Sanders's face grew red, and he stood, leaning over her desk.

"Dr. Victor, if a three-year-old, in a few minutes, I might add, can ascertain this much about the United States Senate and its dealings through the Internet, then somebody else is bound to figure out a way to use that expertise to compromise and damage the security of our country."

"You still have not answered my question of how I fit in."

"It's very simple, Dr. Victor," Sanders said, rubbing his eyes once again. "We need to know as much as possible about your patient, her—for lack of a better word—condition, how she knows what she knows, essentially everything about her, down to her favorite color, if you will. Please, I implore you; don't make me force your cooperation, Dr. Victor. And believe me, I can accomplish that in mere minutes. We must have your cooperation, and we must have it now. Please save us both a lot of headache and red tape and cooperate."

She hesitated, rubbed her hands together, and then reached again for the intercom.

"Let me get my office manager to reschedule my appointments—"

"We've arranged for that."

"You've what? How—"

"Dr. Victor, in about ten minutes Dr. Andrews from our DC office, an expert in child psychology, will walk through the door and begin reviewing your patient files on schedule for today. And let me ward off your concern." He held a hand up. "He has the security clearance to do that. You need only to have your office manager gather the files for him to review."

After a moment, she took a deep breath. "Okay, where do we start?"

"We start by getting your suitcase. You can brief us on the plane."

"There's no need to go to my apartment."

Sanders wore a smirk on his face and shook his head.

"I was planning on joining Sean…Mr. Sampson—"

"Forgive me, Dr. Victor, but there's no need to play games. We know about your relationship with Mr. Sampson."

"What relationship? What do you mean?"

"Dr. Victor, we have about six hundred photographs of you, Mr. Sampson, and his daughter, taken all over New York City. It doesn't take a rocket scientist to see that you two are…shall we say, enamored with each other."

"Are you saying we were followed?"

"As I said, this is a matter of national security."

"So you know I was planning to join Mr.—Sean and Raine in Atlanta for her interview with *World News*?"

"If you're referring to the dark green suitcase in the trunk of your car, yes, we know you are packed and ready to meet up with the Sampsons."

"Is there anything you don't know about me, Sanders?"

Sanders stifled a yawn and then fought off a smile. "Not much, Dr. Victor," he admitted, looking at his watch. "Not much at all."

****

An hour into the flight the panel of experts continued to fire questions at her via a large TV screen attached to the bulkhead of cockpit area.

Her patience was wearing thin.

"Doctor Victor, does the child display any signs of malevolent behavior?" The question came from one of the suits. Either the color balance was questionable, or the man was an immediate candidate for a stroke or heart attack. His face glimmered as the teleconference camera zoomed in. The placard in front of him indicated his name, followed by a string of letters depicting a variety of degrees.

"Dr. Vance, if you read my notes in Miss Sampson's file, which all of you have in front of you, you would find there is no need for that question. Miss Sampson is one of the most nonaggressive children I've had the pleasure to evaluate."

Another woman in business suit spoke up. The camera panned to her mid-sentence. "Dr. Victor, we should keep our personal opinions at bay and stick to the facts."

A flash of anger overtook Noelle. She stood and moved closer to the camera in front of her seat. "How dare you imply my professional opinion is tainted in any way whatsoever!"

"Now, Dr. Victor," Sanders said. "I'm sure Dr. Wade didn't intend for her question to insinuate any impropriety concerning your patient. Isn't that right, Dr. Wade?"

Silence prevailed. Assisting in matters of national security was one thing. Taking insults was another.

The plane soon landed at Dulles, and Noelle was still seething from the confrontation with the so-called experts. She stepped into a waiting car, which took her to a military-like complex not far from the airport. She was taken to a room with sparse but comfortable furnishings and was told Sean and Raine would be joining her momentarily. In a few minutes, Sean walked in alone. She stood to greet him, happy to be close to him again. As he drew near, his expression said it all. His body was stiff, and the warmth in his expression she remembered from a few days ago was gone. His expression was cold, and he looked through her, refusing to make eye contact.

The tension was palpable as he closed the door behind him.

"What did you tell them?" His voice was tired and angry.

She didn't know how to respond, searching for a reason for his curt behavior.

"I thought you said you wanted to protect her." His eyes were wild and desperate. "We trusted you. You're a doctor—what about our rights to privacy?"

"They told me—" She willed the tears away. It wasn't *what* he was asking; it was *how* he asked it. Her heart broke at the piercing look he shot toward her. She wanted to tell him that they had confiscated Raine's file, against her will, and there was nothing she could say that would not be covered in her many notes in the file. He simply didn't give her a chance.

"They told you that you could break the laws?" he shouted in a mocking, desperate tone. "And you believed them?"

"They gave me no choice."

"Yeah, I see that." His tone was filled with hateful sarcasm. "I see very clearly the choice you made."

He turned, walked out, and slammed the door behind him.

So much for a joyful reunion. She stood there confused as the painful truth surfaced. From his viewpoint, she had fallen in a trap and betrayed them, two of the most important people in her life. She wanted to be anywhere else but there. If she could only turn back the clock. She took a deep breath and fought the tears valiantly. In the end, the situation was just too much.

She wanted to die.

Instead, she gave in and cried.

****

"So, young lady," said the woman with big teeth. Raine thought of the Big Bad Wolf. "As I understand it, you have a very special gift."

"Yes, ma'am, I guess so."

179

"I understand you sort of see things before they happen?"

"I don't know. Maybe kinda."

"Can you give me an example?"

"Well, once I ate a lot of pancakes and beeped."

"Beeped?"

"That's what my Daddy calls burping and farting."

"I see."

Some other men and women in the room laughed. They sat at a table behind the lady.

"So what happened when you…beeped?"

Raine pointed to a large binder, which lay on a table behind them. "You already have all that in those notebooks."

The lady didn't look like she felt so good. She turned around to the man who sat behind the stack of files. He nodded.

"That man is going to tell you." Raine pointed to the man.

The teeth lady looked again at the man. He nodded once again and said, "It's in there. Dr. Victor told us about the incident. Miss Sampson told her dad she knew he was going to tell her how belching—rather, beeping—was a compliment in China. In fact, he did say that to her later in their conversation."

"See?" Raine said. More people laughed. "He just told you."

"Yes, but—" The lady wasn't smiling any more, although Raine could still see her teeth. "How did— Never mind. Let's move on to the talk you had with the senator. You remember that, don't you?"

Raine nodded.

"What did you tell him?"

"I asked him if he was going to give the money back."

"And how did you know he had money that didn't belong to him?"

"Because my daddy was going to tell me he was a shady character. So I started looking for reasons why Daddy might say that."

"Because your daddy was *going* to tell you? Wait, honey, I don't understand. When did your daddy say the senator was a shady character?"

"Right after I talked to that bad man at the TV station."

"But you had already talked with the senator when your daddy said that, correct? When you talked to the senator, you had to have already known about the money. Your daddy didn't say anything about the senator until after you confronted him, right? How did you know about the money if your daddy hadn't clued you to his opinion that he was a shady character?"

"I don't know."

"I'm sorry, sweetie. I don't understand. Can you help me understand?"

Raine shrugged.

"Okay, well, let's try something else. When did you look on the Internet and find out the senator allegedly took the money?"

"He *did* take the money."

"Yes. Okay. When did you discover the money was missing?"

"At home."

"You found out by looking on the Internet at home?"

Raine nodded.

"And when did this happen?"

"I don't know."

"Was it after you got home from the TV interview?"

"Duh," Raine said, smiling. These people were silly.

The lady with big teeth looked around at the other people. "Duh, what does that mean? Duh?"

"I haven't been home since the interview."

"Oh, I see. Then you made the discovery about the money while you were in the hotel before the TV interview?"

"No, ma'am. I found out about the money while I was at home."

"But you said you haven't been home since the interview?"

"Yes, ma'am."

The room got very quiet.

"Are you saying you discovered the money was missing while at home *before* you went to New York for your interview? And as I understand it, you made the Internet search ahead of the time when your daddy said the senator was a shady character, not after?"

Raine smiled and nodded. Finally, she got it.

After that the lady with big teeth looked sick, like she might throw up. She left the room. She didn't even ask to be excused. Another man from the table cleared his throat and walked over and sat in an empty chair across from Raine.

"Hello, honey. My name is—"

"Welks," Raine said and laughed.

"How did you know—?"

Another man from the table laughed and

interrupted, "She's got your number, Welks, might as well sit down and let somebody else try."

Raine smirked. "I knew he was going to say that."

"Got me." Welks smiled, but then shook his finger at Raine. "Let's take another tack, shall we, Miss Sampson?"

"Okay."

"Right now, at this particular time, do you know of any other money that's missing, or any other bad man...or woman in the Senate? Or even in Washington?"

"I don't know."

Another lady at the table spoke next.

"If we were to give you some names, could you tell us if there is anything...bad going on with those people?"

"You can't ask her that," said a man in the corner of the room.

"What are you doing, asking that kind of question?" asked another.

Raine had enough of all the silly arguments. "I don't know."

"Is there anything else you can tell us? About anyone in the government or anyone anywhere we should know about?"

"Maybe some things I will tell them at the Congressional hearing."

"What Congressional hearing?" asked a new person, an older man sitting at one of the tables.

"The one they will ask me to talk at."

"Who?"

"I don't know."

"What did, I mean what *will* they ask you?" So

many people were talking now, she couldn't tell who had asked what question.

"Mostly stuff about reform and how to get stuff done. Oh, and how to get some laws passed so everybody doesn't hate the people in Washington so much."

"Good luck with that," someone at the long table said. This made a lot of people talk at once.

She wanted to laugh at them. But Daddy wouldn't approve.

So she smiled and listened to all the crazy people talking at once.

****

He should have known better. Why did he let himself be fooled? Noelle might as well have stabbed him in the chest. Why did he think she—or any other woman besides Patty—would want to protect his child? She didn't know how it felt to lose somebody. Did she? How could Sean think she would? *She* hadn't lost the one *she* loved. *She* had no clue what it was like to be helpless in preventing the one you love from being torn from you or how it was like losing part of your soul. He had let it happen once before, but by God he wasn't letting it happen again.

And then she goes and practically hands my daughter and everything she knows about her over to the Feds.

And now his daughter was being interrogated. What did that mean?

He paced back and forth in the room outside where Raine was being questioned. He clenched his fists and wanted to storm the room. He should take her away somewhere where no one could find them. But he had

184

to keep his cool. He was all she had now, and he couldn't afford to do something stupid and lose her, too. He wanted things to be like they were at Ono before all this happened. Raine was doing fine adjusting to life without her mother. It hadn't seemed as if she needed anyone but him. And he was fine, too. He didn't need anyone, especially someone who would fold at the first threat and fill the Feds full of ideas about her gift. Those clowns had no clue as to what was or was not a threat to national security. They especially didn't know how this interrogation might damage his little girl.

She was so brave when they told her they wanted to ask her some questions. And then when they asked him to leave, Sean resisted. He gave them ultimatums, but they seemed unfazed. And then Raine told him it would be all right. He relented and told her he would be right outside if she needed him. Walking out the door was the hardest thing he had ever done.

After what seemed like hours, it was over. Raine was escorted back into the room. She seemed to be fine and didn't show any outward signs of stress or trauma. But it didn't matter—his mind was made up. Heads were going to roll.

Sean settled Raine into a waiting room with a TV and demanded to talk with whoever was in charge. He was taken to a room and asked to sit in a seat across from a table. Several uniformed as well as plain-clothed men and women sat behind the table. Sean bypassed the chair and leaned over the table, scanning left and right as he spoke. "I want a plane readied to take us back home and I want it now."

Several at the table looked uncomfortable and leaned away defensively. A man directly across from him opened his mouth to speak.

"We're not done with our interviews, Mr. Sampson," said a woman next to him.

"Like hell you aren't." Sean leaned closer. "If you don't want to see a mad man go berserk, somebody needs to tell me exactly why you're detaining a three-year-old child like some criminal. Why exactly are you holding my child, and what is she charged with?"

"Mr. Sampson, there's no need for hostility." A woman at the far end of table spoke quietly.

"Lady, you haven't begun to see the hostility I am capable of," he scoffed. "If somebody doesn't release us in the next ten minutes, every news agency in this country is going to hear from my attorney, who happens to have instructions to do that if he doesn't see me in the flesh later this afternoon. And if you don't think I mean it, go ahead and ignore my demands."

His statement created some commotion, as several along the table began conferring with each other. After a short period, the man in the center of the table cleared his throat, and directed toward Sean, "Mr. Sampson, you and your daughter are free to go. We will arrange your transportation first thing in the morning."

"Now," Sean said and met the man's eyes. "You arrange our transportation now. Maybe you didn't hear me say my attorney expects to see me later today?"

"Very well, Mr. Sampson," he said. "But as a compromise, we would like to arrange for a meeting later this summer with some select lawmakers. And we need the assurance you will comply."

"As if I have a choice," Sean said.

"Mr. Sampson, I don't think you're aware of the gravity of this situation." The man looked left then right, scanning the faces of his colleagues. "We are sympathetic to your rights, but you must realize we must protect the interests of the citizens of this country for whom we work. If you think for one minute the task of setting up this meeting is going to be easy, think again. Convincing the highest lawmakers and executives in this country to sit in front of a three-year-old child and try to decipher exactly what she might know that would protect this country is a formidable task, to say the least."

His words hung in the air around the silence of the room. What he had said made sense, but what about Raine? Again Sean leaned over the desk.

"I get it, folks. I really do," he said softly. "But does anyone of you have a clue as to what all this might do to my child?"

From the expressions across the table, Sean knew he had struck home. After a moment, a woman to the left spoke up.

"Mr. Sampson, I have three children." She spanned the room. "Most of us have children and grandchildren. I think I speak for the group when I say the welfare of your daughter is paramount in our minds as we endeavor to set this meeting up."

She paused and took a deep breath.

"We're not monsters, Mr. Sampson," she said quietly. "We're just people, trying to do a job."

Sean leaned away from the table. "I want to talk to Dr. Victor before we leave."

She looked left, then right. "I'm afraid Dr. Victor is on her way back to Pensacola."

Outside the room, Sean placed a call to her on his cell phone. The call went directly to her voice mail.

If Sean were in her place, he probably wouldn't answer either.

****

The attendant offered food and drink, but Noelle refused.

"When will we take off?" she asked. "Is anyone else going to be on this flight?"

"No, ma'am," the man said. "Only you. We will be airborne in a few moments."

Noelle released a sigh of relief. She couldn't imagine sitting in the same plane with Sean. Not now, after what she had just gone through.

She felt numb and deflated, grateful no patients were scheduled for the rest of the week. She couldn't fathom facing any, and certainly not Connie, although her friend had called frequently since she departed the office earlier. To avoid a call, Noelle sent a text to let her know she would be taking a few days off. The only pressing issue was the suicidal patient, and she would visit her troubled teen during her time away from work. But no one else. Thankfully, the last time she called the hospital, the teen was doing much better. She planned to do everything in her power to help continue that progress.

When the plane landed in Pensacola, a man was waiting for her. He drove her to her apartment, asked what else she might require, and when she said nothing, left.

Noelle was reminded of a time two years ago when she arrived at her apartment. The memories dredged up when she walked in the door. A lot had transpired since the eye-opening trip to Atlanta, when she had witnessed Scott's betrayal. She walked into the kitchen for a bottle of water. She needed to get away. She would pack a bag and head to the beach house.

She couldn't hate or resent Sean for his stinging words. After all, he was right. She had been scammed into complying with the NSA agent's demands. She felt so helpless, aware an arrest on her record would not bode well for patient relations. Not to mention the damage it would do in her quest to help Raine.

She missed Raine, and she missed Sean too. It was a Catch-22—a scenario with no solution. She had let them down, and now she had to deal with the pain of stepping out of their lives. Given her mistrust of Sean and men in general, she should have been happy with the outcome of the situation.

No such luck.

She dropped her overnight bag on the front seat next to her and turned the key.

Nothing.

A red light blinked. She had no clue what it meant. She leaned her forehead onto the steering wheel and wanted to cry. Instead she called Connie.

"Hey," she said softly as her friend answered.

"I take it things didn't go so well in Washington?"

"No." She fought to keep her voice steady. "I really don't want to talk about it now, okay?"

"Of course, sweetheart. Whenever you're ready, you know I'll be here."

"Thanks," Noelle said. "But I need a favor."

"Anything."

"Will you call the service department at the Audi dealership and get someone out to tow my car in for service? It won't start."

"Of course," Connie said. "Do you need me to

189

arrange a loaner?"

"No, thanks. I'm going to the beach house for a few days."

"I'll be right over to take you."

"Connie, you know I love you, but no thanks. I'll call a cab. I don't want to talk right now, okay?"

"Of course, just tell me you'll be all right, and I'll leave you alone until you are ready to talk."

"I'm okay, really."

"Let me worry about your car. When you're ready, and when it's ready, I'll bring it out to you. But you'll owe me dinner. And don't worry about the office. I've rescheduled all the appointments for this week. And if that's not enough, let me know, and I'll move more back."

"I'm sure that will be fine." Noelle was relieved her friend was so understanding. "I'll call you soon, I promise. Love you."

"You, too."

After hanging up, Noelle called a cab.

She sat in her car for a while contemplating her situation.

Thanks to her training, she was a master at analyzing the psychological aspects of situations like hers. She could systematically identify what had happened, what could have been done to prevent it, and what to do about the psychological effects of no longer having Sean Sampson in her life. The man had changed everything, had touched part of her never touched by anyone before.

She had the clinical solutions for dealing with this type of trauma at her beck and call. She had all the answers on how to deal with the delicate issues concerning the loss of a loved one.

But what on earth would or could she do about her broken heart?

Chapter Fifteen

The few days since Washington seemed like an eternity. It was time to shake it off and get back to life with Raine. Time for some fun. The day was tailor-made for fishing. While Raine dressed in her room, Sean took the opportunity to call Noelle one final time before putting it all behind him.

"Dr. Victor's office," came the familiar greeting from Connie. "How may I help you?"

"Connie, you would help me immensely by letting me speak with Noelle."

"Oh, hi, Sean." She was gone for only a second or two. "I'm sorry, Mr. Sampson, she is unavailable currently. May I take a message?"

"Do you think it would do any good?" Sean allowed his frustration to show and immediately backtracked. "I'm sorry, Connie. Yes, would you please ask her to return my call?"

"Of course," she said.

"Thanks, Connie."

"Got to go, other line ringing."

He hung the phone up as Raine jumped into his lap.

There was no way he would show the hurt he felt for all the times he had reached out to Noelle to no avail, especially not to his daughter. And she hadn't given him the courtesy of a response to all his efforts to contact her. He must have apologized a dozen times for being such a jerk in Washington. And she had done nothing to acknowledge his efforts. Just a cold, flat letter stating she was backing away from treating Raine. Of course, there was the note for his daughter but not so much as a word to him. It did much more than put a dent in his ego. It cut into his heart.

He had thought there was something between them, much more than the physical chemistry. He understood the hurt she must have felt when he had his meltdown in Washington. But couldn't she see what the issue had done to him? All his instincts to protect his daughter were on full alert. He wasn't going to chance losing his child. Couldn't she see? He had driven her away. Away from what they had, away from that night in New York, away from the bond he thought she had with his daughter. He took a deep breath and forced a smile.

"Ready to catch some big ones, little lady?"

"Yippee! Let's go."

Soon they were settled in chairs on the dock, lines in the water.

"I think I'm getting a nibble, Daddy."

Sean glanced at the red and white float at the end of the line from Raine's Snoopy rod and reel. It swerved and bobbed in the docile waters. During the many times they had fished, Raine had never been able to bring a fish in, although she had gotten many nibbles.

"I think Mr. Fish is playing with you. Let him take the float all the way under the water, and then pull back on the rod."

Raine watched for a few seconds and when no other movement occurred, she began reeling the line in. "Must've eaten the worm."

The mid-May morning weather was as perfect as could be. A light south wind hummed softly in Sean's ear, bringing a sweet melodic promise of salt and sea. It was the type of day that stirred the wanderlust he often felt. A complex yearning for points south tugged at his gently flapping sleeve, reminding him of the yet unseen and undiscovered tropical treasures that on occasion haunted him. He had felt this tug since the first time he set sail, soon after the delivery of the sailboat.

Raine swung the rod in his direction. and he fished a worm from the small paper container. He caught the line in the breeze, negotiated his hand carefully along the line. and threaded a worm onto the hook.

"Eeeew." She made a face. "Yucky, slimy worm guts."

He looked at his slimy fingers, licked his lips, and faked a move toward his fingers. "Yeah, but the fishies love 'em. Wonder what they taste like. Slurp, slurp."

"Daddy, don't. You're gonna make me hurl."

"Hurl? And where did you hear that word?" He laughed.

"I really don't remember," she said, smiling slyly. "Maybe from you just now?"

"Of course." He nodded but didn't want to dwell on the subject.

He took her rod and tossed the line a short distance out from the pier. It plunked into the water, and the float bobbed up and down before settling on the surface. She held the rod close, waiting for a bite. He fixed his gaze on her profile as she intently watched the float. She sat in a smaller version of a chair like his on the finger pier as *Time for Raine* listed in the breeze behind them, her lines popping and creaking.

Until that moment, he hadn't noticed she had chosen the same color shorts and T-shirt as he wore. The only difference was Sean's Atlanta Braves baseball cap paled in comparison to her red Elmo cap, one she had spotted at a gift store not so long ago and had to have. Silent but comfortable moments turned into minutes. As his mind drifted, she broke the silence.

"I miss her." She never looked up from her fix on the float.

Sean missed Noelle, too. He had tried to call her most every day. In fact, for several days he had called every number he knew to call, including her office. The mailbox for Noelle's apartment phone quickly filled up from his calls. Her cell phone went straight to voice mail each time. Once, under pretense of a joyride with his daughter, he had shamelessly driven out to her beach house. But there was no sign of life, no car parked in the space under the house.

The toughest part since returning from Washington had been dealing with Raine on the subject of Miss Noelle. He had avoided the issue with her and had gone to great lengths to make up excuses for why Noelle had not called. Though her absence hurt Raine, it certainly wasn't Noelle's fault. He couldn't blame her, given the manner in which he had placed the blame on her shoulders.

"I know. I miss her, too," he said. It was time to face up to the truth. "Sweetie, Daddy wasn't very nice to Miss Noelle in Washington."

Raine frowned and looked up at him, but remained silent.

"In fact, Daddy said some mean things to her."

"Is that why she sent me the letter and hasn't

called?"

Sean nodded.

"Why did you do that, Daddy?" Raine turned away from watching the float and now stared at him with contempt.

"I'm sorry, sweetie, I really don't have an excuse. I made a bad choice."

She turned her head away. "It's not fair, Daddy. I like Miss Noelle. Will we ever see her again?"

It would be easy for him to produce a little white lie, but it wasn't the best long term action. "I don't know, sweetie. She's disgusted with me right now. I'm sure she misses you, because she's not mad at you, just me. And besides, she's done the job I asked her to do for you, and there's nothing else she can do to help. I don't know if we'll ever see her again."

"Maybe you should buy her some flowers for Mother's Day."

Sean was taken aback by the suggestion. Why hadn't he thought about the significance of the upcoming Sunday? The more he thought about it, the more painfully obvious the answer became. His mother had been gone for some time, and since Patty died, he had a ready-made excuse for avoiding the holiday. Then again, why would Raine make such a suggestion concerning Noelle, who had no children? "I don't think Miss Noelle is a mother, sweetie."

"I know, Daddy. But someday she will be."

He could think of no response. Or maybe he didn't want to respond. Was this another one of Raine's prophecies? He found himself wanting to move on to another subject, and quickly. Yet he wanted to probe his daughter's statement. A big part of him was terrified at what answer she might give. Given the fact he and Patty had been unable to conceive, this epiphany was unsettling. In the end, his curiosity got the best of him. "Dare I ask for details, little one?"

"I don't know."

"You don't know what? The details, or if you should tell them to Daddy?"

She shrugged. A moment later, her float disappeared beneath the surface of the water. The line became taut, and the sudden hit jerked the rod from Raine's hands. Sean sprang forward, caught the rod in midair and guided it back to her hands as she stood from her chair.

"Hold on tight, sweetie. Feels like a big one."

The strong pull of the rod pulled her toward the edge of the pier. Raine wasn't going to let go of the rod and, from the looks of the bend in it, the fish wasn't going to let up pulling on it. Sean hooked his arm around her waist and stood. He moved slowly along the pier in the direction the fish was taking the line. This gave Raine slack to start bringing in her catch. After a few moments, the fish tired, and she was able to slowly reel in the line. As the fish broke the surface of the water, it flapped and began its fight anew. Raine fought valiantly and brought it again to the surface. With his free hand, Sean grabbed the net and skillfully scooped her catch into the mesh. He lifted the net from the water and onto the pier.

"It's a whopper!" She laughed. "Wow, look at it!"

They sat for a moment on the pier and watched the fish flop in the net. Although it fought as if it was much bigger, in reality he would guess it weighed under a pound. But it was her first fish. After a few seconds it stopped fighting. Its gills expanded and contracted, in search of water. His daughter's expression changed from elation to excitement to a confused frown.

"Let it go, Daddy. Okay?"

"Sure, sweetie." He freed the fish from the net, removed the hook from its mouth, stooped, and gently dropped it into the water. The fish seemed confused for a moment and hesitated on the surface, before slowly swimming into the depth of the water and out of sight.

He knelt before his daughter and wiped his hands on a towel. "Are you okay?"

"I don't want to fish any more today, Daddy." A tear meandered down her rosy cheek.

He lifted her into his arms and held her tight, as if he could alleviate the pain she felt from the realities of life. The absence of Noelle probably also played a role with her sudden display of emotions.

The future might offer much tougher demons for him to slay in protecting his daughter from the harsh dealings of life. He resolved to take them on one at a time. He turned toward the sailboat. Right now, he needed a diversion. "What say we take her out?"

"Really, just me and you take our boat out?"

"Well, why not? But I'll need some help, matey."

"Aye, aye, cap'n. What do I need to do?"

He stepped on board and gently set her on the deck. "Safety is always first, sweetie, so go below and get that funny-looking stretchy line that's hanging on a peg near the ice box."

When she returned, her eyes were wide with anticipation. They had talked about sailing before, but she had always been too small. He promised one day she would be old enough. It was hard enough to sail the boat alone—although it was rigged and laid out for that—and he didn't want to get into a situation where he would have to tend to Raine instead of navigating the boat. The events of the last months had changed his mind about her readiness to listen and her ability to at least do no harm concerning the sailing process. He had been thinking a lot lately about taking the boat out with her, so he had bought a harness and tether line as an extra precaution. When she returned he put the harness over her life jacket and tethered the line to the mast.

"First we prepare the sail. I think we only need the mainsail today. Do you think you could help Daddy take the sail cover off and then wad it up for me and stuff it in the deck locker?"

The day and weather were perfect for the maiden voyage. He put his own safety line and jacket on and lifted her to the ties for the mainsail. She untied them and helped him pull the cover off the main.

"You're doing great, matey." He set her down and guided her to the engine controls at the wheel. "Now we start the engine, so we can free the lines. Once we have the lines untied, we can shove off. You think maybe you can steer the boat out into the sound, away from the dock?"

"Can I?"

"Absolutely." He had never seen her so enthusiastic. He had always hoped she would love sailing as much as her mother had and prayed the enthusiasm wouldn't fade with time.

Away from the dock, Sean idled the engine and helped Raine turn the wheel until the boat headed into the light wind. He clipped both their tether lines to the wheel pedestal and instructed her to keep her eyes on a point directly lined up with the forward mainstay.

"Try to keep us headed right toward that power pole across the water while I hoist the mainsail."

She was so cute, sitting in the pilot's chair, straining forward to reach the wheel as it moved back and forth, keeping the heading perfectly straight. She was a natural. Once the mainsail was up and secure, Sean took the pilot's chair, picked her up, and sat her in his lap. He helped her turn the wheel to port. When the wind filled the sail, the boat heeled to port and began moving forward. He killed the engine and all was quiet, except for the sound of the wind and the water lapping against the hull of the boat as it moved through the ripple of waves.

"Wow," she whispered, keeping the wheel steady as the boat moved east along a reach from the southern wind. "It's so nice out here. And quiet."

Sean glanced toward the heavens and smiled as he tightened his grip around her waist. His first sail with his daughter was turning out better than he could ever have hoped. He cradled his chin on the top of her head and took a deep breath.

"Your mom would be so proud. I'm proud of you, matey," he whispered in her ear. "You are quite the good sailor."

"I love it, Daddy."

She got it. Not everyone did. It was something you either loved, or you became impatient to get to your destination quickly via a power boat. He was so happy she seemed to be one of the former, not the latter.

The incident with the fish was only a distant memory.

****

Noelle put the marker in another one of his books, closed it, and laid it on the small table next to her chaise. She took her cell phone from the table and called Connie.

"Hey lady," she said after she answered. "I think I'm ready to talk now. Can you bring my car out?"

"I'm there," her friend said. "Look for me in an hour."

"Thanks. See you then."

She felt a tinge of guilt at deciding to hide out at the beach house. Sean had been so persistent in trying to reach her, but she didn't want to have to deal with him showing up. The open car port offered little place to hide a vehicle, so if he drove by, he would know she was there. For the entire week since returning from Washington, she had sought the solitude of the beach house, using it to unclutter her mind. And she was so proud of Connie, honoring her reluctance to talk about the situation. But now she was ready. It was time to buy Connie dinner for taking care of her car woes.

She adjusted her sunglasses and leaned her head back to face the heat of the sun. The warmth of the breeze caressed her. She had forgotten what it was like to relax. The stress, as well as the sweet memories of the last day in New York, were ever so slowly beginning to fade. If only she could find the secret to turning off the pain in her heart. She picked up the book and turned to the back cover. There Sean was, a hint of a smile on his lips, looking back at her. The photo alone could have sold thousands of copies of the book. Had she not known him or anything about his writing, she would have bought the book just to look at the photo. She would bet many other women would react the same.

She had purchased all of his books. In the last few days, she had read four of them and was into the fifth. To say they were good stories was an understatement. She understood why his books were so popular. He was a gifted writer. It was a shame the average reader would never know how he managed to capture a piece of himself in every one of his protagonists. Yet they were all very different.

The anomaly, Noelle surmised, was that the leading ladies in his stories were all cut from the same mold. They were all beautiful, successful, erotic women, and all of them were fiercely independent—at least until they met the protagonists. Reading his books gave her a better understanding of the man with whom she had spent wonderful days and one magical night. As popular as all his fictional male characters were, none of them had the exact complement of attributes he possessed. His readers would never know the full extent of his talents and qualities, except for perhaps one lucky woman someday. The full array of those qualities would be impossible to capture by any author, although Sean had done a good job sprinkling his heroes with some of his best traits. She could see his selflessness, his stability, even his temper in some of the characters. Of course, all his heroes were good lovers, but none could compare to his actual prowess in that category.

As independent as the women in his books were, none could resist the lure of his leading men. They became putty in the hands of his protagonists. One day, the writer might well find his perfect real-life heroine again in a story. That woman would no doubt encompass the strongest and best attributes of all the characters he created in the stories so many people loved. It was no wonder the stories had died.

Had they forever died with the woman he fashioned them from? Could anyone ever measure up to that woman again?

Noelle had assumed since he had loved once, he might love again. And that the woman he chose to love again might be her. Was it a pipe dream? In spite of enjoying his books and the fantasy world they related, she was keenly aware she lived in a much different world. In her world, there wasn't always a happy ending. Instead, her world consisted of lost loves and failed relationships, always ending with the same heartache.

This episode had cut deeply. It was especially brutal because she had given her heart unconditionally, as well as her body and soul. It had felt so right. Yet it had ended so wrong. Unlike the lost loves in her past, this time things had changed, and now she couldn't change them back. This was the end for her, the end to ever hoping for true love. Could she ever recover from losing Sean? She certainly couldn't picture having the courage to risk putting herself out there again. Nothing could make her believe there was any reason whatsoever in trying to find love once more. Even if she did give it another try in the future, it was going to take a lot of time—not to mention self-analysis—to find her way back to love.

Future. What an obscene word. Who was she kidding? There *was* no future, at least not romantically. There were very few Seans out there in the world, and she had been lucky to find one, if only for a while. Then she had promptly lost him. She couldn't expect him to ever trust her again. And she doubted she would ever trust him again. She had in fact sold Raine out, just as he had accused her.

She loved his daughter as if she were her own, and as surely as she loved him. Her love was so strong she had lost sight of her logic and had erroneously thought that answering the agency's questions would help Raine. How idiotic that assumption had been. Those feelings made her cross a line—a line someone like her should never have crossed. Her weak, misguided moment had cost her the love of her life. She had let herself be intimidated by the NSA agent, and it had meant losing the only true love she had ever experienced. The strength of the brief relationship with Sean made it so clear to her. It emphasized how meaningless her other relationships had been.

She stood from her chair and made her way to the beach. Perhaps a swim in the Gulf could wash away her mistakes and the fog that distorted her thoughts. It was, after all, time to get back to reality. Connie would soon arrive.

She was reminded of the dinner she owed Connie. She wasn't looking forward to going out in public until she was back in Pensacola at the beginning of a new work week. She was no closer now to gearing up to face her patients than when she had arrived at the beach. She dreaded going back to the office. It would remind her of the time she had spent with Raine and Sean, getting to know them and working with him to evaluate her.

The thought of going back to work had always been something she had looked forward to. Now it was the very last thing she wanted to do.

****

Sean stared at the dustcover and wondered if he would be opening a different can of worms by removing it from the dormant desktop computer. The corner desk, his writing haven, had been collecting dust for two years. Why should he disturb it now? Removing the cover, looking at the keyboard and monitor might dredge up more than a few painful memories.

Yet it felt like the right thing to do.

Raine was in her room with her laptop, continuing her feeding frenzy for knowledge. Since the issue of the July meeting in Washington was confirmed, she had spent a lot of time on that laptop. He hadn't interfered with her desire for answers to questions—except to install some parental controls—mainly because he didn't understand it all, and doubted anyone did. He simply had faith she was doing what she was supposed to be doing.

As much as he tried to block out all the questions about where he fit into all she might know, his curiosity continued to hound him. He wanted to believe if she knew something about his or her own future, she would come to him with it. She was a very intelligent little girl who possessed uncanny wisdom. Maybe she did have some knowledge of what lay ahead for them but instinctively knew he wasn't ready to hear about it.

In particular, he was curious about her suggestion about a Mother's Day gift for Noelle. Had she known something about Noelle's future and didn't want to verbalize it? Could he assume, if Raine did know something concerning the subject, that he was a part of Noelle's future? Did she know Noelle was to have biological children? He found this particularly disturbing, given his own situation. Although the tests proved conclusively that Patty was unable to have children, the tests concerning his virility were less definitive. The doctor was very specific in the delivery of the prognosis concerning *their* inability to have children *together*. He had continually emphasized the possibility of the two of them producing children was remote. He had not pressed the doctor concerning his own ability to conceive, given the diagnosis of Patty. He had merely accepted they weren't destined to have biological children.

"What are you looking at, Daddy?"

Sean flinched and swung around toward his daughter. "Whoa, you gave me a start, little one."

Raine giggled, and then looked at the desk. "What's under that cover, Daddy?"

"Oh, just a computer and an old monitor I've had for a few years."

"Is this where you used to write your stories?"

Was she now reading minds? "Yes, sweetie."

"When are you going to write another story, Daddy?"

He hesitated for a moment and then sat at the desk. "I guess maybe I'm going to start right now."

He removed the plastic cover, folded it neatly, opened a drawer, and placed it inside. When he turned to speak to his daughter, she was gone.

Once again he had underestimated her. Had he been nudged into something he had thought about for days? It wasn't inconceivable, given her talents, that her short conversation with him was based on more than random curiosity.

He flipped the computer and monitor switches to

the on position and settled into the chair. When the computer screen came to life he opened Word. The white screen appeared before him. In the upper left hand corner of the screen, the cursor blinked.

He took a deep breath, cracked his knuckles, and started writing.

Chapter Sixteen

Surrounded by the sanctity of her routine, Noelle's apprehension eased. Although she had not looked forward to returning to work, it had turned out to be exactly what she needed. In a matter of days her caseload of patients had increased dramatically, bolstered by her appearance on the morning show, which was confirmed by all the new patient referral sheets. It seemed everyone wanted their child to be the next Raine.

In spite of taking the days off with her and Sean, the business was growing. Each new day found her spending more and more time building and accommodating her ever-growing patient list. For the first time she added Saturday morning appointments to her schedule. There was safety and security in becoming immersed in work. It also helped to kill the sting of recent events, giving her less time to contemplate things lost. The pain and loneliness dulled with each passing day—if only to some minute degree.

The intercom buzzer startled Noelle.

"Yes, Connie?"

"You know who is on line four," Connie said tiredly.

She hesitated for a moment she fought a smile. "And what do we do when you know who calls?"

"Tell him you aren't available?" Connie whispered.

"Correct!"

In a lower volume, Connie pleaded, "Come on, Noelle. He's so cute, and he sounds so dejected. Won't you speak to him? Just for a moment?" After a few moments of silence, Connie reapplied her business voice. "Very well, Dr. Victor. I'll tell Mr. Sampson you aren't available at the moment."

Sean had been persistent in trying to reach her. During the first few days. there was a plethora of messages on her voice mail systems for both her land line at home and her cell phone. He also called the office repeatedly, of course never getting past Connie.

He chose to ignore the referral letter she had mailed him and had tried to make an appointment for Raine. The wording of the letter had been clear, informing him that she had completed her evaluation. It also explained that, due to her heavy caseload, she was discharging Raine as her patient. If additional services were required he would have to make an appointment with another doctor. She had suggested several good ones for him to choose from, including a few of the best.

In a note she sent to Raine in care of her father, Noelle explained she wouldn't be able to see her any more for a while. At the time, the "for a while" part caused her pain because, in truth, it would most probably be a permanent separation. But she didn't want to hurt the little girl and instead stretched the truth for the sake of the child's well-being. It was a long and carefully constructed note, meant to let her down gently.

Surprisingly, she received a hand-written note back from the child, in which she said she understood. The note was more upbeat than she had expected and was written in a tone that strongly suggested the parting was indeed temporary and not at all permanent. The words the three-year-old had skillfully constructed, without literally spelling it out, implied Noelle would continue to be in her life. As much as she refused to believe it, she suspected there was more to Raine's words than could be derived from the note. Aware of the depth of the little girl's perception, Noelle might not have a clue how insightful the note could turn out to be. And in a strange way, Noelle took comfort in that.

After having no success with the calls, Sean had resorted to other tactics. The gifts continued for many days. Each gift was something thoughtful that brought a lump to Noelle's throat and tears to her eyes. All the gifts came with a note. Although she deemed it unfair given his propensity for words, she found she could not help but read them all. She had once laughed through her tears, surmising each new note and gift was a continuation of a prior one. He was writing a story, one gift at a time. His message was clear—he was sorry. He was a jerk. He didn't mean what he said. He missed her. He wanted another chance.

She wanted to send her own message back to him—she forgave him. He wasn't a jerk. She understood why he said what he did. She missed him, too. But she couldn't bring herself to do it. Time might heal wounds, but it doesn't erase the scars. The mind can never forget what the heart remembers. She had made a serious mistake with Raine, and she wasn't going to compound it by taking him back or taking Raine as a patient again. And no amount of time could change the way things were. It wasn't in the stars for her to be in a happy relationship. Like Raine in some ways, she had a gift, but one that only allowed her to fast forward to the end of her romantic relationships. And the end for her was always the same, and most definitely never happy. When all was said and done, it was hard to accept the possibility of any other outcome, so why take a chance?

****

Well into the story, Sean knew he was spending too much time at his desk and not enough time with his daughter. A few days earlier, he had tried to remedy his guilt by offering to move her small desk into his room and situate it right next to his writing desk. She told him that she needed her own space, so she declined and opted to keep her laptop in her room.

He was astonished at how much he had written in the last few weeks.

It felt good.

Although he wrote mostly at night after Raine settled into bed, he found himself writing more and more during the day. He compromised by taking frequent breaks and spending time with her at the beach, on the boat, or at the library. Raine was becoming quite the first mate on short sails. Sean was so encouraged by her propensity for understanding the principles of sailing, he was thinking about a longer trip. The planning was of a selfish nature, but she seemed to enjoy the time on the boat as much as he did, though she was still too small for a trip of any duration. But in a few years, who knew? In the meantime the short sails were a good way to escape the hordes of people who wanted to get close to Raine. In the boat, Sean could anchor near more secluded beaches to give them some much-needed downtime and privacy.

He looked at his watch. He saved his work, stood, and stretched. A growling noise from his stomach validated his need to seek sustenance. Though Raine never missed lunch, he often skipped it. He was so engrossed in the writing he hadn't heard as much as a peep from Raine in a long while.

"Raine?" He slipped his feet into sandals and padded toward her bedroom. "Are you getting hungry? Daddy is starved. How about—"

At the door to Raine's room, he froze. She lay on her stomach, in front of the laptop screen, with her face buried in her hands. As she lifted her head, he could see the tears.

"Honey, what's wrong?" He knelt by her bed and pushed a wet strand of hair from her face. Her skin was damp with perspiration. "Are you all right?"

She simply looked again at the computer screen. On it was an article from the *Boston Medical Journal*. The title of the article made his heart feel as though it might stop.

"Lymphoma." Her whisper revealed a fear he had never heard in her voice.

"I'm not going to ask how you knew what your mommy...had."

"That's not it, Daddy."

"Isn't that why you were reading about lymphoma?"

"I don't know."

Sean stood nervously and then quickly sat back on the bed, taking his daughter in his arms. "Honey, you know you can talk to Daddy about anything."

"I know."

"I know this may sound funny, given you probably know much more about this disease than I do. But the doctors did everything they could to make Mommy better."

"I know," she sniffled and then from nowhere, asked, "Daddy, who is the Castle Man?"

"The Castle Man?"

She lowered her head in her familiar brand of resignation. He paused for a moment and then squeezed her. "I think someone has been looking at the computer too long."

"Daddy, are you afraid of dying?"

A freight train, head on, would have had less effect on him. For a moment he hesitated, knowing full well that hesitating was something he should not—could not do. "Honey, why are you asking this? Are you afraid you're going to die?"

"I don't know."

"Does this have anything to do with lymphoma or the Castle Man?"

"I don't know." She took a shuddering deep breath. He was aware she probably *didn't* know. She looked very confused, as if she didn't understand what her own feelings were about. In spite of efforts to ignore the inevitability of it, his stomach growled loudly.

She giggled. He smiled and shrugged. The rumble continued, and her giggle turned into a laugh.

"Did you swallow the Castle Man, Daddy?" She laughed her renowned belly laugh. Sean laughed as well. "Should we get you something to eat, Daddy?"

"You stole the question right out of my mouth," he said and pretended to put the words back. "As you can tell, I'm very hungry. How about a pizza?"

"I want popcorn shrimp." Her eyes lit up. "Can we go to the Crab Trap?"

"The Crab Trap, hmmm." He rubbed the stubble on his chin. "An evening of beach dining, perhaps? Why, that's an excellent idea, little one. We haven't eaten there in a long time. What made you think of the Crab Trap?"

"I don't know."

He goosed his daughter. "Perhaps if we have to wait for a table, you can build me a *castle, man*."

"That's not funny, Daddy." Her face was serious. He could see he had hit a nerve.

"Sorry, sweetie." He stood.

She smiled. "Just kidding! Gotcha!" She jumped from the bed and ran for the door.

In his best wicked-witch-of-the-west voice he cackled, "I'll get you, my pretty."

The little girl squealed all the way into the den, as if she might have a chance to escape.

****

"Oh, come on, lady." Connie curled her arm around Noelle's elbow and forcefully guided her from her desk to the office door. "Whatever it is you're doing can wait until tomorrow. I'm starved, and you owe me dinner. Remember? Your car? You never bought me the dinner you promised."

"I bought you dinner that night at the beach."

"Take-outs don't count."

"Okay, okay."

"Honey, you've been working so hard. And my God, look at you. You look like you haven't eaten all week. You're the only woman I know who can gain *or* lose five pounds and look more gorgeous."

"I will take you to dinner, but I won't give you a raise," Noelle promised, smiling. "So stop with the flattery. At least I think you were flattering me?"

"I was." Her friend laughed, still holding tight to Noelle's arm. "But apparently it wasn't enough if you aren't going to give me a raise."

"So where would you like to dine, Miss Constance?"

"I'm feeling kinda beachy tonight," Connie answered.

Noelle gave her a startled look.

"I said beachy, girl, not bitchy. How about the Crab Trap?"

"All the way to Perdido Key?"

"Oh, my goodness, a thirty-minute ride? Forgive me for asking you to drive so very far. Okay, I'll do the driving; you make sure you bring your debit card."

"Okay, okay. And I *will* let you drive."

During the first part of the drive to the restaurant, Connie talked nonstop about the practice and new patients. After pausing to catch her breath, Noelle sensed Connie's attention had shifted as Noelle continued to stare out the window. The last light of the day faded quickly as they chased the western horizon.

"You know, it sounds as if he really *is* sorry."

"I know."

"I really hate to see you lose out on something so good because Mr. Perfect slipped up once."

"Connie, it's much more than that."

"But does it really have to be?"

Noelle remained quiet. She didn't have to wait long for her friend to continue.

"My love, I think you might be losing sight of the

forest for the trees. Hmm?" She hesitated, and when Noelle didn't respond, she continued, "You think maybe your standards might be a tad high?"

She shot Connie a quick, piercing look.

"I know, I know. It's none of my business. Honey, I hate to see you so down."

"I'm fine," she lied and forced a smile.

Connie opened her mouth to speak but said nothing.

"Well, maybe I do need to talk."

"I'm all ears. I knew you weren't spilling all when we talked earlier at your beach house," her friend said. "We have plenty of time before we reach the Key."

"I've been having emotions that are so unfamiliar to me."

"How do you mean?"

"Well, never before had I thought about turning over control of any aspect of my life to anyone. Yet at times I yearn for him to take control of me…well, as he did the night in New York. That night was wonderful. I really have nothing in my life to compare with it. Granted, I *loved* Scott, but strangely, I was never *in love* with him. Certainly not to the point where I wanted him to take control of my life in any form or fashion. One moment I'm okay—even excited—about this fantasy of letting Sean in, and the next moment I want to run as far away from him as I possibly can. Maybe it's because of *his* history, not mine, I don't know. Maybe I'm scared of giving myself totally to a man who has been through such difficult times in losing his wife. And from what I know, it was a very good relationship. How am I supposed to compete with her? And with what's going on with Raine, he certainly doesn't need the extra pressure of taking me on, does he?"

For once, Connie was quiet. Noelle was grateful for the chance to talk it out and use Connie for a sounding board.

The last five minutes of the drive were quiet, as the horizon ahead of them yielded to the deep purple of dusk and the inevitability of night.

****

Directly on the beach at Perdido Key on the western Florida Gulf Coast, the Crab Trap was located about eight miles from the Alabama state line. Although most of the dining area was indoors, there was a large area of wooden picnic tables out back under a roof but in the open air. The popular family restaurant often meant a wait time, but a small bar and adjoining playground adjacent to the outside dining helped patrons to pass the time while waiting for a table.

Sean barely heard the announcement over the playground banter. Raine had picked a swing set farthest from the dining area.

"Sampson, party of two."

"That's us, sweetie."

Raine had already slowed the swing. He stepped over and gently stopped its motion and took her into his arms. He made his way up the wooden walkway, past the outside diners and into the restaurant.

"Can we eat outside, Daddy?"

He smiled. "I figured you would want to. That's why I gave the greeter that as our preference."

"Goody!"

Their server, a slender young woman, gave him an overly animated smile. "Mr. Sampson, please follow

217

me."

He couldn't help but notice the server put on a performance with exaggerated movements of her hips. Apparently, Raine noticed it, too. Following in the server's footsteps, she mimicked her walk. When he noticed, he scooped her into his arms. An older woman sitting at a table watched them as they passed. She laughed and gave him a knowing smile. Since their arrival earlier, several people had recognized them but thankfully had not made a scene. A whisper here, a pointed finger there, but nothing blatant. This waitress was determined to be different.

"Okay, you comedian," he whispered to his daughter. "That's about enough."

"Sorry," Raine giggled. She whispered in his ear. "She walks funny."

His suspicion concerning the server's special interest in him proved true. She lingered for a long time after seating them, theatrically delivering the specials of the night and taking the drink order. She never took her eyes from him and bent low to point out the specials from the menu, flaunting her cleavage. He buried his face in the menu, politely shaking or nodding in response to her narrative. Raine looked back and forth between him and the server and giggled the entire time. Blonde with Swaying Hips ignored Raine, and continued to zero in on him. After a few more grueling moments, she must have picked up the chill. She left, and he took a deep breath of relief.

"That lady was funny."

"Yeah, well…"

"Why didn't you want to look at her, Daddy? I think she likes you."

"I, ah, well. Never mind. You figure out which sides you want with your shrimp, shrimp."

"Don't be so such a crab, crab." Her belly laugh was back.

He laughed with her, glad he had shaken the server. He reached across and lightly pinched her cheek. For a long moment, he couldn't look away from her face as his love for her flooded his emotions.

She looked at him and made a funny face. "What's that face all about, Daddy?"

"I love you." He felt compelled to say it to her at that moment. He struggled to further label how he was feeling, and his throat closed. He took a sip of water. His thoughts meandered.

In a matter of seconds, his mind took him on a blinding fast review of his life with her. From China, the first day he held her, to the Green Room at Global, to where she lay on the bed in her room earlier as her tears flowed. He couldn't put his finger on it, but he suspected this moment would be something he would someday look back on and realize that things could not be any better than they were at this very second. He promised himself he would be better at grabbing and holding on to these kinds of moments. So many of his friends and acquaintances had told him how lucky his daughter was to have been chosen to come to her forever home in America with him. They had no clue it was he who was the lucky one. He looked across at her once again, to ingest her image, and frowned at what he saw.

Tears glistened in her eyes. "I love you, too," she said, barely able to get the words out in a whisper.

"Why are you crying, little one?"

"I don't know, Daddy. I'm just sad all of a sudden."

He took her hand and tried to ignore the fear that nibbled at his soul. He struggled to identify the feeling of impending dread that haunted him. Her face seemed to reflect a reciprocating fear. For a long moment, her tiny hand squeezed his, as if she might never let go.

****

Connie slowed to make the turn into the full parking lot at the Crab Trap. Noelle knew there might be a wait. She thought about suggesting another restaurant, but then decided against it.

"Perfect," Connie said. "I say we check in with the greeter, then head for the bar out back so we can get a dose of the beach air before we eat."

The idea sounded good to Noelle.

The heavy smell of summer permeated the late June night. A prevailing southern breeze caressed Noelle's face as they made their way inside. After registering, they moved through the dining area and outside to the bar. Both the playground and the outside dining area were full, but the small bar was virtually abandoned. The greeter had said it might be more than a short wait, but this gave them more time for drinks. In no time, she was working on her second Chablis. The first one had given her a quick but welcome buzz. After all, Connie was right on the mark about her observation. Noelle hadn't eaten very well lately.

Her friend seemed to enjoy the mixture of fine wine and the night. She couldn't seem to stop talking. The conversation was again one-sided, and she found it amusing how Connie jumped from one subject to another without the least bit of concern that she was continually interrupting herself.

"I love this place," she said and took another sip of her wine. "How come you don't take me here more often? And the weather is getting so nice, I could stay here forever. Well, at least until the wine ran out. I have never seen so many different types of wine on the board over there. Have you? How come I'm the only one talking?"

"I am enjoying watching you enjoy yourself. Maybe you're right, maybe we don't get out enough."

Connie wound up again, and Noelle gave special attention to listening to the public address system that would eventually summon them, since her friend was lost in drink and talk. As the night progressed, the noise from the playground and dining area got louder, making it much harder for her to hear.

However, the next announcement rang through loud and clear.

"Sampson, party of two."

Connie heard the announcement also. She wore an apprehensive look. They watched as Sean and Raine passed across from the bar, making their way to the front. Thankfully, he never looked toward them. Noelle's heart fluttered as he moved confidently and with determination through the outside dining area, chatting away with his beautiful child, whose arms were wrapped around his neck.

With the sight of him she plunged back in time, to that morning at the Hilton, having breakfast. Watching him walk by made her want to leap from the bar stool and run to him. It took every bit of her courage to sit still.

How could any man do this to her? Was it simply a

physical reaction to seeing him? Was this the basis of her attraction to him? Without a doubt, that part of her feelings for him could not be denied.

Would she always be in love with him? Would time ever be kind enough to allow her love for him to fade? She only knew when she saw him—even after all these weeks—the feeling was still there and if anything, stronger than ever.

It wasn't fair.

Connie was kind enough to remain silent as she watched them emerge from inside and make their way to the picnic area. There he was, following a beautiful, slender, big-chested, long-flowing bleached-blonde hussy who practically displayed a *Do Me* sign on her backside as she led him via the scenic route to their table. Had he shown interest in her blatant display of flirtation? She honestly did not remember. Then the witch proceeded to throw herself at him, totally ignoring his child. Then she noticed he *did* indeed ignore the server and looked very uncomfortable as he buried his face in the menu. Great, another reason to love him more. Nine out of ten men would have stared down that cleavage and had her number so quick it would make her head spin.

"Well, that was interesting."

"Can you believe how that…woman threw herself at him?"

"Oh, I wasn't watching her, honey." There was a big smile on Connie's face. "I was watching you."

****

In spite of the emotion Sean felt, the next announcement rang out very clear.

"Victor, party of two. Victor, party of two."

Sean almost choked on a bite of crab claw. Raine's eyes lit up as she stood on her chair and looked around. "There they are!"

There they *are, she had said. Party of two. Party of two.* The words swirled around his head and his heart pounded. Try as he might he couldn't take his eyes from his daughter to look toward where she pointed, petrified he would see Noelle with another man. The anger welled in his chest and the adrenaline surged, making his ears burn and his teeth grind. In spite of trying to avoid it, he ventured a look. There she was— looking even better than the last time he had seen her. The simple movement of her standing from the bar stool looked sexy. A tall bald man stood close to her. Sean's first thought was that he was looking at a dead man. He would simply kill him, thereby eliminating the competition.

Then he saw her step away from the man and move toward Connie.

Thank God.

Then a different emotion took control, a mix of anger, pride, and defensiveness. After all, she had avoided him like the plague.

I can handle this.

Raine was off to the races, running around tables and chairs toward her. As she reached her, Noelle knelt and scooped her into her arms. Her smile couldn't hide the tears that formed in her eyes. It was obvious she had missed his daughter. For a moment, he couldn't get his mind around that. He caught up with them and stood awkwardly before Raine and the two ladies.

"Hi." Noelle timidly offered her hand. He reluctantly took it and ignored the jolt his body felt from his first contact with her in what seemed like ages.

"Noelle," he said with a cool, forced smile and then glanced toward her office manager. "Connie."

Connie nodded. She stood quietly, biting her lip.

"Will you sit with us, Miss Noelle?" His daughter's invitation made him uneasy. He stammered for a moment before Noelle spoke.

"Thank you for asking, honey. But we don't want to intrude on your Daddy time."

"Please, we would love to have you join us," Sean said and immediately wondered why. In spite of all the emotions surging through him, he swallowed his pride for the sake of his daughter.

"Why, we'd love to join you two." Connie stepped up. "I don't know about anybody else, but I'm starved. There ain't no use in the two of us taking up a whole big table, when you have so much room at yours."

Noelle looked at Connie and forced a smile.

Soon after they all sat down at Sean's table, it was apparent Blonde was not happy with the new seating arrangements. Having two more lovely women at Sean's table slowed the service and iced her smile. Although she wasn't the primary server, she was influential. The longer it took to get service, the more conversation was needed to fill the gaps.

"Daddy, did you tell Miss Noelle about us going sailing?"

"Haven't had the chance to talk to the doctor lately, little one. You know between her practice and my writing, busy, busy, busy." Not a chance he was going to hide his sarcasm. Noelle passed right over it.

"You're writing again?" She blushed, stammered, but didn't wait for him to answer. She looked at Raine.

"You helped your daddy sail that big boat?"

"Uh-huh," she said. "And I caught a big fish, too."

"Really?" Her eyes were wide, her lips pursed. Perhaps his slight about not being able to speak with her was soaking in. "Let me guess. He threw it back, didn't he?"

Sean opened his mouth with a comeback but was cut off quickly.

"Wonder where our server is?" Connie strained to look around with a desperate look on her face. "They aren't usually this slow. We ordered a while ago, didn't we?"

"Perhaps your daddy can get his little blonde friend over to help us out? She seemed eager to help earlier." Noelle's implication was venomous.

"Raine, sweetie, why don't we go back to the playground for a while, until the food arrives?" Connie asked. "I'm sure your daddy wouldn't mind, would you, Sean?"

"Of course not." They quickly left, and Sean prepared to unload, but he didn't get the chance.

"Please stop calling me," she said quietly, leaning across the table.

"Done."

"And please stop sending me gifts."

"Done."

The food arrived. The server took one look at Sean and then Noelle and quickly dumped the food and left, as if the plates were suddenly too hot to handle.

"Excuse me," he said. He dropped his napkin on the table and stood. "I'll get the others."

Before she could reply, he was gone.

****

Noelle rode in silence on the way home. The meal had been stressful. She hardly touched her food. Raine took care of the leftovers. Apparently, Sean wasn't hungry either. He looked as though he could have used a stiff drink, but he would never allow himself that luxury. She knew him well enough to know he would never drink and then drive with a child in the car, even the few minutes to Ono Island. She was suddenly jealous of Raine. He was much better at being a father than at being in a relationship.

The night had been a total bust. She had hoped to have some time to talk with him, but pride and anger got in the way. There was so much she wanted to say, so much she had wanted to clear the air about, so many feelings she needed to resolve.

In spite of being on the outside looking in, Noelle couldn't fault Sean for going to great lengths to build his life around Raine. He protected his little girl at all costs, obsessed with guarding her in every sense of the word. Noelle didn't need to be a specialist to know exactly why he felt this way. Plain and simple, he didn't want to lose her as he had lost his wife. The conversation in New York left little doubt where his priorities were. There were a couple of times she had wanted to chime in, but she resolved she wouldn't do that, not without his asking for help.

He never asked.

So, instead she had just listened, all the while wanting to tell him there was nothing more he could have done to save his wife. She wanted to say Patty would have resented anything he had forced her into doing and would have never forgiven him if his insistence had caused a delay or suspension in the adoption proceedings. From the sound of how advanced her cancer was, his efforts would have served to only postpone the inevitable.

He loved his daughter very much. He would never have forgiven himself if his insistence had contributed to their losing Raine. Her heart went out to him and the impossible situation his wife's illness had put him in.

Noelle was mired in guilt from resentment. How could she ask him to love her, when his struggle every day with the past and his fear of the future were so strong? Yet, what she felt for him was so powerful and so deep that no matter how she tried, she couldn't control it. The situation was impossible. If she gave in to those yearnings, she might never be able to survive, especially if someday he decided to walk away. This was a definite possibility. His inherent, instinctive protection for his daughter was so strong, it trumped everything else in his life. All the sum total of her experience and studies told her to cut her losses and run. Unless he could properly control his guilt and obsession with protecting his daughter, she would always live in fear of losing them both. She couldn't take that chance. She had to face reality; she wasn't on the right side of history.

And yet she loved them both.

Deeply.

"Do you want to talk about it?"

She glanced at her friend. "I'm not sure what it would accomplish." The tears flowed. Connie touched her shoulder.

"I understand. Just know I'm here for you."

Noelle forced a smile. In spite of everything, she found comfort in her friend's words.

****

"So, I was wondering if you had forgotten about your best friend."

"No, Derek, I talked to him the other day. He says to tell you hello."

"Funny."

"Jerk." In spite of the anger that still consumed Sean, it was good to lighten things up. Raine was tucked in, and his head was still spinning with the events of the night. He felt he was losing grip on life. In his gruff, comical way, Derek always seemed to know what to say to set things right—something he definitely needed at the moment.

"From what you told me about the New York trip, it's obvious you care for Noelle. You know, I think there's hope for you yet, buddy. But then you tell me the two of you ignored each other all night?"

"Pretty much. She seemed more interested in talking with Raine."

"And you just sat there? You didn't put your napkin down, stand, take her hand, and ask Connie to watch Raine while you took her to a dark corner and had your way with her? And by the way, can you get this chick Connie's number? She sounds hot."

"Jeez, man, is that all you can think about?"

"Oh, that's easy for you to say, bud. But remember, I'm divorced." He barked and then brought down his volume to a whisper, as if there were someone else listening. "What else have I got but fantasies?"

"You see, that's what I mean. How am I supposed to know she's the one in the first place? You thought Marie was the one for you, and that didn't work out. I had the love of my life, and that didn't work out. How can I possibly think I could find another Patty?"

"You won't."

"What do you mean, I won't?"

"You'll never find another Patty."

"Then why try?"

"Because you've found a Noelle instead."

"Look, call me dense, but I don't get it."

"You'll never have another relationship like you had with Patty. The next one will be different. It will be better in many ways, maybe not so good in other ways. I don't know. But it will all be worth it, my friend."

Sean thought about this for a moment.

"I do know this. If you don't continue trying to see if this will work out, you will regret it for the rest of your life. She may not come around tomorrow, next week, or next month, but you shouldn't give up on her. You have to figure out what exactly you feel for her. Look, I remember every word you said during our conversation when you got home from D.C. In fact, I recorded it and am selling it to Simon and Schuster as your next work. The advance check is in the bank."

"Very funny."

"Shut up, ya big jerk, and listen. Seriously, these things take time. She needs time. You need time. You may not agree with that, but you do. Although you ain't gonna believe this is coming from me, but I really don't think you're ready to open your arms and take her back. Never thought I would say this, but I think you need more time to really let it sink in that, whether or not you believe it, you can't control and protect everything and everybody you care about."

This hit home for Sean. He thought about arguing, but his friend was right. "I miss her."

"And you will continue to miss her. But it's time to move on."

"I meant Noelle."

"Oh. Look, I believe with all my heart Noelle will be back. You need to give her space and time. Just wish you hadn't pissed her off before I got to meet her and this Connie babe."

"Well, I'd love for you to meet her, but given the circumstances—and in case you haven't noticed, I am giving her plenty of space and time. Hell, this is the first time I've seen her in weeks, and it was by accident."

"Hey, I wouldn't be too sure about that."

"What are you talking about?"

"I'm saying maybe it was fate you two hooked up tonight. Even if it wasn't much of a hook-up. I still think you should have taken her away behind a sand dune."

"Oh, so we were destined to meet at the Crab Trap?" Sean asked, ignoring Derek's last suggestion. "Like there are so many seafood restaurants along the Redneck Riviera?" As he said it, he became aware how ridiculous it sounded. There *were* a lot of seafood restaurants along the beach.

"I'm just saying…" Derek retorted, closing in for the kill.

After a moment's silence, Sean yawned.

"Let me know if I'm boring you."

"You're boring me. Later."

"Hey!"

"Yeah, what is it? I'm tired."

"Two of your books are climbing the best seller list. One is seventy-fourth and the other is number eighty."

"Yeah, yeah. That's great," Sean replied. "And, by the way, I'm writing a new story."

"No kidding?" The excitement in Derek's voice rose a few decibels. "That's great. Your timing may be finally right. By the way, did you hear the news about your buddy the senator?"

"My buddy the senator?"

"Blane. He was arrested today. Don't you ever watch the news?"

"Not if I can help it." He tried to sound disinterested, but in fact this news made him uneasy.

"I'm surprised that little genius of yours didn't tell you. You tell me she's on the Internet all the time."

"If she knows, it's probably old news to her, now. She's on to bigger things. Passing bills, balancing the national budget, advising Congress, economic summits, lobbying for world peace, and the like."

"Go to bed."

"Later."

Sean hung up the phone and literally staggered to bed.

He was too tired to worry about lymphoma or arrested senators.

Or the Castle Man.

****

The loud ring of the phone sent bolts of pain through James's head. He fumbled in the dark for the night stand and knocked the receiver from the cradle. He tried to sit up from the bed, but his head throbbed. He reached over and turned on the bedside lamp. An empty bourbon bottle lay on its side near the edge of the table. Had he drunk the whole bottle? His head and stomach suggested he had. He found the receiver and lifted it gently to his ear.

"Yeah?" The sound of his own voice did little to sooth his miseries.

"Did you hear?" The tone of the voice of one of his closest friends did little to alleviate his near panic.

"Hear what?"

"Senator Blane was arrested."

"What!"

"Yesterday. Something about him stealing some money or something."

James was silent. No words could express what he was feeling.

"Somebody figured out he was funding the Cause."

"But how?"

"No idea. Hell, nobody in the club could figure it out, but we all knew it was him footing the bill. Must have been some sort of genius that put the pieces together."

James thought back to the morning Blane was supposed to appear on that morning show. Then he thought of the Chinese kid. Could his no-show somehow be related to that smart Chinese kid? "It ain't right, man."

"Somebody needs to pay, man."

James was thinking the same thing.

"They will, man." His hand shook. The adrenaline was surging. He had some vacation time coming up soon. He swore to himself he would get to the bottom of who sent Blane up. "They definitely will."

Chapter Seventeen

The cloak and dagger continued.

A call from the National Security Agency came three days later. An agent, who identified himself as Wayne Worley, gave Sean a special secure phone number, and asked him to call back from his cell phone. Sean got the agent back on the line, after glancing in on Raine, who was asleep.

"Mr. Sampson, the agency would very much appreciate your and your daughter's cooperation in the continued investigation of the alleged misconduct of Senator Blane. I have been instructed to escort you and your daughter to Washington to speak with the ethics committee."

"Look, Agent Worley, my daughter was very specific concerning what she learned about the issue. I see no reason to drag us back to Washington to go over the same stuff. Besides, we'll be there in a couple of months."

"I understand your concern, Mr. Sampson, but this won't wait. In matters as high-profile and important as this one, you must understand we can't hesitate in our efforts to cross every T and dot every I. It is imperative you cooperate in matters—"

"I know, I know," Sean interrupted. "In matters of national security. Would it make any difference at all if I refused?"

"Quite frankly, no, sir."

"Fine, then fill me in on the details."

"On Wednesday, an escort will arrive at your home and take you to waiting transportation at the Naval Air Station in Pensacola."

Sean thought of the threat he had received from the senator in the Green Room.

"Agent, is there any reason I should be concerned about my daughter's safety?"

"Mr. Sampson, as you may or may not know, we have made every effort to isolate your daughter from this incident. In the press releases, we state information relative to the implication of the senator was from undisclosed sources. We are aware of no immediate threats to your daughter or from the press connecting any dots. This interview is to wrap this matter up."

Sean suspected the matter might never be wrapped up. As powerful as Blane was, he would likely have many more friends than enemies. It didn't take a rocket scientist to tie Raine to the senator. There were a lot of crazies out there, who could easily put the two and two together concerning the senator's failure to make his appearance on the morning show, and then Raine's appearance afterwards.

"Sir, I am breaking a few rules here, but I will tell you that an agent has been assigned to support you and your daughter."

"You mean protect, don't you?"

"Let's think of it as extra insurance. As far as the agent goes, you won't ever see him or her. But know they're around. Our men and women are the finest anywhere, so you can rest assured you will be safe."

Sean thought about this, but the agent's

reassurances did little to ease his mind.

"Mr. Sampson, again we have no credible intelligence of a threat to your daughter. This is a precaution only, and I would appreciate if you keep this under your hat."

"How long will we be in Washington?"

"You might want to pack some extra clothes. Your presence there could, of course, be brief, but better safe than sorry. The department will provide for you any needs you might not anticipate."

He ended the call, turned, and found Raine standing behind him. He replayed the conversation in his mind and wondered how much she had heard. If he had said anything that might alarm his daughter, it was now water under the bridge. He smiled and touched her cheek. "Well, sweetie, looks like we get to go to Washington, once again."

She seemed to think about this for a moment. "When?"

"On Wednesday."

"For how long?"

"A few days, I would assume."

"Why?"

He thought carefully about his response. "Honey, I think they want to hear it again about how you figured out the appropriation scheme."

She seemed to chew on this comment for a moment, and then took a deep breath and smiled. "Do you think I could get a snack on the plane?"

He stifled a smile. It was like her to worry about food, first and foremost.

"Of course, sweetie." He knelt. "I would imagine you can have anything you want. They're sending one of their planes to take us there. I'm sure there will be lots of food on board."

With this, her eyes grew big, and her smile widened. "Wow," she mouthed, silently.

"Yeah, wow," he agreed. "Are you ready for all this?"

She shrugged. "I don't know."

He drew her close, lifted her into his arms, and headed for their favorite chair in the den. He sat and positioned her on his lap, so he could clearly see her face. Based on the wisdom she possessed, he could be more frank with her than someone might normally be with a child her age. "Are you sure you're okay with this meeting? I really don't know what to expect. Maybe you do, maybe you don't; I don't want you to be nervous or anxious. But let me tell you, if they start acting ugly, the meeting's over."

"It's okay, Daddy. I'm not nervous. I'm glad we're going. There are so many questions I want to ask them. And so many things I want to tell them."

His pulse quickened. "Such as?"

"Things I think might help them with their jobs."

"Forgive me, sweetie, I don't understand."

"I don't either, Daddy. But I think…I think I will, when I get there."

"I know you've been looking at a lot of things on the Internet. Anything else you and I might need to prepare for?"

"I don't know, Daddy." Her nose wrinkled. "Just be there for me."

"Always." He hugged her. "I will always be there for you."

She held out her little finger. "Pinkie promise?"

He wrapped his finger around hers. "Pinkie promise."

She smiled and made no attempt to leave his arms. Neither moved for a long while.

****

Noelle walked onto the plane, and Sean's mouth flew open. He glanced at Raine, surprised she hadn't seen the doctor first. The child was absorbed in a *Washington for Dummies* book he had bought for her.

He stood. "What?" Words eluded him. Was it the shock of seeing her then and there, or the shock of seeing her at all?

She looked incredible. No matter where or when he saw her, his heart reacted with a flutter. She was such a beautiful woman, in every way.

The attendant brought luggage in behind her and lifted it into a storage bin.

"So you didn't ask that I come?" Noelle asked.

"No. I mean yes. I mean no. I mean I wanted you to come, but I had no idea you would consider it."

"If it's any consolation, I didn't ask to come either. The NSA showed up at my office. Again."

It took Raine no more than a few seconds to jump from her seat and run to Noelle. "Miss Noelle!"

Noelle knelt and embraced her. She squeezed his daughter tightly. "Oh, look at you." She made no attempt to let Raine go. "You look so pretty, and your hair is so beautiful and long."

"Just like yours, Miss Noelle. I missed you."

"I missed you too, sweetie." Tears filled Noelle's eyes. She quickly wiped them away.

He stood silently, dumbstruck. Until Raine's comment, he had not realized his daughter had wanted to grow her hair out because of Noelle. Although the thought touched him, he remained cautious. He didn't want to read too much into this reunion. Raine's show of affection reminded him of the scene at the Crab Trap but with much more emotion. He kept reminding himself of what Derek had said, about being patient. Just because the two were peas in a pod didn't mean anything more than they were fond of each other. A crew member joined them from the cockpit and removed his cap.

"Folks, I'm Captain Greer. I wanted you to know we'll be shoving off in a few minutes. If I could get you all to take a seat and buckle up?" He turned his attention to Raine, reached into his pocket, produced a shiny plastic wings pin, and handed it to her. "All except you, little miss. How would you like to come with me up front to the cockpit for a couple of minutes?" Then to Sean, "Agent Sanders will be along in a few minutes."

Raine looked to Sean, and he nodded his approval. She took the pilot's hand and walked forward. The flight attendant disappeared aft. He was alone with Noelle. She moved toward a seat across the aisle, sat and buckled up.

"Sean, I want you to know I won't be discussing anything about Raine with Sanders, or anyone else without talking with you first or without you in attendance."

He shook his head, before she finished her statement. "It's all right. I was wrong to react the way I did before. I've thought about it a thousand times. You did nothing I wouldn't have done myself. I am so sorry for the way I reacted."

He thought he detected a slight smile as she looked away. "I'm not sure I can process an apology without a bouquet of flowers, or some sort of extravagant gift I've grown so accustomed to. Your apology doesn't seem as sincere, somehow."

Sean returned the smile.

"You are crazy, you know?" She gave him a look that melted his heart. "And for the record—thank you for all those gifts. You really shouldn't have."

"It didn't seem the gifts worked very well."

She took a deep breath and looked at him. Her smile was gone, replaced by an expression he couldn't read. "I think you should know I really meant it about your taking Raine to another doctor. The one I had in mind was Dr. Barton. He's excellent with cases similar to hers, although I'm not quite sure if there are any cases exactly like Raine's. But…well, he's better equipped to deal with her situation than I am."

"I'm not buying that," he said. "Raine wants you, not anyone else. And so do I."

****

Noelle unbuckled and loosened her seatbelt and fought the urge to run. Her heart beat wildly as he continued to look at her as if he might devour her at any moment. Was there hidden meaning in what he had said? Should she believe he had meant much more than just wanting her there for Raine in the plane at the moment?

He looked so handsome in khakis, white golf shirt, and navy blazer—larger than life and sexy as hell. She felt a familiar warmth, so easily triggered in his presence. What control he had over her! All he had to do was look at her. Or speak to her. Memories from the

---

intimate night haunted her. She had to look away.

"I'm—I'm flattered, but nonetheless I believe strongly that I won't be able to deliver the treatment and advice my colleague will."

"Then why are you here?" His question was steadfast, unyielding. This served to turn her on more, and she fought a desire to give in to him.

"I'm here because Sanders told me you hadn't secured another doctor. I'm here because he thought Raine might need me." He looked deflated and lost, as if he wanted to hear something else.

He nodded, smiled, and looked away as Raine emerged from the cockpit. He ignored the approach of his daughter and turned to look at Noelle. "For Raine's sake, thank you for being here."

This only added to her confusion, and she was thrown off balance once again. With Raine back, the discussion would have to wait.

The captain, who followed closely behind Raine, looked as though he had lost some of the swagger he had shown earlier. In fact, Noelle was concerned about the expression on his face. He seemed to snap out of a trance as he watched Raine buckle up.

"Mr. Sampson, I must admit I don't recall ever talking with anyone—of any age, for that matter—who knows more about this aircraft and, well, aerodynamics, in general." He glanced at Raine. "Young lady, how do you know so much about flying? And where did you learn so much about this aircraft?"

Raine shrugged.

"She does a lot of reading, Captain," Sean said.

Noelle smiled. The captain took off his cap and scratched a bald spot on the crown of his head.

You have no idea, Captain. Not a clue. Noelle settled into her seat and buckled up again. It was shaping up to be a long flight.

And a longer day.

Once airborne, and in spite of Raine's constant banter, the calming drone of the engines did little to abate the uneasiness that hung in the air of the cabin. Noelle managed a few quick glances toward Sean, who stared out the window. She wondered where his head was, what he was thinking, and where she fit in to any of it.

"Did you know that the Washington Monument is closed?"

"No, honey, I didn't," Noelle answered, uncomfortable. Was it Sean's silence or flying in general?

"I think they need to check it out after they got the baby earthquake."

Noelle ventured a look once again at Sean, but he still gazed out the window. "Where did you hear that, sweetie?"

"I don't know." The child retreated, again deep in thought. Noelle suspected it might have to do with her gift. It had to be difficult trying to decipher what was fact and what was intuition. She hadn't heard about any earthquakes in the area and wondered if this was something that had happened or was going to happen. The very train of her thought did little to ease the mixture of emotions surrounding her.

"Honey, you know it's perfectly okay to be confused sometimes," Noelle said and put her arm around her. "When grown-ups ask questions, it doesn't mean they're upset with you."

"I know." She snuggled up. "It's hard."

In spite of the admission she had heard from Raine, she smiled. This was a big step—talking about her tendency to shut down.

As she glanced across the aisle, she could see Sean's smile as he continued to look away.

****

Raine monopolized most of Noelle's time during the flight. The ladies had no trouble mending the relationship severed by several weeks and the incident during the last trip to DC. Sean spent most of the time in his seat across the aisle, looking out the window and contemplating Noelle's words. As much as he would like to think he could shrug her cool demeanor off, he knew better. Too much water had flowed under the bridge now, and he was in too deep. It was becoming clear to him now that the situation had changed since he first met Noelle, and he had passed a point of no return. He had no idea where their volatile relationship was headed, and he couldn't gain clarity at the moment concerning it, given the situation with Raine. He resolved to table the issue and focus on his daughter, as Noelle seemed to be doing.

As Sean stepped from the aircraft onto the tarmac, the temperature and humidity seemed higher than in Pensacola. The heavy air was stifling. He held tight to Raine's hand as he helped Noelle down the steps. A black SUV waited, steps from the aircraft. An agent in a dark suit and shades was positioned at the bottom of the steps. Another was at a rear door of the SUV. Both spoke into their wrists. In spite of the unsettling feeling that gripped him, Sean couldn't help but find humor in the scene. It played out like a movie, the kind he had pictured in his mind when plotting his stories. The first agent nodded as they passed, and Sean found it strange that he looked totally in control, as cool as a cucumber. Not one bead of sweat was visible anywhere on his face, in spite of the heat. Void of expression, he lifted an arm, indicating the door to the SUV.

Once they were inside the vehicle and their luggage was loaded into the back, the driver wasted no time in departing. The vehicle sped along the Potomac River. Raine was the first to see the Washington Monument, which stood tall in the hazy distance across the river. That sight was the one and only hint of the locale before the vehicle pulled up to a suburban motel. Sean was paying more attention to the ladies in the rear seat next to him than the route, so he had no idea where the vehicle had taken them. The agent in the front passenger seat asked them to wait in the vehicle while he checked them in. The NSA certainly seemed to be making good their promise concerning taking care of the details.

Sean glanced toward Noelle as they were escorted into the hotel elevator. *A penny for your thoughts.* He wanted to say it aloud during the short ride up. Noelle seemed so uncomfortable. Was she feeling closed in by the confined space in the elevator, or by him? He'd had time to think it through. It might be dangerous putting all his cards on the table, but so be it. He wanted to explore the true extent of his feelings for her and more importantly, what she felt for him. That wasn't going to happen unless he made the first move. He planned to do just that at the first opportunity. Like it or not, Noelle was going to hear him out.

"Daddy, my head hurts." Raine tugged on his hand.

Her face looked flushed. Was it because of the weather?

"I'm not surprised, little one. You haven't slowed down all day long."

"And I'm hot."

"Well, I think it's going to be dinner, a quick cool bath, and bedtime for you. You've got at least a couple of long days ahead of you."

"But I want to stay up with you and Miss Noelle."

"I don't think so, sweetie." He immediately felt guilty. His true motive for putting her to bed early was more than concern for her rest. "Eight o'clock is lights out for you, little lady."

"Ahhhh." She gave him that heart-wrenching pout that always tugged at his conscience. But this time it wasn't going to work.

****

Noelle fought to control her nerves. The ride in the elevator seemed endless. She wondered what sort of accommodations awaited them. She had posed this question to Sanders earlier. His response was short and to the point, assuring her of adequate privacy. In spite of the promise, she remained uneasy. Her uneasiness came not from lack of trust concerning Sean, but from wondering if she could trust herself. Why did he have so much power over her? He wasn't a pushy man; he had never done anything to bully her. Yet she was very much aware of the old adage, "The closer to the flame, the hotter it gets." The question wasn't *when*, it was *if* she could get Sean out of her heart. His very presence made the task formidable.

A loud *ding* made her flinch, as the elevator reached the top floor. She stepped out, and her heart leapt, in anticipation of reaching the rooms. All these thoughts about control—giving it up, keeping it—were playing on her nerves. She stood on the precipice of where she most feared to be. Falling into an unknown abyss with him couldn't be that bad, could it? Was being close to him again even possible now? Had she ruined it all with her aloofness? Had she seemed ungrateful for his efforts to reach her and for all the gifts?

Had she gone too far and shut him out of her life for good?

She was relieved to see that the room layout was more conducive to privacy. The three rooms were interconnected, with Raine's in the center. Sean unpacked in his and Raine's rooms, and Noelle offered to help Raine with the room service.

"And what would you like, little missy?" In spite of everything on her mind, it was always fun to witness Raine's enthusiasm for food.

"I don't know, Miss Noelle," she said, and her little shoulders slumped as she sat on the edge of her bed.

"Wow, they have a lot of good-looking items on the room service menu. Wanna take a look?"

"Okay," she said and took the menu as Noelle handed it to her. "Can I have a hamburger and fries?"

"You can have anything you want." Noelle waited for additional items, but they did not come. "Is that all? No dessert? No fruit? What would you like to drink?"

"Coke, I guess." She laid the menu down and yawned.

She ate with little enthusiasm. To Noelle's surprise, the tired little girl couldn't finish her burger.

True to his word, as Noelle unpacked after dinner with the door open to Raine's room, she could hear

Sean getting her ready for bed at precisely eight o'clock. She stepped into the room and blew the little girl a good night kiss.

"You sleep tight, missy," Sean said and looked toward Noelle as his daughter smiled and blew a kiss back. He kissed her forehead and hesitated. "Are you still hot, sweetie? Will you turn the thermostat down, Miss Noelle? I guess maybe I got her bath water too warm, considering the weather."

As fate would have it, the thermostat was next to the door to Sean's room. Noelle walked cautiously around him. She quickly adjusted the thermostat, as he tucked Raine in and then turned off the small lamp by her bed. Noelle smiled politely as she walked past him on the way to her room.

"Good night," she whispered and turned away.

"Can I talk to you for a minute?" It wasn't really a question; it sounded like a command.

She had almost made it. "I'm kind of tired—"

"This won't take but a minute." He indicated his room. "Please."

He didn't give her much of a choice, so she followed him into his room. As she left the safety of the central room, she glanced through the dim light of Raine's bedroom. The little girl was motionless, apparently worn out from the long day's events. She stepped into Sean's room, and he quietly closed the door. She felt awkward, unable to decide what to do with her hands. She tried not to look, but the bed loomed in the background. It seemed larger than it had a right to be, and an image of her in it, lying beside him, flashed through her mind. She moved quickly to a small desk and pulled out the chair, facing the escape route to her own room, which now seemed an impossibly long hike. He stood on the other side of his bed, next to two chairs, but did not sit.

Instead, he walked to a small refrigerator and opened it. "Would you like something to drink?"

"No, thank you," she replied, with hopes the words sounded steadier than they seemed coming from her mouth.

He retrieved a bottle of water and took a sip. He stood for a moment looking at her, as if he hadn't a clue what he would say next. He took another sip of the water. Was he buying time? He studied the bottle for a moment, took a deep breath, and looked at her. Her heart skipped a beat as his gaze burned its way into her heart. He wore a little boy vulnerability that softened her into mere putty. She could meet his eyes for only a moment, and then had to look away.

"I'm not one for speeches." He seemed to have trouble swallowing. "But there are some things I have to say."

Okay, play it cool. Don't look at him. Remember the real world. Remember the real world. Men don't really know how to love you back. Relax.

Her palms grew sweaty as her resolve slipped with every word. She forced herself to lean back in the chair and cross her legs and arms, silently cursing for allowing herself to feel so uneasy. Her self-control waned. Every fiber of her body and mind wanted this man. Options other than totally giving in to her love for Sean quickly dissipated before her eyes. He looked as if he wanted to bolt and run more than she did. He again studied the water bottle while twisting it in his hands.

"I'm in love with you, Noelle Victor. I—There's

no use in saying anything else at this moment, because I am totally and idiotically in love with you. Like I've never been in love before—"

She couldn't remember getting up from the chair. Her legs wrapped around his waist, and her arms surrounded his shoulders. Her mouth found his as her tears flowed. His arms took possession of her as her breathing became erratic. The taste of him sent a jolt through her. "I want you," she whispered. He immediately turned toward the bed. Some sanity returned, and she whispered in his ear, "The door."

"I'm in love with you, too." She managed to utter those words as the door closed behind her.

He didn't have to say a word. She felt his smile on her shoulder—he had acknowledged her words in the only expression she needed.

Chapter Eighteen

Hanging by his fingertips, Sean tried desperately to keep from falling into the darkness of the bottomless abyss. Raine was on a narrow ledge above, calling for him, just out of his reach. A tall, sinister stranger, dressed in a suit and shades, edged along the ledge toward her. If Sean loosened his grip and reached out for his daughter, he would fall and there would be no one to save her from the Castle Man. He refused to panic at the hopelessness of the quandary, and instead was determined he'd find a way to save her and himself. Then they needed to get the hell away from the man who so desperately wanted to get to his daughter.

"Sean?"

He could not determine where the woman's voice came from. As he looked around, searching for a way out, he became aware of the futility of the situation. Then, when he closed and reopened his eyes, the ledge was gone, as was Raine and the man in the dark suit. He awoke, lying on his stomach with his fingers wrapped tightly around a corner of the mattress. He sat up, his body in a cold sweat and looked around at unfamiliar walls.

Noelle shook his shoulder. She stood next to the bed, searching for her clothes. "Sean, wake up." She pointed to the door. "Raine's calling for you."

He jumped from the bed and struggled to dress.

"Daddy!" The call from behind his closed door became frantic.

He unlocked the door and expected to see his daughter walk through, catching him in the room with Noelle. Instead, still in a stupor, he hurried into the adjoining room and saw his daughter thrashing around in her bed. Noelle donned a robe and followed him. When he got to the bed, Raine's eyes were closed. She rolled back and forth under the cover. Her face was beet red.

"Honey, Daddy's here." He took her into his arms. She was blazing hot.

Noelle returned quickly with a wet washcloth. "Do you have a thermometer?"

"Yes, it's in the small plastic zip-bag next to my shaving kit." Before he could turn to look at her, she was gone again. She returned in a matter of seconds with the thermometer. He switched it on and placed it gently in Raine's ear. In seconds, numbers were displayed.

"Jeez, 104.6."

Noelle had a bottle of children's ibuprofen in her hand. "I found this with the thermometer. How much? The directions say up to two milliliters."

"That's fine." He took the plastic syringe and lifted his daughter's head. "Here, sweetheart, open up."

With her eyes still closed, she opened her mouth enough to take the red liquid. He squeezed the syringe, and she swallowed.

She moaned and opened her eyes in alarm. "Daddy, did you see the Castle Man?"

It took every bit of strength in his arm to maintain his grip on her. "Yes, sweetie, but he's gone. Daddy told him to leave."

"Thank you, Daddy." She smiled.

Sean glanced at Noelle, who wore a confused look. She handed him a plastic cup with ice water. He managed to get a few sips down his daughter before she gagged. She mumbled something, and closed her eyes again, and smiled. In a matter of seconds, she was asleep. He lowered her head gently onto the pillow and adjusted her cover. He left the lamp on dim and stepped back into his room, giving Noelle an evasive look before he walked past her. She quickly followed him.

"What's wrong?"

"Nothing," he said, but he couldn't hide the feelings that gripped him.

"Sean, don't do this." She closed the door behind them.

"Do what?"

"You know exactly what I'm talking about. It's okay, you didn't do anything wrong. You couldn't have known she was sick."

"Oh, yeah? Well, I look at it differently. Hell, I couldn't wait to get *her* in bed, so I could get *you* in bed. You don't see anything wrong with that?"

"No. No, I don't." Her voice broke. "Wanting me doesn't make you a bad father, and this doesn't make you negligent. Children get sick, Sean. No matter what you do after you put them to bed."

He paced for a minute and then stopped and took a deep breath. He couldn't stop the tears as he moved toward her. She met him halfway.

"I'm so sorry." He held her close. "You're right. Please forgive me. I didn't mean to cheapen what happened—"

"Shhh," She placed her finger over his lips. "It's all right."

They stood next to his bed for several minutes, holding each other. He drew away from her and kissed her passionately. He tasted her tears as his lips pressed against hers.

"I think we're going to need some coffee."

He nodded and yawned.

The digital clock on the table by the bed displayed 2:30. They had been asleep only a few hours. Sean fell into one of the chairs on the other side of his bed. She switched the coffee maker on and sat in the other. He reached for her hand.

He smiled. "I'm really sorry."

"It's okay."

"Thanks for helping me with her."

"Sure."

"And thanks for the reality check."

She smiled.

"I wonder what brought the fever on," he said and rubbed his eyes.

"Probably just a bug or something. I noticed she was cranky while eating her dinner. I thought she was just tired."

"Yeah." He frowned. "Her face was red even then. Never thought about her getting sick. She hardly ever does. Can't remember the last time she had so much as a sniffle."

"I'm sure the ibuprofen will help bring her fever down."

"Yeah, we'll give it an hour and check again."

"So, do you want to talk about it?"

"About what?" he asked.

"The Castle Man."

He nodded. "Ah, the Castle Man. I'm really not sure what to say about this. That's why I haven't mentioned it before. I'm not real comfortable with situations I can't explain."

He told her about the incident in Raine's room, about her asking him who the Castle Man was, as well as about the dream he had. Noelle was quiet during the entire time. It was a coincidence, wasn't it? The coffee machine finished. Noelle walked over to it. "You know, I don't even know how you like your coffee."

He yawned. "Black."

She poured two cups, handed one to him and sat again. They sat in silence, sipping the steaming brew. He couldn't help but admire how she looked, even at that late hour, and especially after all they had been through in the past few hours. He couldn't seem to get enough of her. Even now, he couldn't take his eyes from her.

"What?"

"You look beautiful."

She scoffed. "I'll bet."

He knelt in front of her chair. She kissed him. In a husky voice, she said, "I guess I *have* been a bit of a distraction to you lately."

"What? No, not at all. You can't be distracted unless you want to be."

"And I'm sorry I didn't notice her getting sick, either."

He smiled. "Well, I guess it's true. I *have* had a one-track mind most of the day."

"It was certainly a good track, though."

"Yeah, I thought about it a lot on the airplane and

was determined to tell you how I feel."

"I felt the same way. I guess I wasn't through feeling sorry for myself."

"How so?"

"Well, I'm not very good at relationships."

"I find that hard to believe." He returned to his chair.

"No, it's true. I guess I've always spent a lot of time trying to be the best doctor I can be, sometimes to the detriment of everyone and everything else in my life. The relationships I've had have not ended well."

He fought jealousy but refused to feed it by asking a lot of questions. "I can't imagine anyone walking away from you."

"Funny you should say that. I must admit it was always me who walked away."

Sean frowned.

"I guess that sounded suspect, huh?"

"Well, it did give me pause for concern."

"I should probably explain."

"Really, it's not necessary."

"No, please. I want to. I don't want you to think I'm a love 'em and leave 'em type of girl."

He raised his eyebrows.

"Wow, I'm the analyst." She shook her head. "And I'm talking to you like I'm the one on the couch."

He held his hands up in defense and grinned. "What you say can and will be used in a court of law—"

"And I can't believe I'm pouring it all out to you."

"Please. I want to hear what you have to say. You might have noticed I'm somewhat interested in you."

She glanced at the floor. Her expression became

somber. "I've had two serious relationships. The first one was while I was in college." She gave him a pained expression and took a deep breath. "My first love. He was my professor." She spoke fast. "And he was married."

Sean nodded but remained quiet as he processed the information.

"I was so young and naïve. Not to mention stupid." She shook her head and laughed. "There was nothing special about him. He wasn't good-looking. He was short and dumpy and rapidly balding. But he certainly knew the right things to say and when to say them. And in spite of his sleazy intentions, he made me feel special."

"You *are* special."

She gave him a grateful smile and sipped her coffee. "Thank you."

"So, did he promise to leave his wife and run away with you?"

"Yeah, the whole nine yards. Hook, line, and sinker."

"You were in love." What he'd intended as a statement ended with the inflection of a question.

She shook her head. "No, I don't think I was. I guess I loved him, sure. But I wasn't *in* love with him. I figured that would come later when he left his wife and we had a quote, normal, unquote relationship."

"But of course he never did?"

"Right. He never did, which turned out to be the best thing that ever happened to me."

Sean was puzzled again and must have shown it.

"If he had made good his promises, I would probably have dropped out of school and be raising three or four little balding professors by now."

"Three or four?" He couldn't hide his surprise.

She took his hand. "Does it surprise you I love kids and that I might want children one of these days?"

"No, no. In fact, it's obvious you do love kids. And they love you. I mean, look how Raine adores you. And your other patients do too. You can't be as good as you are at what you do without loving the ones you do it for." As much as he tried to hide it, the realization she wanted more kids brought a measure of sadness.

"Did I…did I say something wrong?"

He was trapped and forced into a position to make a choice. Should he come clean with her, or was it too early to tell her why he and Patty had chosen the adoption route? He deferred. "You said two. You said you had two relationships?"

"Yes, I did, didn't I?" She took another deep breath. "And then there was Scott."

Sean remained silent as she seemed to be lost in memories.

"We were together four years. Scott's a urologist and was attending a medical convention in Atlanta— one similar to the one where we first met. I had gone with him each year, but that year my caseload was especially heavy, and I couldn't get away. It was the first day of fall, and a mean and nasty stomach flu cleared my schedule for a couple of days, so I decided to surprise him. I caught an early flight, rented a car, bought a bottle of champagne, and made it to his hotel before the first morning session." She seemed to choke up somewhat and paused.

"You really don't have to—"

"No, no. I'm fine." She took a sip of coffee and

continued. "There I was, getting off the elevator on his floor and about to step around the corner to his room, champagne in hand. I heard a bellboy knocking on a door, and peeked around the corner to discover he was outside Scott's room with a breakfast tray. I was about to step around the corner and work a deal with the bellboy to stand in for him when Scott's door opened. And there she was—a blonde in one of the hotel robes."

He frowned.

"Well, naïve me, I thought I had the wrong room. But before I could round the corner and head to the hall phone to call the front desk, Scott appeared at the door, dressed in a matching robe."

"I'm so sorry," he whispered.

"You know, the relationship was on the brink for quite a while anyway. In fact, I don't know if it ever really got started. At least not to a point where the magic was there, you know?"

Sean had no response.

"Then again, I don't guess you *would* know. You had a great relationship with Patty."

"I'm so sorry," was all he could offer.

"It's okay." She took a deep breath. "I think it was over before that day anyway. The whole miserable day confirmed it. At any rate, I flew right back home, dumped all his stuff outside the apartment, and had the locks changed. I haven't seen him since. The next morning, all his stuff was gone."

He took her hand.

"So you see? I haven't had the best of luck with the men I've known."

"Raine's mom and I couldn't have children," Sean admitted after an awkward moment of silence. It came out blunter than he intended. How absurd the words sounded. He laughed. She smiled and joined in the laughter. "That's probably the strangest statement I've ever made."

"It was a double shock, I must admit. But it doesn't matter." She squeezed his hand. "I know what you meant."

After another moment of silence, Noelle's expression lightened. "Ahh, now I understand your reaction to my comment about children."

"Well, you *did* say you wanted to have children, as in more than one."

"I said I *wanted* children. I didn't say I necessarily wanted to give birth to them myself."

"Touché." He needed to clarify his statement. "The doc said she was most certainly infertile. But it most probably would not have mattered anyway, because there was some question about my ability to father a child. At any rate, the doctor was quite certain the combination of those conditions would never permit success in making a baby."

She leaned toward his chair. He pulled her onto his lap and kissed her.

"You know, you're going to have to stop doing this if you don't want me to attack you again."

"Doing what?" She batted her eyelashes playfully. "And who said I don't want you to attack me? And why would you think I want you?"

"Well, for one thing, looking at me like that. And for another, just coming near me." He couldn't help but laugh as his thoughts took him back. "Last time you came at me, you got a good jump start."

"You know, I don't remember what happened. I

only remember jumping you, wrapping my legs around you, and—"

"Okay, okay. Don't remind me." He gave her another kiss. "Hold that thought. Let me go check on Raine."

He deposited her in the other chair, picked up the thermometer, and stepped into Raine's room.

****

When Sean returned from Raine's room, the look on his face spoke volumes. Something was wrong.

"What is it?"

"One-oh-five point two."

"We need to get her to a doctor," Noelle said calmly. Inside, she was in a panic. "Why don't you get some ice, and I'll call the front desk and find out where the nearest hospital is? We've got to get her temperature down."

Sean was on his way out to the hall, where he spoke to the agent. She heard them talking, and then the agent spoke into a cell phone. Sean returned and found a clean garbage bag in a cabinet. "Can you run some tepid water in the tub while I get ice from the machine down the hall? Don't worry about calling the front desk. The agent is getting a doctor."

As she started for the bathroom, the agent called from the door. "Doctor is on the way. He said to get her into a tub of tepid water."

"Way ahead of you," she said and continued into the bathroom.

The wait was excruciating. Sean paced the floor while Noelle tried to console a very irritated child. Minutes seemed like hours. Twice Sean relieved Noelle at the tub, each time threatening to go directly to a hospital.

An hour passed and finally a knock on the door. Noelle could barely hear it over protests from Raine. The little girl wasn't at all happy sitting in a tub of water. Sean had wrapped her in two thick towels to shield the shock of the water, but it just served to make her more uncomfortable. Sean managed to get a reading on her fever, but the cool water had only brought it down to one hundred three. He relayed this as the doctor walked into the bathroom and introduced himself. He looked as though he had literally just stepped from bed.

"Miss Sampson, I'm Dr. Parlow." He pulled her to an upright position. "Let's get you sitting up—" He stopped abruptly and stared at the back of the tub, his hand examining Raine's underarm. He turned to Sean. "How long has she had this lump under her left arm?"

Noelle's heart sank. All the color drained from Sean's face as he whispered, "Lump?"

The doctor didn't answer and instead took a depressor from his bag and asked Raine to open up. With a pin light, he looked at her throat, into her ears, and at her eyes. He then pressed the inside of her lower thighs, her calves, and the side of her throat.

"Dr. Parlow, what lump?" Sean's voice shook as Noelle took his hand.

"Mr. Sampson, we need to get this little lady to a hospital."

"Doc, what's going on?" With every unanswered question, Sean's voice grew more impatient.

"Mr. Sampson, the swelling in her underarm is a lymph node. Could be due to the high fever. I don't know. We need to do some tests. We need to get her to a better place to begin some treatment to get the temperature down."

"Lymph node?" Sean practically dragged the doctor outside the bathroom. Noelle followed close behind, keeping her eye on Raine from the doorway. "What do you mean her lymph node is swollen? What does that mean?"

The doctor smiled. "Dad, it might not mean anything. It simply indicates the need for further examination. Nodes can swell because of an infection. But first we need to isolate the infection and get her fever down and quickly. And I think you will agree this isn't the place to get that accomplished." As he spoke, he wrote something on a script pad. "Take her to the Children's National Emergency Room. Give your greeter this note—it will cut through a whole lot of red tape and get her right into the system."

He looked directly at Sean, as Sean put the note in his pocket.

"Mr. Sampson, relax." He patted Sean's arm and smiled. "It's probably an infection or twenty-four hour viral event. I'm sure there's nothing to worry about. I'll call Mr. Sanders—"

"You work for the NSA?"

"Oh, no, sir. I'm one of the first family's pediatricians. But you needn't worry. Some of the best pediatricians in the world are on duty as we speak at Children's. You won't find a better place to take your daughter. Oh, and by the way, your daughter is a delightful young lady. Been hearing a lot of good things about her. I'm sure she'll be fine."

Noelle wasn't encouraged. All she could think about was the day not so long ago in Raine's room, and how Sean had related the word he saw displayed on her laptop.

Lymphoma.

Chapter Nineteen

Like a lost child, Sean exuded a vulnerability that broke Noelle's heart. He looked numb as he held tight to his daughter in the back seat of the SUV. She wanted to take them both into her arms and tell them it would be okay. Instead, the words refused to come, because she feared she night burst into tears. She was often around stressful situations concerning children. But this time, it was personal. She felt a very real connection to the man and child sitting next to her. Like Sean, she felt helpless. For now, all she could do was hold his hand. Someone had to stay strong, not only for the short ride to the hospital, but for the duration of what could possibly be a long, bumpy ride.

An attendant awaited the SUV when it pulled up to the emergency entrance. She was a dark-skinned woman with a clipboard and a smile. She opened the door before the driver had a chance to come to a full stop. "Mr. Sampson?"

Sean nodded.

"And you must be Raine." The woman's face lit up, which caught Noelle by surprise. She was a beacon of brightness amid a sea of sour expressions. "My, but aren't you a beautiful young lady!"

Raine was awake now but seemed as subdued as her father. She managed a smile, which was quickly shaken away by a wrack of shivers. Sean drew her closer and tucked the blanket in around her.

"My name is Sheila, and I'm gonna make sure you get the best of care, little lady. In fact, we're gonna take such good care of you, the short time you'll be here will fly by."

"Thank you," Raine said. It was the first coherent words that had come from her mouth since going to bed hours earlier.

Hours earlier? It seemed like eons ago. And it seemed even longer since Noelle made love with Sean. Stress could stretch time to a breaking point. Noelle had been in similar situations in the past. And she was aware how easily elation can give way to fear and uncertainty with little warning. Cruelly, a high can slide so quickly to a new low and can change the playing field to a vast wasteland of uncertainty, crushing the mere memory of joy in the wink of an eye.

In spite of the late hour, the emergency room hummed with activity. One child's sobbing was lost in the hurting moan of another. They followed Sheila to a bed inside a curtained area near the end of a row of cubicles. A team of health care professionals entered and went to work. Before Sean could dress Raine in the provided gown, a nurse had taken her temperature, blood pressure, and pulse, jabbering to her the entire time. It all seemed staged to Noelle, a well-rehearsed scene delivered by well-trained actors in a sleight-of-hand effort to distract from the tension of being sick.

Noelle managed to catch at least part of the thermometer display. Although the nurse pasted her best poker face on while she wrote the numbers onto a clipboard, Noelle could tell that the number was a four-digit one. A simple nod to an assistant quickly brought on a metal box on wheels, which the technician plugged into a nearby socket before extracting a bulky sheet from inside. Frosty air escaped as he pulled out the fabric and placed it on top of thick towels and then over Raine. He gently pulled her arms from under the cool blanket, placing them on another layer of towels.

"Has the child recently been given any medication?" another attendant directed toward Sean. For a moment, Sean seemed confused, unable to remember. Noelle quickly responded.

"About an hour ago, we gave her one teaspoon of children's ibuprofen."

The nurse smiled and spoke softly to another assistant. "Let's give her—how much does she weigh?"

"Thirty-two pounds," Sean managed.

"The doctors says we can give her ten milliliters of pain reliever. The ibuprofen doesn't seem to be having much effect." After Raine swallowed the liquid, the nurse returned to her with a cup. "Sweetie, I want you to drink as much of this water as you can." She lifted Raine's head and held the cup to her lips. The little girl tried to swallow, but choked and gagged and spat it back out. The nurse grabbed a small tray and held Raine's hair while she lost the contents of her stomach, including the red medicine she had taken.

A clown with a red rubber nose and large, floppy shoes bounded into the room. "I'm Dr. Wendell Wells," he announced. He approached Raine. "Hi, I understand you're not feeling so well."

Raine was hardly amused by his apparel. He glanced at the chart and, after the nurse filled him in, began examining Raine, similar to the manner in which Dr. Parlow had.

When he was done, he turned to the nurse. "Let's get her started on an IV…" He paused and studied the clipboard, flipping sheets, and then turned to Sean. "Any allergies?"

"No, none that I know of." Sean stepped up to the bed, moved a strand of hair from Raine's face, and gave her a smile. Noelle wanted to cry at the little girl's vacant expression.

The doctor gave the staff in the room instructions for a myriad of treatments and tests, including blood work. As quickly as he had arrived, he moved out into the hallway with the only indication of his presence the flapping of noisy shoes.

Noelle glanced at Sean, who was doing his best to stand back and let the medical team handle the situation. He swallowed hard and watched them but continued to look lost. As strong as he appeared, she wondered if he was hanging onto the edge by a thread. She placed her arm around his waist. His startled look suggested he wasn't expecting the gesture. He forced a smile.

"She's going to be fine." She squeezed his slim waist. He draped his arm around her shoulder and leaned his head onto hers. As they continued to look at his daughter, she couldn't help but say another prayer, one of many she had said during the long night. As she did, Raine closed her eyes and the smallest of smiles brightened her pale lips.

"Daddy and Mommy, I think this little gal is ready for some rest now." The nurse stripped her latex gloves and tossed them in a garbage bin. "Give her a night-night kiss, and I'll grab the doctor. He'll meet you outside to chat."

The nurse's mistaken assumption she was Raine's mother took her by surprise, but it was true she couldn't have loved the child or worried about her more if she were her own.

So this was what it felt like to be a mother.

"How soon do we get the results of these tests, Doctor?" Noelle took the lead as Sean sat in the waiting room, elbows on his knees and head in hand. Before the doctor could respond, Sean looked up. The doctor's left hand worked nervously on the red nose he had pulled from his face.

"Doctor," Sean said. "I hear them talk about all these tests, and I understand why you are doing them, but I want to know what you think. Why is her lymph node swollen, and what does it mean? And why have the ibuprofen and pain reliever not helped with her fever?"

The doctor hesitated for a moment and took another look at Raine's chart. He pursed his lips, pinched the bridge of his nose, and cleared his throat. After a moment, he placed the chart on a table in the empty waiting room and sat down next to Sean.

"Mr. Sampson, first of all, ibuprofen and acetaminophen are not always one hundred percent effective. Secondly, many conditions can cause the swelling of a lymph node, most of which are benign. It's far too early to speculate which of these conditions are affecting your daughter."

"Your best guess, doc. That's all I'm asking for right now. With her symptoms, and based on what you know about them, what can this indicate? I need to know if this could be serious." Sean lowered his head for a moment to gain his composure. "Her mother died of lymphoma. Patty wasn't my daughter's biological mother, but as you might imagine, this is a concern for me."

When Sean mentioned Raine's mother, the doc glanced toward Noelle but didn't comment. The doctor took a deep breath and fidgeted. "Mr. Sampson, we can't rule anything out at this point. I'm sorry to give you a short answer, but unfortunately, any number of factors could be causing any one or more of your daughter's symptoms. Now, it will take around twenty-four hours to get all the test results back, at which time we hopefully can give you a better picture of what's going on. That's really the best I can offer at this point."

During the entire statement, Sean stared at the floor. He folded his hands in front of his face, as if in prayer. He rubbed his face and looked up, his eyes wet with tears.

"Thank you," he said and lowered his head again.

"I will be in touch the very moment I learn anything from the tests."

Sean nodded but didn't look up.

The doctor walked away slowly, as if trying to minimize the noise from his shoes.

****

Raine rested well for the remainder of the night, despite the traffic in and out of the room constantly, and considering Raine's left arm was secured to a padded metal rail so as not to compromise the IV. Getting the small needle into her arm was fairly painless. Raine fell into and out of sleep during the short process. The process seemed to pain Sean more than it hurt Raine. He went to great lengths to ensure the nurse didn't hurt

268

her, to the point where the nurse was getting visibly nervous and annoyed. Afterwards, Sean looked worn out.

Noelle made him take a break around five a.m. Raine was sleeping, and his stomach was making enough noise to wake her and to strongly dispute his claim he wasn't hungry. She assured him she would not leave Raine's side while he found something to eat and convinced him he needed to go so he could bring back something for her to eat. She wasn't hungry either, but this sweet man needed a break. Who knew how long their vigil would continue? At the rate he was going he wouldn't last twenty-four hours, not without some serious rest. Rest was not something that could easily be procured for him, not when he reacted to every movement and sound from his daughter's bed.

Noelle schemed to find a way to get him to at least consider a shift arrangement for staying with his daughter, although something told her he wouldn't venture far away for very long, under any circumstances.

Minutes after he left in search for food, Raine stirred. She tossed and turned, hampered somewhat by the restraints on her arm, and began mumbling. Noelle moved closer to try to decipher what she was saying.

"At the beach, Daddy…can I have some more of those…it's a boat…where is the sand castle?" Raine thrashed around, restrained only by the IV splint.

In her sleep, Raine went through the motions of eating. She rambled about shrimp, crab, and other seafood. Most of her mumbling was not unpleasant. However, at times she sounded fearful, as if she were running away from something or someone.

"Daddy, help me, Daddy," she called. "Miss Noelle."

Noelle moved closer. Taking Raine's hand, she stroked her hair and talked calmly, reassuring her that everything was all right. Raine quieted down for a few moments and even smiled, soothed by Noelle's voice.

Just when Noelle thought she had drifted back into sleep, Raine opened her eyes. Her face was wild with alarm. She squeezed Noelle's hand tightly and looked directly into her eyes, yet straight through her. "Please tell them about the Castle Man. Please," she said in a whisper.

A chill went down Noelle's spine. Before she could say a word, Raine closed her eyes and fell asleep once again. During these few seconds, she was aware of someone entering the room. Deep in thought about Raine's words, she flinched as someone touched her shoulder. She jerked her head around to see Sean standing beside her.

"Did you hear?"

"The Castle Man?"

"Yes."

They stood silently next to her bed, as she searched for the right words to explain her apprehension. She dug deep, calling on all her expertise and studies for something to explain Raine's obsession with the Castle Man. There had to be a reason why.

She could think of none.

****

It wasn't hard for James to spot the agent. The big man was never very far from the little girl or her doctor and father. He had to give it to him—he was good. He, and the other two who relieved him, made sure none of those he was protecting knew he was around. Whether behind a newspaper or in the floor waiting room, they blended in nicely.

Not to James. He could spot the law a mile away. God knew he had experience with their type. He was, as far as he knew, still on probation, so he would need to lie low.

But it didn't matter. The cause was much more important than the possibility of spending more time behind bars. The risk was worth it. Taking out the Chinese kid would serve a couple of purposes. First and foremost, it would avenge the damage she had done by exposing the senator and getting him arrested. True, he had no proof that it was the little girl, but it just made sense, the more he thought about it. She had been waiting to come on that morning show and would have at least seen the senator before he bugged out. He wasn't sure how the kid had found out about what Blane was doing, but it didn't matter. The damage was done. And taking her out would go a long way to deter others from messing with the Cause.

And he sure wasn't about to let no little brat get away with it. She and her dad and doctor would pay, and pay dearly. Nobody stands in the way of the Cause and lives to tell about it.

Especially a foreigner.

But first he had to deal with the agent.

****

"Daddy?"

Sean jumped from his chair and took her fragile hand in his. "What, sweetie?"

"I'm hungry."

He smiled. As he reached to touch her face, he

found her hair soaking wet. Her fever had broken! At some time while he dozed, the cold blanket had been removed, and fresh, clean linens and blankets were on her bed. A chilled paper container of apple juice sat on the tray next to her bed. He picked it up and forced the straw into the top. She practically ripped it from his hand and began sipping it.

"Easy now, sweetie. Your stomach is empty. Too much in it, too fast, might not be so good." For a moment, he could barely speak through the lump in his throat. Her eyes were so bright, and color had returned to her face. Her forehead was warm, not hot. And she was hungry! He pushed the call button. A voice answered quickly. He informed the nurse his daughter was awake, soaking wet, and ravenous. The nurse assured him food and dry linens would soon be there.

For what seemed like the first time in two days, Sean took a deep breath.

He heard her before he saw her. When he turned, Noelle stood at the door with her hands over her mouth, watching as Raine drank the juice. The child's eyes lit up when she saw her.

"Miss Noelle," she whispered and smiled. "When did you get here?"

"Miss Noelle has been here with Daddy the whole time, sweetie. I practically had to force her go to the cafeteria to eat, to keep her from withering away."

"You're teasing me, aren't you, Daddy?"

"Wow, I am so happy to see you're feeling better." Noelle joined Sean at her bedside. "Daddy and I have been worried about you. You've been a sick little girl."

An attendant wheeled in a tray with a covered plate and carton of juice and placed it on the larger bedside tray.

"Yippee!" Raine said as the attendant removed the cover and exposed meatloaf and potatoes, along with veggies and a small slice of cake. As she forked the first bite, the door opened again.

"Well, well, young lady, you sure look like you feel better. Do you remember me? I'm Doctor Wells." The doctor looked spent. He wore no costume.

Raine shook her head, more interested in her food than anything else at the moment. The doctor took a moment and examined each side of her neck, under her arm and the inside of her legs. None of the poking and prodding fazed Raine. She continued to eat all through the short examination.

"Let's leave this little lady to chow down for a few minutes while I talk with Mom—Daddy and Doctor Victor."

Raine nodded and took another big bite of mashed potatoes.

Outside, the doctor directed them to the same small waiting room, several doors down. He motioned for them to take a seat, and at that moment, Sean's heart sank. The doctor sat, wearing a weary expression. For a moment the doctor focused on the clipboard, flipping back and forth between documents.

Noelle must have sensed the dread also. She grabbed Sean's hand and squeezed it.

"I'm afraid the news is not as good as we had hoped." The doctor licked his lips and swallowed. "Although the tests are not totally conclusive, and I want to stress that—they are not conclusive—the initial indication is of a viral nature, and to an extent, unfortunately points to lymphoma as a possible diagnosis."

The doctor continued to talk, but Sean could not get past the first statement. His mind raced and began playing tricks on him. *Was the spot on the carpet a soda stain, or coffee? Could be grape juice. Hard to tell.* The doctor continued to talk, but Sean couldn't put the words together coherently. *You would think a hospital as good as this one would not allow that spot to remain for very long, wouldn't you?* It was sad, actually, and a tear dropped, joining the stain, darkening it for a moment, before soaking in and disappearing.

"Mr. Sampson?"

Noelle was plastered to his side, her head leaning against his shoulder. When he looked at her, she smiled, but her lips trembled. He needed to assure her he would mention the stain to the staff and get it cleaned up. Nothing to cry about, certainly. Was there?

"Mr. Sampson?" The doctor stood and moved closer to him. He touched his arm. "Sir, did you understand what I said about the treatment?"

"No—no, I'm sorry. What did you say?"

"Mr. Sampson, there are excellent new, tested, and proven treatments available that are both effective and have shown very few side effects, especially in cases like your daughter's, having been diagnosed very early. And as I related, because the diagnosis is not conclusive, we would like to conduct a few more tests over the next few days to get a clearer picture of what is going on with her. Please understand your daughter's profile is not a perfect match for the suspected diagnosis. As I said, at this point we have to assume lymphoma is what we are faced with. But either it is very, very early in its stage—which in itself is good—or we *could* and let me emphasize *could* be dealing with something other than our suspected diagnosis."

"Are you saying there's a possibility it might not be lymphoma?" Noelle formed the words before he could voice them.

"I realize this is very confusing. Quite honestly, it's not totally clear to us either. I don't want to give you any false hopes. But yes, that is correct. It might possibly be something else. However, the possibilities we are correct about the initial diagnosis are high at this point. That's why we have to continue to do a few tests in the next few days. The other good news is, if your daughter continues to improve, you can take her home. Her fever has broken and that's good, but I must warn you it could come back. And the intensity of the fever could be lesser or greater than the last couple of days. While we are doing the tests, we need to watch her for another forty-eight hours. If the fever doesn't come back, then we can release her."

"And if the additional tests confirm the diagnosis?" Sean could barely get the question out.

"Well, she can go home either way. If we confirm the diagnosis, she can begin treatment at a hospital near home. And Children's Heart Hospital in Pensacola, I can tell you, is one of the best for this type of treatment."

There was silence as Sean thought through all he had heard. Many questions raced through his mind, but he still wasn't thinking clearly.

"I know this is a lot to throw at you two. I want you to know I am available twenty-four seven for any questions you might have, beginning right now, if you want."

Noelle forced a smile at Sean. He turned to the doctor.

"Thank you, Doctor. I think I would like to speak with Noelle for a few moments. I know I'll have questions later."

The doctor produced a card from his pocket and wrote on it. "This is my card. I've written my cell phone number on it. Call me any time. If I don't answer right away, I'm probably in surgery or with another patient. But leave a message, and I'll call you back as quickly as I can."

"Thank you." Those were all the words Sean could muster at the moment.

He had to pull himself together. His daughter needed him now, and he wasn't going to flake out on her. *Remember, if the tests do confirm lymphoma, according to the doctor, her prospects are very good.* That mantra went through his head. He had to get his smile back before stepping into her room. Raine must never sense the torment he felt. She was feeling much better now, and they would celebrate that. The mindset had to be that she had something else less threatening, and more tests would prove it.

When they returned to the room, Raine greeted them with a belch. She had pushed the tray away and lay against the elevated head of the bed.

The burp garnered a big smile as she slapped her free hand over her mouth. "Excuse me."

"Well, that must have been good," Noelle said. The plate was shiny clean. "Who said hospital food isn't good, huh?"

"I'm still hungry, though."

"Uh-huh. I think we better wait before putting anything else in that tummy," he said and sat on the edge of the bed. "Let's make sure that little tummy is ready for all that food. But I'm glad you're feeling better."

"The nurse said my fever is almost gone. When can we go home, Daddy?"

Sean glanced toward Noelle before answering. She had plastered a smile on her face.

"Sweetie, they want to keep you for another day or so, to make sure your fever doesn't come back. Then we can go home."

She thought about this for a moment and then looked first at Noelle, then back to him. "I don't have what they think I have."

The blood drained from Sean's face, and he gripped the side of the bed, glad for the support.

"What do you mean, sweetie?" Noelle touched his hand. For a moment, he fought back a lump, overwhelmed by his love for both these ladies. He shot Noelle a relieved glance that she had asked the question, for he was unable to utter as much as a word at the moment.

"The bad thing," Raine murmured and looked down at the sheet covering her. With her free hand, she took her index finger and moved it across the smooth white sheet, as if spelling a word. "They think I have the bad thing, but I don't."

"What bad thing, sweetie?" Noelle continued to take the lead.

"The limp-oh-my?" She carefully and slowly pronounced the words. "Or however you say it."

In spite of the lump in his throat, Sean smiled.

"Who told you that's what you have?" he asked.

"Nobody."

"Then sweetie, why would you say that?"

"I just know I don't have that." Her face cleared. "The Castle Man told me."

His pulse quickened. He squeezed both of their hands and smiled. "That ol' Castle Man. He won't go away, will he, sweetie?"

"He's not a bad man, Daddy." Raine frowned but seemed confused. "I mean, I don't think so. At least not *all* bad."

The little girl shook her head, as if trying to summon clarity.

"I don't know," she said and continued fiddling with the sheet. "Sometimes he's bad, and sometimes he's not so bad. It's like he's two people."

"Now I'm confused." Noelle shook her head. "Am I missing something here?"

"She dreams about the Castle Man, right, sweetie?"

"I don't know."

"Is he your imaginary friend?" Noelle asked.

"He's not imaginary, Miss Noelle." Raine pointed to her own chest. "He's right here."

"You're the Castle Man?" He couldn't hide his shock.

"No, Daddy," she replied, sparing them a *duh*. She pointed once again to herself. "He's right here, inside me. At least I think he is."

Sean was inclined to touch her forehead, afraid the fever had returned. Instead, he smiled and squeezed her hand. He searched Noelle's face for clues to the interpretation of his daughter's strange comments. "Maybe we can talk about this again, some other time.

What do you think, Miss Noelle?"

"I think that sounds like a good idea. But do you know what sounds like a better idea to me?"

"What?" Raine asked, with anticipation in her smile.

"Ice cream." Noelle smiled.

"Yippee!"

"Only if the doctor says it's okay," Sean added.

"Okay."

He retrieved the button and handed it to Raine. "Would you like to press the button?"

Without hesitation, she did.

Chapter Twenty

Noelle left for a shower and a change of clothes. Sean insisted she sleep at the hotel and relieve him in the morning. As a compromise, he agreed to do the same the following night. Soon after she left, a nurse and assistant entered the room.

"Hello, little girl," the nurse said, approaching her bed. She turned toward Sean. "Daddy, you might want to help here. We need to get a biopsy of your Miss Raine's bumpy node." She turned and smiled at Raine. "Sweetie, this might pinch a little bit, but I promise it won't last long."

Sean made his way to the other side of the bed. "Why don't you tell this nice lady how you helped me sail our big boat? I'll bet she wouldn't believe you are such a sailor."

Raine began a step-by-step dissertation about preparing for and sailing a boat. Sean was amazed at how she had memorized the entire routine after only a few times out on the water. Her voice faltered occasionally as the nurse and assistant worked, and tears filled her eyes, but she remained strong. Sean tried to draw from her strength. Soon, the procedure was done.

The nurse pressed a piece of tape over the bandage she had positioned under Raine's arm. "That wasn't too bad, now was it, Dad?"

Like hell. He smiled and moved a strand of hair from Raine's face. It was red and hot.

The fever was back.

With a vengeance.

He glanced toward the nurse.

She nodded. "I'll let your floor nurse know this little one needs something more for the fever."

The nurse and assistant were gone before Sean could answer.

Afterward, Raine ate a light dinner and fell asleep. An hour later, she was tossing and turning.

What was he going to do now? With every move she made, he flinched. Every fiber of his body tensed. How long could she maintain such a fever without some sort of damage? He walked quietly to the call button. Sean met the nurse at the door and asked her to step outside.

"I'm worried about this fever," he said without waiting for a greeting. "She's had so much in the last days; could it cause some other problems?"

The nurse smiled. Sean failed to see the humor. His expression must have shown his irritation, and the nurse touched his shoulder. "Mr. Sampson, children can tolerate a great deal more and much higher fever than adults. She may have this fever for a long period without worry of permanent damage. We'll make sure she has all the treatment we can possibly administer. Her body will eventually fight it off. Your daughter is a very strong young lady."

The reassuring words did little to help Sean's apprehension. He stood looking at the tile floor, trying to find strength to accept the situation and to believe the nurse was right.

"Mr. Sampson, let me talk with the doctor and we'll do everything we can to step up the treatment. I'm sure your daughter will come through all this and be fine."

"Thanks," Sean said and forced a smile. The nurse stepped to the station and picked up the phone. Sean moved back into the room. He was exhausted. He fought sleep as the activity in and out of the room picked up.

With the return of the fever came another round of IV treatment and cold blankets. Even so, her fever refused to loosen its grip. Most of the night, her temperature hovered around 104 before elevating to 104.5 for a short but tense period. By four in the morning, the fever had dropped to around 102. She slept easier. Sean could barely keep his eyes open. He resolved to close them for a few moments to rest.

****

It was time to make a move. Over the past two days, James had watched the change of command. Three agents alternated eight-hour shifts. He figured the one with the least seniority—and hopefully least experience—would have the midnight to eight shift. Fortunately for James, this agent was also the smallest. Make no mistake, he was probably trained well, so he had to be on his toes to take him out. James's years in the Corps and combat experience in the Middle East would give him the edge. He'd teach them for dishonorably discharging him. He doubted this kid agent had served in any of the armed forces. Besides, at that late hour, it would be easier to accomplish his mission of clearing the way to the kid.

He timed the "accident" perfectly. The agent went

for coffee, and when he turned the corner to the waiting room, James made his move, bumping the guy and making sure the hot coffee spilled on the agent's shirt.

"Jeez." The agent stumbled backwards. James grabbed his arm and prevented his fall.

"Oh, man," James said in his most polite tone. "I am so sorry. I should've been watching where I was going."

The man surveyed him. "Forget it. No harm done."

"I was looking for my aunt. She was supposed to be here doing the night shift for my nephew. He was in an accident."

"Sorry to hear that, man." The agent threw the empty cup in a can.

The waiting room was empty, so James knew the agent might fall for the next part of the plan, but only if he left.

"Anyway, sorry again, man. I'm double parked, so I've gotta split."

James made his way to the elevator and pushed the button. The agent watched him get in. The door closed. He punched the floor below and waited. In a moment, the elevator reached its destination. James quickly punched the button to close the door and hit the button to return to the floor above. If the agent was still there, he would feign looking for his keys, which he had placed under a chair in the waiting room.

The door opened. He walked the short distance to the waiting room to find it empty, as he had hoped. He quickly retrieved his keys and made his way to the men's restroom, quietly pushing open the door. He glanced around the corner toward the stalls and sinks. As he suspected, the agent was standing at the sink, cleaning the coffee from his shirt. When he was done, he made his way toward the door.

The agent never knew what hit him. James jabbed the knife in the center of his chest and then twisted it. James watched with pleasure as the life drained from the young man's eyes.

He grabbed a stack of paper towels and stuffed them against the puncture wound. He dragged the agent's body into the far stall and propped him on the toilet and against the wall. He quickly latched the stall door and slid under it.

No more agent. No one else in his way.

The little girl was next.

****

"Hey, mister."

Her words brought a smile to his face.

Like father, like daughter.

Noelle found it amazing he could, in every situation, continue to exceed any expectation she could possibly have for a man. For four days, he had given no thought to himself. His slim physique was thinner now, but he still looked all man, strong and sleek. Most people would be banned from public after four days of no showering or shaving, but it only made him look sexier. Although she would have thought it impossible, his cologne still lingered, counteracting some of the working-man scent. Instead of being repulsed, she found it quite erotic. There he sat, sprawled in a chair not nearly the size his tall frame required, wild-haired, unshaven, and causing her heart to fill with desire. Under different circumstances, she'd lead him to the nearest bed.

"Hey, big guy."

He stirred, changed position, and dropped away again. She laughed. His eyes opened, and he smiled at her. He mumbled something, glanced at the bed where Raine slept peacefully, before he turned back and reached out for her. As he touched her hand, a jolt shot through her. Funny how a long bath, a glass of wine, and a few hours of sleep helped to refresh the desire she had for him. Was it that or his primal scent?

"You look fresh as a daisy," he said and covered his mouth. "And I bet I'm an array of pungency. At least, my mouth feels that way."

"You have no idea how good you look and smell to me."

"You must be kidding."

"Not in the least." She leaned over to kiss him.

"Oh, no," he growled and backed away. "I don't think you want to get much closer."

Fully awake, he took another look toward Raine. He stood and lightly touched her forehead. "Thank God." He sat once again. "It was a rough night for her."

"I heard. I spoke to the nurse before I came in. She's been much better for a couple of hours, since around four."

"Yeah, that's when I leaned my head back for some rest. What time is it?"

"Six-thirty."

"You're kidding? I slept three hours in that...box?"

"It would appear so."

"Well, my back knows it." He stretched, and his joints issued a few pops and cracks. "Let me go splash some water on my face and we can talk."

"Oh, no, you don't." She grabbed his arm and pulled him toward the door. "A deal is a deal. I had my luscious bath and snooze and now it's your turn. Besides, if you don't get a shower and some real rest soon, they're gonna ban you from the hospital premises anyway."

"But—"

"No buts. I'm a doctor. And those are my orders. Raine is resting fine. Her fever is way, way down, and you need a break. I'll be right here by her side. I'm all fresh and rested, fed and pottied."

"You smell good." He leaned into her.

"And you don't," she lied.

"I'm hurt," he replied and smiled.

"You'll get over it." She pushed him down the hall and then remembered she had the suite key. "Think fast."

He turned in time to catch the card key as it slithered through the air. She watched him walk along the hall toward the elevator and noticed she wasn't the only one looking at him. During the long walk down the corridor, he turned a few female heads and received his usual stares. She would bet it had nothing to do with his scruffy look and everything to do with how sexy he looked.

In a dirty way, of course.

Several hours later, Noelle was well into the last book she had purchased, another Sean Sampson bestseller, when Raine awoke.

"I feel better, Miss Noelle." Raine bounced upright in the bed, as far as the restraints would allow.

"And you look much better." Noelle stood and patted her hand. "And I bet you might be hungry?"

"A little. But mostly I'm thirsty."

Noelle poured apple juice into a fresh cup with ice

and pushed a straw into it.

"Mmm. That's good."

"Slowly, please."

"Okay." After she took several sips, she handed the cup back to Noelle.

"Would you like some breakfast?"

"Could I have oatmeal with honey?"

"Let's see."

"Can I press the button?"

"Of course."

In a short time, the oatmeal arrived. Raine dug in. Noelle picked up her book and read while Raine ate. "Daddy says someday I can read his books."

She put the book down. "And you'll love them. He is a very gifted storyteller."

"I know. He tells me a lot of good stories all the time. I think he makes them up as he's telling them. They're funny."

"Well, I hear you are pretty good about making up stories, too."

"Yeah, sometimes Daddy and me share a story."

"Oh, yeah?" Noelle shifted in her seat and leaned forward. "What do you mean?"

"It's fun. Daddy starts with a sentence—about anything. Then I add a sentence. Sometimes I make him laugh. He always tries to get the story back on track, but I say crazy things, making it hard for him to keep the story going."

"Sounds like fun."

"It is."

After a short silence, the intercom, out in the hall, called a doctor's name with instructions to call an extension.

"I'm glad I don't have the bad thing."

Noelle could think of no immediate response.

"I'd glad I don't have limp-on-my." Raine slowly formed the words and smiled.

Noelle's pulse quickened. She glanced at the door. "Has the doctor seen you this morning, sweetie?" Maybe he came while Sean was asleep. But that didn't make sense; the doctor would have awakened Sean.

"No, he hasn't told me yet."

"Is this something you dreamed?"

"Uh-uh. It's the Castle Man. I have the Castle Man's disease inside of me. Not the limp-oh-my."

"The Castle Man's disease?"

"Yeah, when I woke up I just knew. You can look it up on the Internet."

Raine's matter-of-fact tone sent a chill down Noelle's spine. Her hands shook as she took out her cell and opened the search engine. It took her several attempts to type the words *Castle* and *Man*. When she finally succeeded, she felt faint. She quickly scanned the information, enough to see there was indeed a disease termed Castleman's. A lump formed in her throat, as through her tears she read about the disease and how closely it resembled lymphoma. She quickly fumbled through her purse to find the card Dr. Wells had given them. She managed to punch the numbers onto the phone pad. After a few rings, the doctor answered.

"Doctor, this is Dr. Noelle Victor, Raine's—"

"Doctor Victor, I am on my way to the hospital to make my rounds. I have good news for you."

That was all she needed to hear. The tears flowed unchecked. She found she could barely speak. "I know.

It's Castleman's disease. It's a benign condition of the lymph nodes and completely curable and treatable."

"Yes, but…but how did you know?"

Without answering the doctor, she told him she needed to call Sean, so he could meet them at the hospital when the doctor arrived. The doctor said not to hurry, it would be a couple of hours before he made his way around to them. She told him okay and hung up the phone, as a pretty young girl came through the door with a cart in tow.

"Time for your bath, Miss Sampson."

Raine wrinkled her nose.

Noelle regained her composure and took Raine into her arms. "You were right, sweetheart. You're going to be fine. The doctor said so. I'm going to step outside and call your daddy. I made him go back to the hotel for some rest and a shower."

She frowned once again.

"Is that okay?"

"I think I might have pee-peed on myself."

"Oh, honey, I don't care. That's okay."

"I don't want to hurt you, but I kinda want some privacy, if that's okay, Miss Noelle?"

The nurse smiled. "I'll be happy to stay with her, if you want. If your hotel isn't too far away, I'm sure you'd have time. It will take me a while to get this little one all fresh and clean."

"Is that all right, sweetie?"

"I guess," Raine said.

"Are you sure?"

Raine nodded and squirmed.

"Okay, I'll go tell Daddy the great news, and we'll both be back in a while."

She yawned. "I might take another nap after my bath, so you don't have to hurry back, okay?"

"I see." This little girl might have more motive than Noelle was giving her credit for. She kissed her forehead. As she hurried out the door, she felt like a child, granted permission by a parent to go out for the night. She ran squarely into a tall, slender man in a dark suit.

"Excuse me," Noelle pleaded. "I'm so sorry, I wasn't watching—"

The man smiled and removed his shades. "My, my, you must be the famous Dr. Noelle Victor?"

"Yes, and you are?"

"I'm Derek, Sean's agent and good friend."

Noelle smiled and took Derek's hand. "I am so happy to finally meet you. To say I have heard a lot about you is an understatement. Did Sean know you were coming?"

"No, I thought I would surprise you all." He grinned. "I figured you guys were tired by now and could use a break."

"Well, as a matter of fact, we could. I was about to ask the nurse's station to look in on Raine and the attendant while I leave for a few minutes."

"Nonsense." He shook his head. "Not necessary. I'm at your service."

Noelle started back toward the room. "Come on, I'll take you in to see—Oh, I forgot, the attendant is giving her a bath."

"That's perfectly fine. I'll just hang out for a while until I'm sure the attendant's done."

"Are you sure you don't mind?"

"Of course not, what are friends for? You run

along, get some rest. And tell Sean I said hello and will be here when ya'll get back."

"You are a godsend." Noelle rose on her tiptoes and kissed his cheek. She continued down the hall, before remembering the good news. She turned back toward Derek, who had taken a chair in the hall. "Oh, Derek, our little girl's going to be fine."

"Wonderful," he called back.

Noelle picked up the pace toward the elevator. There was much good news, and she couldn't wait to get to Sean to tell all.

****

Noelle's heart beat wildly. She removed the extra card key she had gotten from the front desk from her skirt pocket. If only her shaking hands could hold it long enough to get to the room and insert it. She nodded to the agent when he stood from his post next to the suite door. The green light flickered. She quietly opened the door and stepped inside to silence. She passed Sean's bed, which was still made. A light shone through the bathroom door. She quietly pushed open the door and caught a glimpse of him wiping the fogged mirror. He had a towel wrapped around his waist and shaving cream on his face.

He caught her movement and turned defensively. "You scared me. What? Why are—"

She hurried to him. "Everything is fine. Raine is fine. She couldn't be better. In fact, I have such great news."

His facial features softened as he stood motionless, apprehensive.

"I know I said I wouldn't leave her side, but please hear me out before you jump to any conclusions. And besides, Derek is with her."

"Derek?" Sean's face lit up. "When did—"

"He arrived as I was arranging for someone to stay with Raine."

"Great. I had no idea he was coming, although that's just like him to show up unannounced. So what's the news?" He leaned against the counter. He may have lost a few pounds, but his slim, tan frame was still rippled with muscles. His shirtless torso and wet hair made him look delicious. It was all she could do not to attack him before delivering the message that would surely make him very happy.

"She doesn't have lymphoma." She choked on the barely audible words. His eyes filled with tears, assuring her he had indeed heard her.

Visibly shaken, he sagged against the counter. "How?"

She relayed the narrative about Castleman's and her conversation with the doctor. He literally staggered to her and put his arms around her. For a long moment he held her, his broad shoulders heaving from silent sobs of joy. She held him as tight as her arms could muster.

He took a deep breath, pushed her away, and gazed into her eyes. Tears streamed down his face, and he nodded. "You can bring me news like this any time you want." He kissed her. As he withdrew, he laughed, and wiped a finger across her face, removing shaving cream. Before long they were both laughing.

"So my sweet little angel was okay with you leaving and told you not to hurry back?"

"Yep. Wanted her privacy and a nap."

"I think we've been duped. She is such the little

Cupid."

"No doubt. Too bad you're so tired. I suppose you need a nap, huh?"

"For some reason, I'm not really sleepy anymore."

"Then whatever will we do with our free time?"

"I can think of something," he said, as the towel around his waist fell to the floor.

****

Lying in the bed afterwards, Sean broke the comfortable silence.

"Marry me, Noelle."

"What did you say?"

"I said, marry me, Noelle," he answered and grinned. "You would make me—and my lovely daughter—two very happy people."

"Your daughter?"

"Well, she doesn't know I was going to ask you to marry me—wait, let me rephrase—as far as I know she doesn't know, but she's certainly been nudging us together." He squinted his eyes. "And you would have to be blind not to see she loves you, too."

The tears came hard and fast, and Noelle couldn't wait to take the little girl in her arms. But first, she couldn't wait to give him her answer.

"Yes, yes, yes. Yes, I will marry you." She laid her head against his chest. She had never been happier.

****

While the nice lady gave her a bath, Raine tried to make sense of her apprehension about the Castle Man. The doctor told Noelle the tests proved she was right about having the not-so-bad thing instead of the real bad sickness. So why was she still feeling as if there was something else about the Castle Man that made her scared? She should be happy and relieved she would get better. Why did she think something else was wrong? Of all the feelings she had in the past months, this one was the hardest to figure out.

Getting clean felt good. She refused to let the silliness spoil everything good that had happened recently. She had caused so much trouble by being sick; it had to be the right thing to do to ask Miss Noelle to go see Daddy. Wasn't it? She loved Miss Noelle so much and hoped she would never leave again and she would be with her and Daddy forever. Daddy was so lonely, and Miss Noelle was so good to him. It was okay to ignore a bad feeling to get them to spend some time together, wasn't it?

The lady finished bathing her and smiled as she prepared to leave.

"Is there anything else you need, little miss, before I get someone to come sit with you?"

"No, thank you," she said and remembered her manners. She stifled a yawn. "Thank you for bathing me. I feel so much better."

"You're very welcome," the woman said and laughed. She handed Raine the call button. "You looked tired and sleepy. Why don't you relax? And if you need anything, just push the button. Someone will be in soon to sit with you until your doctor and daddy get back."

This sounded like a good idea. She could hardly hold her eyes open enough to turn her head on the pillow.

Although it seemed like only seconds, when she awoke a strange man was leaning over her. The mean look on his face scared her.

Her heart beat fast, and she struggled for breath.

She reached for the button, but it was gone. The bad man lifted his arm and revealed the call button.

"Looking for something, brat?"

She wanted to scream for Daddy, but no sound came from her mouth, as the pillow covered her face.

She struggled, and it all became clear to her.

She remembered the other bad thing about the Castle Man.

****

The cab couldn't get there fast enough. Although Noelle relished the time alone with Sean, she was anxious to get back to Raine. She flinched as his cell phone rang. The hospital came into view.

"Hello?" Sean answered and smiled. "So I was wondering when I'd hear from you again. When did you get in?" Sean paused for a moment and then frowned. "What do you mean, what do I mean?" He winked at her, as the cab pulled up to the hospital entrance. "Showing up out of nowhere and then offering to sit with Raine. Since when did you turn so nice?"

She watched his expression turned to horror. His cell phone fell to the floor of the cab. and in no time he sprang out of the car, turning to her in the process. "That was Derek—calling from Gulf Shores. We've got to get to Raine!"

He darted onto the sidewalk and broke into a run toward the door.

Noelle managed to pass him inside the entrance. Although Raine was on the third floor, she didn't wait for the elevator. She took the steps two at a time and flung open the door to the third floor.

The imposter flinched as she burst into Raine's

room. The blood drained from Noelle's face as she saw him standing over her on the opposite side of the bed, and the pillow over Raine's face.

"She's resting." The man pulled the pillow away and fluffed it before moving toward the door.

Although the scene took only seconds, her heart sank at Raine's sweaty pale face. Her little body was too still. He glanced between Noelle and Raine, then whipped a knife from his jacket pocket. Noelle ignored the knife and rushed to Raine, pulling her into her arms as the man stabbed the mattress. As he drew his arm back for another strike, Sean darted in and dove for him, catching the blade of the knife on his forearm before taking control of the intruder's arm. He slammed him against the wall, knocking the knife onto the floor. It slid across the room.

Sean grabbed the stranger's thin neck and yanked him forward, slamming him face first into the wall. The imposter struggled away from Sean and staggered toward the door but quickly dropped face first onto the tiled floor. The impact made a sickening crunching noise as blood gushed from the man's face.

A hospital orderly rushed into the room.

Noelle laid Raine back onto the bed. The child wasn't breathing. She breathed air into her mouth. Sean's heart beat wildly as he watched the woman he loved and her desperate attempt to breathe life back into his little girl. His head spun with dizziness as the sheet on the bed before him turned bright red. For a moment he feared the man had cut Noelle or Raine, until he looked at his arm and the blood gushing with each rapid beat of his heart. As shooting flecks of lights invaded the corners of his eyes and his balance spun out of control, he fought to hold onto consciousness. Tears streamed down Noelle's face as she spoke softly to his daughter.

"Come on, baby." Her voice cracked. "Breathe, sweetheart. One time for Miss Noelle, little one. You can do it."

Sean sank further into the black abyss that threatened the edge of his sight and he became aware of someone tugging at his other arm. Another staff member was guiding him onto a gurney. He reached in vain toward Noelle and Raine as he was wheeled away. Images of the ladies he loved faded, as he fought valiantly to hold on to consciousness.

The last sound he heard was Noelle's scream. "Please, baby, please, breathe! Just once for Daddy."

In spite of his efforts to stay with them, the world around Sean went dark.

****

Darkness spilled through the blinds as Sean opened his eyes. The world spun. Where was he? Pain shot though his left arm when he tried to move. Efforts to release his bandaged arm from the restraints were futile, so he resolved to close his eyes for a few moments more and try again later.

So sleepy. He allowed himself to slip down, down into the need for rest, and thought of his sweet daughter. Memories of her lying motionless on the bed flashed across his vision.

"Raine?" He opened his eyes. Noelle appeared beside the rails of the bed and took his free arm.

"Easy, baby." She touched his face gently. "You've been through a lot. You don't want to rip open those sutures."

"Raine, where is she?"

"She's fine," Noelle smiled. "She's sleeping. It's very late. You've been out for several hours."

"The man?"

"He's dead, Sean." Her voice broke. "It's over, baby. Raine's okay. We were able to revive her. She's fine. There was no damage; she had stopped breathing for less than a minute."

The tears flowed from his eyes. "Thank you."

"It was a team effort," she whispered. "Lucky we were here when that man…"

"How did he—"

"You rest," she said. "There will be plenty of time for answers later."

Sean opened his mouth to speak, and the door opened. In came Raine in a wheelchair, guided by a nurse.

"Daddy!" she shouted and tried to stand. The nurse restrained her.

"Hang on," demanded the large nurse. "Your daddy is fine, sweetie, but he needs his rest."

Noelle was having nothing to do with protocol. She lifted Raine from the chair and gently placed her on the side of Sean's bed. The nurse shook her head but remained silent.

Raine leaned gently into her father and hugged him. Sean reached out with his free arm and held her close.

"I thought we had lost you," Sean whispered.

"I thought we had lost you, too, Daddy. Thank you for saving me."

Sean looked toward Noelle. "I think you can thank Miss Noelle, our award-winning sprinter for that, sweetie. I still don't know how she got to your room so fast."

Raine turned and held out her arms. "Can we have a group hug, please?"

Noelle leaned forward and wrapped one arm around Raine and the other around Sean.

In spite of the pain, he realized nothing felt better than holding the two ladies of his life closely.

It was just what the doctor ordered.

Epilogue

On the beach, across from Ono Island
Three months later, the first day of fall…

Noelle knelt on the sand and tightened her sandal strap. The day slipped into a cool and misty dusk. It was still shorts weather on the coast during the warm days, but nippy enough for sleeves after the sun set. A cool, brisk northern breeze pushed across the dunes and out into the Gulf of Mexico. The warm water felt good to her toes, as she watched and listened to the docile waters. A wave chased a periwinkle bird away from the surf, as it scurried along the beach ahead of her in search of a meal.

"One, two…three!" Sean counted as they lifted Raine from an encroaching wave, then set her back onto the beach to witness the salt water fizzle away. There was no doubt in Noelle's mind he was repeating the newfound ritual just to hear Raine laugh. It was a glorious sound. In her three-and-a-half years on this earth, a lot had happened, including almost losing her. It was good to hear her patented belly laugh. The stress and pain of the summer months were all but a memory now.

The Castleman's was cured. Sean had picked the doctor's brain apart in determining the detailed prognosis for his little girl. Yes, she was totally cured.

No, there was no reason to think it would ever come back. No, having had the disease was no indication of a more serious risk. It was the most benign form of Castleman's and was remedied by simply removing the lymph node affected. Because it was a relatively simple surgery, it was done as an outpatient procedure. The whole ordeal transpired in Pensacola and was painless. In a few weeks, Raine was back to her normal self. There wasn't any indication to suggest she had any problem with her underarm, as evidence by her game of dodging the waves.

Like her father, she was hard to keep down.

In more ways than one.

Even after losing half the blood in his body from the sliced artery while deflecting the man's second attempt to stab Raine—an attempt that most probably would have hit Noelle also—Sean had pulled through. It was touch and go for hours, but he made it.

Noelle thought about what might have happened if they had caught even one more traffic light driving back to the hospital. Or if it had taken even seconds longer to reach Raine's hospital room. Sean had dwelt on this aspect more than she and had several times expressed his thanks that Noelle was fast enough to earn those trophies still residing in the display case at Pensacola High. Her speed was the difference in Raine's avoiding serious injury, if not death, from the knife.

Try as she might, she couldn't help but think of the many, many what-ifs that could have yielded a much different outcome. But the past was gone, now, along with the horrible monster that day.

James Castle, the man who posed as Derek, was

dead, putting an end to the last piece of the Raine's confusing premonition about the Castle Man. When he hit the hospital floor, a shard of bone punctured his brain, killing him in seconds. How lucky they were to have escaped this ruthless man, who had murdered the FBI agent assigned to Raine and hidden his body in the men's room. Castle's involvement prompted more investigation from the Feds. They discovered the man was linked to an association tied to Senator Blane. The group's radical ring of corruption was busted wide open, and the associated white supremacy organization was rendered ineffective.

In a matter of weeks, father and daughter had completely recovered, and life was almost—almost—back to normal.

Noelle had returned to her practice, at Sean's insistence. Although he needed help with Raine, especially after her surgery, he refused Noelle's assistance, turned her around, and pointed her toward her office. Derek—the real one—insisted on coming over and helping out, and Sean had taken him up on his offer.

Getting back into the swing of things made the hours go faster. In some ways, going back to her old life was torturous. Not being with Sean and Raine around the clock was worse. But keeping separate living arrangements was at her own insistence. She wanted to do the right thing. So days were spent working—her with patients, him with his writing—and early evenings after Raine's bedtime were spent stealing away, whenever possible, for intimacy. She longed for the days when she could be with him—and Raine—all night. Thankfully, she wouldn't have to wait much longer, as the wedding was in eight days. Between her practice and his finishing the new book, which he appropriately entitled *Time for Raine*, there was little idle time.

The story this time was indeed semi-autobiographical. They say "write what you know," and that's exactly what he had done. Sean told her there was no longer any doubt concerning the details of his heroine for the story, because she was actually Noelle.

His publisher was very impressed with the synopsis and partial manuscript. Because of Raine's popularity and extraordinary psychic gifts, Hollywood had jumped all over the story. Plans were in the works to turn the story into a made-for-TV movie. Noelle cried when the publisher told them about the call he had received from the director of the proposed film, who happened to be an Asian man. It seemed he had followed Raine's story, and after hearing of their engagement, insisted on footing the bill for the wedding and offered his own vacation home in Malibu for the event. The director was a supporter of foreign adoption and had adopted two Chinese children himself, one from the same province where Raine was born. In addition, the best man, Derek, and maid of honor, Connie, had teamed up to help with the details. And from what Sean had told Noelle, the two were teaming up in more ways than one.

It was all a dream come true.

The coming year promised to be very interesting and hopefully a joyous one. The NSA and ethics committee had agreed, in light of all the events, to postpone Raine's hearing. They had more than they needed, thanks to Raine, to put the senator away for a very long time.

In the meantime, Raine's calendar would be as full as time allowed. She had offers from literally all over the world to make appearances. Several award ceremonies were scheduled, including the one from the testing institution, which was to be a nationally televised event. Pleas for endorsements from every imaginable product and service poured in. The most amusing one was from a vitamin company that made gingko biloba supplements. For a substantial endorsement fee, Raine had to agree she took the supplements and that they enhanced her astonishing mental powers. Sean had presented this to Raine, but she had simply frowned. She proceeded to inform Sean exactly what chemical elements the supplement was composed of and although it did have some benefits, it didn't exactly have anything in it to make people smarter. Her father thought it prudent to turn the offer down.

And then there was the Dalai Lama. He wanted to meet with Raine, convinced she might be his successor. Sean respectfully nixed the successor idea but agreed to allow her to meet with him. That event was scheduled for the spring.

After her brief setbacks, Raine continued her uncanny pursuit of knowledge. She soaked in everything the limitless reach of the Internet had to offer. Noelle spent a lot of time with her on the weekends and evenings, supervising the activity. During one of those sessions, while Daddy had slipped out to pick up dinner, Raine told her someday soon Noelle would be a mommy.

"I'm already a mommy, sweetie," Noelle had said.

"I'm your other mommy."

"But I'm going to have brothers and sisters," Raine insisted.

How right she was.

It was still difficult for Noelle to think in plural terms relative to the babies that grew inside of her. More astounding, she had no idea there was a possibility of becoming pregnant. And then, after Raine's revelation, some things that were going on with her body all made sense. After her first breakup with Sean, she had stopped taking the pill. Looking back, she wasn't sure why, other than she considered her love life over. And in the back of her mind she had always assumed Sean was sterile. Thus, no need for the pill, or at least so she thought.

Then, synchronistically, she was late for her period. Nausea came next. The mood shifts. The sleepiness. She seemed to have every symptom at once. Last week, it was confirmed. The doctor had then asked if there were twins in the family. Not in hers, she had said. She learned that there were in Sean's family. Definitely two individual heartbeats, the doctor had said.

Oh, well.

The honeymoon sail to the Caribbean would have to be postponed for a while. And he was so looking forward to heeding the call for points south! She wasn't looking forward to dropping that news on him.

She watched the little girl frolicking with her daddy on the beach ahead of her and hoped Raine would not connect too many dots. And she certainly hoped the child wouldn't say anything about her condition before Noelle could tell Sean, which she planned to do before the wedding. Fortunately, if Raine knew about the birds and the bees, she wasn't telling, and Noelle hoped she hadn't figured out exactly how or when the babies got their start. She'd cross that bridge when she came to it. Sean slowed his pace and allowed her to catch up.

"I finished the book," he said, looking over to her. She smiled at him. Raine released their hands and started chasing a crab along the sand.

"Oh, yeah? How does it end?"

"I think you know."

"Tell me anyway."

"And they lived happily ever after. Oh, and the happily ever after part officially starts in eight days."

He got quiet as they started walking again.

"Penny for your thoughts," she pleaded.

"Okay. It occurred to me we haven't decided where we will live. Ono or the beach?"

"Well, I think I know Raine's choice." Noelle brushed a strand of hair away from the little girl's face as she rejoined them.

"Why not both?" Raine offered.

Noelle and Sean laughed.

"Problem solved," he said.

The three of them continued on slowly.

"Something else on your mind?" she asked.

He stopped suddenly and dug his toes into the sand. "Okay, I've been thinking maybe we ought to put off our sailing trip."

She stopped again and gazed into his eyes.

"Yeah? Why?"

"I don't know, it doesn't seem quite right this soon after our ordeal this summer. Raine's schedule is pretty full. There will be edits to deal with on the new book."

Noelle smiled and nodded. "I agree, Mr. Sampson." She did her best to hide her relief. "I would feel better if we wait until Raine gets a little older anyway."

"You really mean that? I know you were looking forward to the trip as much as I was."

"I think I can find other things to do until we can reschedule."

He took her into his arms and kissed her. "I love you, soon-to-be Mrs. Sampson."

"And I love you, too, soon-to-be famous author again," she said, instead of *soon-to-be daddy again*, which she'd have to say soon enough.

"Ooooh, I see you," Raine shouted from a distance ahead and shook her finger at them.

"Oh, I forgot to tell you the rest of the story. Then they adopted three or four more of those," he whispered, and inclined his head toward Raine.

"Nice ending." She kissed him again and winked at *their* daughter. "And three or four more isn't a bad idea, the more I think about it."

Raine gave Noelle a knowing smile. She could almost read her little mind.

Duh, at least he got part of it right!

"Okay, what's going on with you two?" Sean stopped.

"Nothing, Daddy."

Noelle winked again at Raine.

Raine's giggle turned into another one of her belly laughs.

Noelle would never tire of hearing that sound.

A word about the author...

Barry lives with his wife Karen and their two daughters, Abby and Ally, on Florida's Nature Coast. He holds a BSBA and MBA from Webster University.

He has served as VP Finance for TMC, a health care corporation, since 2002.

He is a member of Sunshine State Romance Authors, a chapter of RWA, where he served two terms as Treasurer. He obtained PAN status with RWA last year.

http://cbdenham2003.wix.com/first